Crime in Cornwall

The British Book Tour Mysteries | Book 2

Emma Dakin

CAMEL PRESS

PRESS

Seattle, WA

A Camel Press book published by Epicenter Press

Epicenter Press
6524 NE 181st St. Suite 2
Kenmore, WA 98028.
www.Epicenterpress.com
www.Coffeetownpress.com
www.Camelpress.com

For more information go to: www.camelpress.com
www.emmadakinauthor.com

This is a work of fiction. Names, characters, places, brands, media, and incidents are the product of the author's imagination or are used fictitiously.

Cover art by Teresa Hanson
Design by Rudy Ramos

Crime in Cornwall

ISBN: 9781603816106 (trade paper)
ISBN: 9781603816090 (ebook)

Printed in the United States of America

To the gaggle that keeps me flying
Nancy, Janice, Glen, Jill, John, Ian, Diane, Libby,
Maria, Sandy and Charon

ACKNOWLEDGEMENTS

My thanks Kathy Ackley who, when she revealed her mystery book tour business, inspired me to give that occupation to Claire. Thanks also to Robert in Penzance who offered me care and attention during my stay there, the bookstore owners in Fowey and Penzance, the librarian in Penzance, the bus driver who took me from St. Michael's Mount to Falmouth and explained why the Cornish people are so independent. My thanks also to the many tourists and locals in Cornwall who helped me find information and experiences. I returned with Janice, John and Wren. We had a car and I am grateful for the many times they good-naturedly detoured at my cry of "It's in my book, I have to stop here." Checking facts, is what I told them, but it was really to get another satisfying taste of Cornwall.

AUTHOR'S NOTE

The historic spots and the settings where Claire takes her tourists are real, as are some of the guest houses and hotels. I have peopled them with staff and guests who come straight from my imagination. I hope you enjoy the tour.

CHAPTER ONE

The walls were shaking again. The noise level from the neighbor's back garden rose like the roar of a football crowd and had reached that stage of raucous shouts mixed with wild music that made sleep impossible. I'd tried ear plugs. I'd tried putting my head under the blankets. I gave up.

I considered phoning over. "This is Claire Barclay from next door. Could you tone it down?" I doubt they'd pay any attention to that request and I'd end up looking like an interfering neighbor.

"That's twice this month, Gulliver."

Gulliver, all twelve pounds of beautiful King Charles Cavalier Spaniel, stirred and sat by my head. I knew those big brown eyes were watching me in the darkness. I could *feel* them. He shook himself, stood and sniffed my ear. He wanted out.

"I know. You're still a puppy." I yawned and swung my legs to the floor. Bass beats thudded through the floorboards. 2:30 a.m. Time for all partygoers to leave.

The Stonnings were rarely in our semi-detached. It would be a duplex in Seattle, but here in England, it was a semi-detached. I imagined the two halves of the house pulling apart until they were attached only by a few bricks. That wasn't going to happen. It had stood here for several hundred years. When the Stonnings came down from London for the weekend, they tested the solid construction of the house by bringing guests who partied. Patrick and Rita were about my age, but I'd stopped that kind of partying years ago. Did that make me virtuous or dull? I was too sleepy to pursue the thought.

I escorted Gulliver to the kitchen door and waited while he made his mark at the far end of the garden. The noise was much louder here. It rose and fell in waves, the low percussion compressing the air until I could not only hear it but feel it. The volume of the music suddenly lowered. The change was a little startling. I heard a bellow of laughter, a screech of response, then the noise receded to the constant blur of many conversations. Comments floated over the fence.

"I *told* her that she had to show us some presence on social media. Does she think she can get published without that?" The voice was young and scornful.

"Authors! They think they're omnipotent."

The vocabulary was sophisticated. I imagined the person who used a word like "omnipotent". Young, blasé, wearing jeans and a suede blazer. I used to teach English to executives. That conditioned me, so at times, I paid more attention to how people spoke than what they said. I admired the syntax and vocabulary and occasionally missed the meaning.

"Without us, you'd be out of a job," a deep, older voice said.

Patrick worked at a publishing house. I think Rita worked there as well, but I've never had much conversation with them. I knew Rita's brother, Robert Andrews, who was Gulliver's vet and my friend, and his daughter, Sarah, but, somehow, Rita faded into the scenery and I had never had a conversation with her. Patrick was a little friendlier and had come over for coffee once. They were good enough neighbors— rarely there and not at all nosey about me, but their parties could go on until morning.

I made myself some hot chocolate and carried it back upstairs. The only way to endure the party was to wait it out. I sipped my comfort chocolate and read for a while. The music didn't pound through the walls now and I heard car tires spin on the gravel in the driveway. Good. Finally, some of the guests were leaving.

My mobile on the bedside table showed three a.m., about four hours before the October sunrise. Patrick would have to return to London in the morning, leaving our Hampshire village in peace. According to past form, he would be over about nine to apologize for disturbing me before he left.

He came over at nine right on schedule and banged on my kitchen door—but it wasn't to apologize.

Patrick isn't a grand sight on any day. He's about fifty, almost gaunt, with thinning brown hair and a hunched look as if he lived in a closet, fed on junk food and computer info-feed, and dressed in clothes that had seen better weeks, but he was socially aware, inoffensive and, while he talked fast at any time, he usually made sense.

"Claire, you've got to help me."

I stared at him.

Gulliver sat beside me. He knew Patrick and didn't bark at him.

Patrick leaned over and reflexively patted Gulliver.

"He's dead."

I looked at Gulliver. "No, he isn't."

"Yes, he is. Dead as the proverbial doornail. Dead as a dodo. Dead as road kill. Dead as a mouse in a trap. Dead as...."

In this editorial excess, I tried to pick out the salient fact. "Someone at your house has died."

"Not just someone. Oliver Nott." His brown eyes widened and he blinked.

"The thriller writer?" I'd read his novels. Not my style. A little too melodramatic, but readable.

"The very one."

"I'm sorry," I said. Nott was middle-aged, I think about fifty, a little young for a heart attack, but that can happen to the under sixties.

"I'm sorry as well. Very. It's untidy. Gross. It's murder. I need you to come over and call the police."

Murder? I stood there for a moment, a little stunned. Then picked up my quilted jacket, snapped on Gulliver's leash and followed Patrick through my back garden, out the gate and into the lane.

The murder happened at his house. I didn't see why *he* couldn't have called the police, but he was my neighbor, and he had asked for help, so I trotted behind him. I was going to assist him, but I didn't want any part of a murder. I hesitated in the lane, but curiosity trumped reluctance.

Patrick pushed open his gate. "He's here, in the garden."

He was there. Obviously dead.

"Why didn't *you* call the police?" I stared, morbidly fascinated at the remains of Oliver Nott.

"Because you're the one who knows the police. You're close and intimate with the police. You're our neighborhood conduit to the police."

I was not. My very good friend Mark Evans was a Detective Inspector of the Hampshire Constabulary. We met over the death of a member of the Mystery Book Club and have been meeting ever since. Patrick must pay more attention to my household than I'd thought. But I'm not an emergency dispatcher.

"I don't have a straight line into the homicide unit. In any case, you'll have to call the local police."

"Fine. Fine. I'll do that. You must look at him, though. I need a witness. There were scores of people here last night wandering around, yelling and making a lot of noise. You'd know about that. Sorry."

I don't think he even took a breath, just kept on talking.

"I have no idea who would have done this. Someone must have hated him. In fact, any number of people. Lots hated him. We could create a list."

I've got a little list. He never would be missed. The line from Gilbert and Sullivan floated through my mind. But he would be missed. He was a high-selling writer.

"How did he die?"

Foolish question. It was obvious how he had died. Oliver Nott was slumped sideways in an iron garden chair, his head turned, his cheek resting on the table. One hand was under his head, the other hanging straight down by his side. A long knife protruded from his chest. There was very little blood, but there was no doubt he was dead. His eyes were wide open with that glassy look of absence that removes all doubt.

Gulliver whimpered. I petted him. I agreed with Gulliver. Oliver Nott was a horrific sight.

"For God's sake, Patrick. Call the police."

"All right. I will. I'll do it now. I needed a sane and sober witness." He pulled a mobile from his back pocket and punched in 999.

I looked around. There were three people in the garden—all witnesses. Rita, Patrick's wife, sat in a chair near the kitchen door. She looked as though she'd been up all night, as, no doubt, she had. A younger couple was sitting at a picnic table as far away from the body as they could get. The man, about thirty had his mobile out. I expect he was taking pictures. That age seemed to photograph everything. The couple looked a little dazed.

Patrick had reached the emergency dispatcher and asked for the 'Murder Room.' They didn't call it that, but the dispatcher would know where to send the call.

"Yes, yes. A body. What? What? Of course, I know who it is. It's Oliver Nott. No, he doesn't live here. He came here last night for a party."

Patrick stopped talking long enough to listen for a few seconds. Then he was off again.

"Why am I asking for the Murder Room? Because there is a frigging huge knife sticking out of him, that's why. Do you think I'd report him if he slipped away with a heart attack, although I expect his heart was attacked, if you want to be literal? What?"

Patrick stared at the phone and then shoved it toward me. "Here. Talk to him."

A calm, rational voice which, no doubt, would have infuriated Patrick asked me if I could shed any light on this situation.

I tried to respond in the same tone, although after another quick look at Oliver, I felt a rising nausea. I blinked and breathed deeply.

"Yes, he is dead. There is a knife protruding from his chest."

"Madam, do you think this is homicide?"

What kind of inane question is that? Of course, it was homicide. Well, let me think. Was there any other option? I knew the constable on the phone would call Mark's homicide team if there was any question of murder.

"It may be homicide. It may be an accident. Perhaps Mr. Nott was enacting a play or something, and he was inadvertently stabbed." I tried not to let any hint of sarcasm drip into my voice. "Perhaps he stabbed himself. I couldn't possibility know." I heard my voice rising and struggled to control it.

"Yes, madam. I expect all those things are possible. I will send the local police and then, if necessary, notify the Major Investigation Team."

"Thank you."

"Could I have your name?"

"Claire Barclay."

"The address of the property?"

I gave it to him. It was the same as mine, with one letter different. "The Briars, B."

"Thank you, Madam. There will be someone there shortly. Please ask everyone in the area to stay at that address and to keep away from the crime scene."

"I can do that."

This officer's voice was so calm, it seemed almost robotic. "Thank you."

"One moment, please." I got that in quickly before he disconnected.

"Yes?"

"You might want to know that the man who died, Oliver Nott, is a well-known writer of thrillers. There will be press."

There was silence on the other end for a moment.

"I appreciate the warning." This time, his tone was warmer.

I handed Patrick his phone, and he dropped it into his pocket.

"Coffee. Coffee," he muttered.

Gulliver and I followed him into the kitchen. It was a disaster. A dustbin in the corner was full to overflowing with paper plates, plastic cutlery and napkins. Plates with half-eaten hors d'oeuvres were piled near the sink. No one had attempted to clean anything. I looked quickly for a knife rack. There was one on the wall behind the coffee urn. It had, perhaps, five knives in it. I couldn't see if one was missing without going over to peer at it. I wasn't that keen on finding out.

A huge coffee urn took up most of the counter. I hoped Patrick wasn't going to give me coffee from that. It might have been made hours ago by someone so drunk or stoned he couldn't measure anything. Patrick bustled around the kitchen muttering. He pulled a stainless steel, expresso coffee machine from behind a box, grabbed two small packets from the cupboard and loaded the machine. He handed me the first cup of aromatic coffee. It was excellent. He made himself another and had time to take two sips before the doorbell chimed. I envied him that chime. My doorbell did not chime with melodious bells. It clattered, sounding like pots and pans crashing to the floor. I should replace it with the Big Ben chimes. I sipped coffee and thought about doorbells. I was not going to think about Oliver Nott.

Patrick opened the door to the local beat constable, one of the many community patrol officers in Ashton-on-Tinch. He must have been close by to come this quickly.

He was about six-two and athletic looking. Young, twenty-six or so. He had the regulation black uniform with the black stab vest and various radios, a smart mobile and even a set of handcuffs clipped to his belt. Mark told me the officers carry mace and a collapsible baton, but I couldn't see them. He touched his helmet, but didn't take it off. I could see by the plain metal insignia on the helmet that he was a constable.

"Good morning. I'm Constable Pemberthy. What's to do then?"

Gilbert and Sullivan again.

"Lots to do," Patrick snapped. "Somebody killed Oliver Nott. He's an important author in my publishing house. Somebody killed him in my garden. He's just sitting there, like he's posing for publicity shots. It's bizarre and outrageous."

"He's dead then?"

"Of course, he's dead with a bloody great knife sticking out of him. It's macabre."

"Yes sir, I'm sure it's upsetting. Could you show me? And you are?" He whipped out his notebook. Patrick gave his name and the constable wrote it down. Mark had told me constables had to write everything in a new notebook every day. There is a serial number on the book and they have to hand it in when they go off shift. Inspectors can use tablets.

The constable turned to me.

"I'm the next-door neighbor, Claire Barclay. Patrick asked me to come over."

Constable Pemberthy followed Patrick, but gave me a thoughtful look as he passed me.

Gulliver had found something entrancing on the floor and was licking at it.

"Leave it, Gulliver." For a wonder, he did.

Clutching my coffee cup, I moved in behind the constable.

Constable Pemberthy looked down at Oliver. I approved of this officer's solid stance. He didn't touch Oliver or even get close. He pulled out his mobile and hit one number. Speed dial.

"Yes sir. Constable Pemberthy here. We do have a homicide. Could you get the Major Investigation Team here? Thank you. Yes, I'll hold."

He didn't hold long, as it was only a moment before he spoke again. "White male about fifty, blue eyes, no visible scars, one tattoo visible. No sir, I didn't approach the body." He waited a moment and continued. "Black leather jacket with zipper half-open, red scarf hanging loosely, blue shirt, brown pants, black trainers. Name of Oliver Nott."

He waited. "Hold, please. I'll ask." He turned to Patrick.

"Is he the writer?"

"Of course, he is *the* writer," Patrick said. "He writes thrillers, and they're selling like no one listens to the news and only wants the fictional version of murder, the more dramatic, the more they sell. Everyone knows him. *Murder in Penzance.* Remember that one?"

The constable's eyebrows rose. "Yes, I remember that one. He got the police procedure right."

Patrick nodded. "He was meticulous in his research. Nasty to work with but a genius."

"I'm sorry, sir."

Patrick really looked at the police constable then. "Well. Thank you."

I didn't know if Patrick was upset by the murder, sorry for Oliver, or disturbed that his source of income had disappeared. Perhaps all of that. I listened to their conversation and carefully avoided looking at Oliver.

The constable finished his call and followed us back toward the house. Patrick gestured at the picnic table. I sat with Gulliver on my lap, petting him with my free hand and taking comfort from his warmth. Rita nodded a hello but said nothing.

The constable sat.

"Coffee?" Patrick said to him. "I presume we have to wait until the special unit gets here to deal with this?"

"We do, and I would appreciate coffee. Cream, no sugar."

Patrick disappeared into the kitchen to work his magic with a package and some hot water.

I sipped my coffee. Everyone else had a cup in front of them or on the ground near them.

"Could I have your names, please." The constable had his notebook at the ready.

The young man sighed but spoke first. "Kyle Bradbury. I work at the same publishing house as Patrick. I'm marketing."

I suppose that meant he was the only one in the marketing department.

"Address, please."

Kyle gave it to him. He was a couple of inches short of six feet, blond with streaks not endowed by the October sun, and brown eyes. He looked a little stunned.

Cst Pemberthy turned to the young woman.

"Alexandra Atley," she said quietly. "I work for the publishing firm as well. I'm an executive assistant to the publisher, Nigel Hanson."

"Mr. Stonning is not the publisher?"

"No, he's the manager and editor. Mr. Hanson owns the company."

She was in her late twenties, about five foot eight, a little shorter than me, but much thinner and so blonde her long hair almost sparkled.

The constable wrote her name in his notebook and her address as she provided it. Patrick returned with the coffee and set it beside the constable.

"Ta," the constable said and took a sip.

"This is my wife, Rita." Patrick said. "Rita Stonning," he clarified. "She was Nott's editor."

Rita gave the constable a half-smile.

"I live here." Her voice was soft and a little hesitant. "We also have a London address." She gave it to him.

Rita had to be my age. The lines around her eyes gave that away, but she dressed as if she was about twenty with a stylish short skirt and top.

"Thank you. Now, did any one see anything last night that would help us in this investigation?"

I knew Mark would not appreciate the constable interviewing the witnesses before the Major Investigation Team got here, but I wasn't about to chastise the constable.

"He stayed out here most of the night," Patrick said. "Holding court, granting interviews to the favored few and doing his imitation of a famous author."

"Wasn't it cold in the garden?" I asked before I thought.

The constable looked at me sharply but waited for the answer.

"He had a warm leather jacket, and he wanted to smoke," Patrick said.

Kyle roused himself and leaned forward. "Everyone came to talk to him. He was pretty funny."

"Witty," Patrick said, "Not funny."

Kyle looked affronted. "I bow to your extensive vocabulary." His voice was resentful. I wondered if Patrick corrected him often.

"I wish I hadn't asked him here," Patrick said. "I knew he'd be trouble. He was always trouble."

"What kind of trouble, sir? Something new?" The constable's voice was so soft I wondered if Patrick had heard him.

He had. "This time, the greedy manipulator wanted to leave us. His sales were great, he said. Well, they *were* good. Maxman and Brown would give him a better percentage."

"A rival publishing house, I take it?" the constable asked.

"That's right. They would have offered him more, because they didn't have to put in the promotion money. We'd already done some work on it. It's true he could get a bigger advance with Maxman, but he knew we'd give him a slice of the profits. We couldn't afford not to. Not the way he was gripping the public's imagination."

"So, you invited him to the party."

"He liked adulation. I provided him with a group of sycophants."

I saw a look of active dislike wave across Kyle's face. I didn't blame him. No one wanted to be called a sycophant. Patrick noticed it.

"Oh, not you, Kyle. Sorry. You had to be here to figure out the promotion for the new book. Everything is an ad man's meat, and this party could have added some ideas to the promo package. No, it was all those others. I didn't even know some of them."

The constable reached into an inside pocket and produced a small paper notebook, ripped out a page and handed it to Patrick. I supposed he couldn't tear anything out of his official notebook. There could be no missing pages there.

"I am going to need a list of all the people who were here last night and their addresses."

Patrick groaned.

Rita stirred and reached for the paper. "I can do that—at least, I can put down most of the names. I don't know all the addresses, but I have phone numbers on my mobile."

Constable Pemberthy smiled at her. "Very good. Very good. Thank you."

Since everyone here was a suspect, I wondered at his friendliness. A healthy level of suspicion might be better. However, he wanted a list of partygoers. He'd smiled at Rita and she'd provided it. Maybe he was effective.

"Some of the people whom I don't know came with people I do know. I can phone them for their names and addresses. Would that be okay?"

The constable started to nod. I stared at him. He caught my eye.

"Uh, perhaps not. The detectives may want to do that themselves."

I nodded. They certainly would. Mark would be furious if Rita got to those witnesses before he did.

We sipped our coffee, waiting. The constable wrote in his notebook. Rita checked her mobile and copied names and numbers. She looked up.

"Does anyone know the name of the woman who came with Oliver? She drove him, I think."

There was silence for a moment. Then Alexandra said. "She told me her name was Jane. She tore out of here without him. They had a fight." Alexandra smiled a little, as if she had enjoyed that fight.

There was another silence.

"Does anyone know anything more about her?" The constable asked.

I knew Mark would tear a strip off this constable because he was fishing for information. He could shape the memories of witnesses. Mark had told me how susceptible honest people were to having their ideas influenced by questions. Once they answered a question, they tended to remember that piece of information and repress other observations. All this constable was supposed to do was take names and addresses and secure the crime scene. I frowned at him.

Pemberthy looked at his notebook and then at me. "I need your name and address please." I gave it to him. "Are you also an employee of the publishing house?"

"No. I have my own business." I still felt a frisson of satisfaction in announcing I owned my business.

"And that is?"

"Tour Guide."

"The name of the company?"

"British Mystery Book Tours."

"Books, again."

"True. But I don't produce them or sell them, just take people to the sites where the fictional mysteries are set. We're going to Cornwall in a couple of days."

"That's where Oliver set the last three mysteries," Patrick said.

I didn't appreciate Patrick linking me to Oliver Nott. "He's a thriller writer. My tourists are usually cozy fans."

Patrick nodded. Cst Pemberthy looked confused. I didn't want to explain the difference between the two genres. I wanted to go home. I picked up Gulliver's leash.

"I just arrived a half-hour ago, you have my name and address, I can't do anything more here and I would like to go home. The detectives from Major Investigation Team can find me there."

Cst Pemberthy hesitated.

Patrick stood. "Thanks, Claire. I'll walk you to the gate."

I nodded goodbye to everyone and followed Patrick to the back gate, giving a wide berth to Oliver, slumped in the iron chair and looking like a stage prop. Patrick was right. It was macabre to see this highly intelligent man reduced to a lifeless mannequin.

"Sorry to pull you in. Nasty business. Creepy, really and inconvenient. Just like Oliver to create a mess. He defined the word narcissism. Always has to be in the center of everything."

I glanced at him. No one would choose to be center stage in their own murder. "I suppose he will sell better now." I admit I was a little sarcastic. It had been a rough half-hour. Then I gave myself a mental kick. I could be kinder to him.

"Absolutely," Patrick's face lightened. "Absolutely. I'll get Kyle on it. He's probably already on it."

Patrick wasn't looking for kindness right now.

"The press will be coming, and we need to be ready with a statement. Have to get a promo for the next book in that statement. Hint at the death as a connection to his research."

I was surprised. "Do you think so?"

"No, I don't." Patrick stopped in the lane, momentarily, glanced at me and then continued walking. "I think the woman who drove him and left in a hurry might know something about it. A bit of a bastard with women, our Oliver. But the press can swarm all over Oliver's last research site and give us free publicity. That's Cornwall. Your tour to Cornwall—it starts tomorrow?" He stopped in the lane at my gate and was quiet for a moment. "I could go to Cornwall next weekend—if the police let me. I realize I'm a suspect as well as everyone at the party, but there will be hell to pay at the office this week, and Hanson will be on my neck. It will be my fault, as far as he's concerned. I'll need to get away."

Patrick opened my gate and waited while Gulliver and I went through.

"Cornwall would be a good excuse. In fact, Cornwall will demand my presence what with all the press hoopla. We'll need a promotion event there anyway. TV, press, the works. We could even put a video on line. *Blake in Smuggler's Cove* is set in Cornwall, in the caves around Fowey. It's about smuggling drugs into those caves and then out through a distribution system into the London area. Pure fiction. I don't suppose Oliver met any smugglers, although his research was impeccable. We might play that up. Kyle will have ideas. We can both go down to Cornwall."

My first reaction would be to avoid him if I saw him in Cornwall. But my tourists would find even peripheral involvement in a murder fascinating *and* they would be interested in a publisher. I reconsidered.

"Would you like to give a talk, perhaps at the library in Penzance about publishing?"

He stared at me, blinking a little. "Sure. The library. Paid for by the National Arts Council?"

"If I can persuade the librarian."

"Maybe get Kyle to video it. Could put it on the website. Lots of blitz, media attention, get the book out quickly. It might work."

I left him with his brain buzzing with ways to make money. I waved a goodbye and closed and locked my gate. I must remember to keep it locked. We didn't get much foot traffic along this lane and almost no vehicle traffic. Nevertheless, I locked it. Someone from the party may have murdered Oliver Nott, but it hadn't seemed to occur to anyone that the murderer might have come and gone through the lane gate. The killer might be anyone.

CHAPTER TWO

I knew Deirdre was either interviewing a client in her office, arguing with the desk clerk at the jail, prosecuting in court or preparing documents for court, but I needed to talk to her.

"What's up?" My sister's voice is curt when she is busy.

"Sorry. I have a murder," I said matter-of-factly.

"What?"

"Do you have five minutes?"

"I have six minutes, then I'm due to meet my client. I'm starting a murder trial tomorrow that should run for two weeks. I'm packing a lot into today. Talk fast."

"My neighbor Patrick came over this morning to report one of his party guests died. Apparently, he died sometime in the night, but they just discovered his body in the garden this morning."

"And it's murder?"

"There's a knife sticking out of his chest." I remembered that knife—incongruous, grotesque.

"Uh. Oh. And you are involved why? Did you know him?" She sounded censorious.

"No, I didn't. I didn't *ask* to nose into this, Dierdre. Patrick thought I was 'sane' and he wanted someone sane to be a witness to what he saw and did." I was defensive.

"Implying no one else was sane?"

She flung questions at me so quickly I felt I was under some kind of cross examination.

"That's right. They'd been drinking and doing drugs. Patrick was fairly clear-headed himself but didn't trust anyone else."

"There is no question of the police blaming you?"

"I don't think so." That hadn't occurred to me. "Why would they?"

"Trust me. The law picks some strange scapegoats. Are you all right?"

I took a deep breath. "Yes, I think so. It was just startling."

13

Deirdre murmured, "It would be." She rattled off more questions.

"Are the police there yet?"

"Just a local constable," I said.

"Not Mark?"

"The constable was going to inform Major Crimes Investigations, but there's no guarantee Mark will be assigned this case. "

I heard the alarm on her computer ring. She had her life divided into fifteen-minute segments. Her client was waiting.

Deirdre said, "I have to go. Let me know what happens and if there is anything I can do."

"Thanks. Good luck with your case."

"I'm going to need it."

I heard the weariness in her voice. She didn't sound like that often. The evidence against her client must be substantial. My sister, nine years younger than I, was brilliant. If there was a chance for her client, Deirdre would find it. I shed the big-sister-must-protect attitude toward younger sisters quite some time ago, probably because Deirdre could deal with almost anything. I left home when she was nine when my reliable step-father came into the family. My mum could relax, my sister could choose any profession she wanted, and I could leave for a life on my own to travel as a teacher with *Executive English and Etiquette*. Bless my step-father Paul. I appreciated him then and even more now. When he died earlier this year, he left me a fortune which Deirdre didn't want to share. She said she was happy, didn't need my money and wanted me to enjoy it. She was a remarkable woman, and I cherished her in my life. I did feel better just having told her about Oliver. I blinked. I hadn't told Deirdre it was Oliver Nott who had died. She'd want to know because she read his books. She said she enjoyed the procedural aspect of the mystery. We differed there. I didn't like his books. No character development. I'd email her as soon as I could.

I poured coffee into a thermos, gathered my jacket, gloves, hat and scarf. The October sunshine held little warmth, but it was comforting, and I wanted to get out into the countryside and that sunshine.

"Gulliver, let's leave before the Press arrives. For sure, either Patrick or Kyle will call them. It's almost parasitic the way they want to capitalize on Oliver's murder. I suppose their minds just run along advertising lines."

Gulliver stood alert, staring at the leash in my hand. He didn't care what I said as long as he was going for a walk. I snapped on the leash and led him out the front door, locking it behind me.

"No one seems to care about Oliver over there. Not personally," I muttered and headed toward the river and the path to the hills.

I heard a car move slowly along the street as I started down the hill. Press, most likely, or the police. I had my mobile with me. If the police wanted me, they could call.

Gulliver trotted to keep up with me as I crossed the bridge over the River Tinch and strode up the other side. Only then, did I feel my shoulders relax. I slowed my walk to an easier pace.

I passed Robert Andrews' clinic, *Riverside Animal Hospital*. He and I often walked with our dogs on Sundays. Since I arrived three months ago, he had introduced me to many dog-friendly paths, historical sites and parks. Today, he was off to London to visit his daughter where Sarah was a student at the university. Gulliver and I were alone on this walk, and it felt wonderful. A slight breeze from the river cooled me as I reached the lookout half-way up. There was no bench there, but a handy stone wall. I banged the wall, as I had seen Sarah do, to disturb any snakes that might surprise me. I waited. No snakes. I released Gulliver from his leash and sat on the stones. Gulliver was much more reliable on recall than he had been and I was reasonably sure that he would come on command. I wouldn't let him out of my sight, though. I poured the strong coffee into the thermos lid and noticed the steam in the cool air. I'd ordered the coffee beans from Seattle—the place that makes the best. It was a habit from my years of working there. The odor was blissful: strong and spicy. I sipped and looked over the Downs, keeping an eye on Gulliver and let the peace of the Hampshire countryside slide into my bones.

We were just off a rutted farm track that led along the side of the hill and up toward more hills beyond. In front of me, the tall grass, brown and dry, rustled a little, still showing green near the soil. Fields fell away to the river below. Willows draped elegant, pale yellow fronds into the river on both sides. Beyond the river lay farmers' fields and woodland. Out there somewhere, Robert had raced to save a calf one morning and Sarah and I had sat on this wall while she told me of her ambitions. The landscape stimulated my memory. I was starting to become like one of those willows, sending roots into the neighborhood.

Ashton-on-Tinch was a large village, close to London where I could take in a show or meet friends, close to my sister and her family in Guildford and close to Heathrow Airport where I collected my tourists. Five clients would be here on Wednesday. I hoped they would be congenial, but I was pragmatic about that. There was usually one who annoyed the group. It's almost inevitable in the business. I enjoyed the challenge of that one dissident and felt as though I'd earned my money when I metaphorically patted them on the back and sent them home at the end of the tour. We were going to be two weeks this time in Cornwall, looking at the sites of mystery writers Carola Dunn, Jeanne Dams, Veronica Black and Janie Bolitho. Now Oliver Nott. Most of my clients wanted to explore the world of cozy mysteries, not thrillers, but because Oliver's murder would be in the press, I would include some references to his books. I'd have to buy a copy and have it available to them, and I'd have to reread at least one. The bright side was that, according to Patrick, the last one was set in a cave. I could make sure my tourists saw a smuggler's cave. I'd already scheduled a trip with a tour guide in the area to explore an old clandestine cave where nineteenth century smugglers ran their business. That would tie in well with the client's need to see something of Nott's world. I finished the coffee and chastised myself. I was as bad as Patrick and his ad man, making capital on Oliver's murder.

Murder seemed distant from this pastoral scene. I rolled my shoulders and casually let my eyes wander. Oh, oh. Where was Gulliver? I had a moment of panic when I couldn't spot him, then saw a splash of white wiggling in the grass near a stone wall below me some twenty yards away. That was too great a distance for him to respond to a "come" command. I slid off the fence and started toward him. His tail quivered like a flag, indicating his position. When I was ten yards from him, I called the command. He lifted his head, stared at me and bounced through the grass to my feet.

"Good boy." I rewarded him with a small piece of dried liver and clipped on his leash.

"Let's go home and hope that the press has come and gone."

We were walking along the river when my mobile chimed. I checked the identifier: Mark.

"What's this I hear about murder?" were his first words.

"Hello Mark. Nice to hear from you. It *is* a lovely day."

"Claire, what's going on?"

I gave up trying to talk to my friend and responded to the police officer. "Did you get the call to investigate Oliver Nott's murder?"

"I did. Of course, I did. I investigated the last murder in your peaceful Ashton-on-Tinch, so naturally the Super gave me this one. What's going on? Your name appears on the message that came to me."

"The man died in Patrick Stonning's garden, and he asked me to come over and view the remains."

"Why?" Mark's brain clicked along in a logical path.

"Why did he die in the garden? Or, why did Patrick ask me to come over?"

I didn't know why both Deirdre and Mark thought it strange that Patrick would ask me to be supportive. I'm a sensible and level-headed neighbor. Why wouldn't he ask me?

"Claire!"

I thought about it and tried to explain. "He didn't trust anyone left from the party to be a credible witness."

Mark was silent for a moment. "And?"

"And he thought I would have influence with the police."

"What kind of influence?"

"You know, the usual 'If I sleep with you, you won't prosecute me or my friends' type of influence. He doesn't have his facts right, but I suppose he's seen you coming and going."

He was silent for a moment and then drawled, "Any chance of testing that theory?"

I laughed. "Not today."

"I'm coming over." His voice was abrupt.

He can switch from friend to an official so fast it takes my breath away. "It would be lovely to see you. Who's coming? My friend or the Detective Inspector?"

There was a moment of silence. "Both."

"Right you are," I said. "See you soon. I'll put the coffee on." I might as well accept he was both friend and officer.

I was home and had the coffee on when I got another phone call. This one from a man called George Baker.

"I saw on the Internet that you are offering a tour of Cornwall to the sites of mystery writers."

"That's right."

"Are you going to the site of Oliver Nott's books?"

He must have heard about Oliver's death. I imagined it was all over social media, no doubt tweeted out by Patrick and Kyle.

"Yes, we will be going to the caves around Fowey."

"Do you have room for one more?"

I had five booked. I would rather have six people than five. Five could be awkward, and six made it more lucrative for me.

"Yes, I can take you." I hoped he would be congenial. At least, he sounded like a mystery fan and that gave him a common interest with the others. He agreed to the rates as well as the single supplement, as I would have to get another room for him.

I was on my mobile, arranging that, when Mark arrived. I waved him toward the coffee pot and finished my conversation. I felt a little irritation toward him, but he couldn't help acting like a detective. The lingering resentment didn't stop me from appreciating his dark, thick, curly hair or his compact build. He wasn't tall, just a few inches taller than me, and he was stocky. I imagined him on the rugby field. I'm sure he must have played at some point in his life. Those shoulders would demand it.

He had his coffee and was seated at the table when I disconnected, satisfied that George Baker was now part of my tour.

"Business is good?"

I nodded. "Just filled up this tour to Cornwall. "

"When does it start?"

"Wednesday."

Mark took a long swig of coffee. He likes my Seattle brand. I sat with him and waited.

"A murder," he said. "Next door."

"I never heard a thing."

He stared at me.

I reconsidered "Except a car leaving in a hurry about three a.m.," I said, inexplicably remembering that fact.

Mark pulled out his tablet. "Direction?"

"No idea."

"Anything else?"

"Nothing. Patrick came to get me about nine in the morning. I stayed at his place for a few minutes until the constable arrived."

"Patrick is next on my list for an interview. I left a constable on guard."

"Pemberthy?"

"No. Wilson. Cst Wilson. The coroner's officer will come with the rest of the team in about a half-hour."

I knew that the coroner's office had to be informed if there was any question of murder. Their job was to establish an investigation, but not actually do it, and to liaise with family.

"You'd better grab Patrick quickly. He and his advertising man, Kyle, are planning to capitalize on all the publicity this murder is going to generate. They will be hobnobbing with the press and tweeting to the wide, wide world of the Internet."

Mark looked thoughtful. "We will have the press down here soon. Patrick will likely stick around to be interviewed by them."

My doorbell rattled and crashed.

Mark rolled his eyes. "Get a new one."

"It's unique. I might keep it."

Cst Pemberthy was at the door. He was as tall and imposing as I recalled from this morning in his black uniform with vest and the accoutrements of the trade bristling around him, adding width to an already large frame. He looked as fierce as an Alsatian. I almost expected him to bark, but he was soft-spoken and polite.

"Good morning, madam. I brought your statement for your signature."

"That was nice of you. Come in. D. I. Mark Evans is here. Have you met?"

I hoped he'd already reported to Mark. He certainly should have.

"Uh, no, I was going to contact him today."

Mark had followed me into the hall and stood waiting. They were a contrast. Cst Pemberthy was about six inches taller than Mark, twenty years younger and had half Mark's confidence.

"I'm Constable Pemberthy," he said, standing at attention.

"Mark Evans, D.I.," Mark said as he reached out to shake the constable's hand.

"Good morning, sir."

"Did you come to give me a report?" The constable looked at me quickly and then back at Mark. "Yes, sir, and to ask Ms. Barclay for her signature on her statement."

I would bet my brand-new pair of Bruno Magli's that he had no idea Mark was at my house but realized he *should* have sought him out.

I acted as the hostess. "Would you like coffee?"

Again, he glanced at Mark as if asking permission.

"Yes, join us," Mark said. "I just got here, and you might as well grab a coffee while you can."

"Thank you." The constable lumbered along behind me.

I poured another cup and sat down. I took the typed statement from Cst Pemberthy and read it while Mark asked questions.

The biggest question in my mind and one Mark didn't ask was: Why hadn't the constable called him earlier?

It must have been on the constable's mind as well, because he addressed it immediately.

"I'm sorry, sir. I wanted to call you when I got back to the nick this morning, but the Super said my report had to go through channels, and I haven't got the release to talk to you yet."

"Owen's your superintendent?"

"Yes, sir."

"A stickler, that Owen."

"Yes sir, he is that. Although," he hesitated, "he says going by the rules saves time in the long run."

"Sometimes."

Not this time, though. Obviously, the sooner Mark got all the details, the better.

"What do you have for me?"

Cst Pemberthy glanced at me.

Mark shook his head. "It's all right. I'll vouch for her."

"Well, sir, I have here..."

Mark interrupted him.

"Call me Mark," he said. "What's your given name?"

The constable looked straight at him. "David."

"Claire," I said.

David smiled. He lost a little of that tense, I'm-in-over-my-head look.

"Okay, David. What do you have?"

David pulled out a typed report and spread it on the table. "I have a guest list from Rita Stonning and telephone numbers. She didn't have everyone's phone number."

"I hope you told her not to contact friends for the phone numbers of the others."

"Yes, sir... Mark. I did tell her that." He shot a sideways glance at me, but I wasn't giving him away. He had stopped her, after all.

"I took fingerprints from the knife, but I didn't remove it. The autopsy surgeon will do that. I have measurements of the position of the chair he was sitting in, and I took fingerprints off the table in case the murderer leaned on it, and I took photos."

"Good idea."

"I've got everything together, sir,... Mark."

It was going to be some time before David Pemberthy was comfortable enough to get past "sir," if he ever did.

"But my Superintendent wants everything sent through official channels."

"He would," Mark said.

David hesitated, then pulled more papers from inside his vest. "I made copies."

Mark grinned. "Good man." He reached for them. "Anything else?"

"I don't know the next of kin," David said. "Sorry about that. I didn't think to ask when I was there."

"I've got it. A man named Harris Nott. Nephew."

David was quiet for a moment and then took a huge breath.

"Sir, could I be seconded to you for this case?"

I imagined David Pemberthy had an ambition to be a detective. Or, he might just want to get away from the punctilious Superintendent Owen.

Mark took a moment to consider this. He had told me that his department was temporarily short two men, one of them his sergeant. He must feel handicapped by that loss. I couldn't see David Pemberthy doing the work of Mark's sergeant, but he'd at least be some help.

"Great idea. I'll ask for you. They might not lend you full-time, but they might part with you half-time. Two detectives in our unit are both away. One's sick and one's on a course."

"Good opportunity for me." David Pemberthy beamed.

It was easy to respond to his genuine enthusiasm, but he was young, inexperienced and probably not much help.

Mark smiled in response. "I hope you're going to appreciate it in a week or so. "Did you take any prints off his clothing?"

David froze. "No, sir."

"Best do that. Check first to see if the SOCO team got them."

"Yes, sir. Right away. I'll let you know."

"If we can clear it with Owen and my department, you can interview this Harris Nott."

"I can?"

"I can't be in two places at once. You can do the preliminary interview with him. Let's go over what we need to know."

I sat quietly, listening to Mark take David through a list of questions. All logical and important.

"I talked to Oliver Nott's solicitor this morning on the phone. He read me the will. Harris Nott benefits greatly," Mark said. "So, this interview is important. If you think he's holding something back, don't push. Just let me know. I'll have to interview him later. Cover the ground and get the basic info."

"Such as where he was yesterday?"

"For sure," Mark said. "Find out his present occupation, his financial situation if you can without upsetting everyone and his need for this legacy. The amount is considerable. Oliver Nott was making a lot of money from those books, and he owned property—a flat in Guildford and a cottage in Cornwall."

"More money to come, I assume, when this new book comes out," I offered. "They are going to really promote it."

Both looked at me, storing that information away.

Mark turned back to David. "Call me when you have the info. The sooner, the better. I have a sergeant I've pulled from a different constabulary who will start the preliminary interviews with everyone on the guest list, but we're all part of the team. We'll meet this afternoon, five o'clock at your nick and pool our information. Arrange an incident room if you can. Call me immediately if you have information you think can't wait until five."

"Anything else, sir?"

"I've got a constable guarding the place, but he'll return to your station after the team takes the body to the morgue. Patrick Stonning will likely want to have a press conference, and we can let that happen, but we need to keep the press out of the house. He can do the press conference on the stoop. I want them away from the crime scene in the garden, and I don't want them coming over here."

"They might come around the lane," I said." They could take pictures over the fence."

Mark groaned. "How many people can the constabulary give us?"

"Just the one, I guess. The auxiliary police might help us."

"Can you ask?"

"I can ask." David said.

"Good."

I signed my statement and handed it back to David. Mark intercepted it, and we sat in silence while he read it. He nodded and handed it over to David.

"All right. So far so good. Here's my card. Send documents officially but call me if you have any questions or any ideas. I'll be at the nick at five. Meet me then. I think the press will be around for a couple of days. We might just need a police car out front periodically tomorrow. The press doesn't usually stay anywhere long."

"Low budgets at the newspapers and TV stations?" David suggested.

"That's right."

I saw David to the door and returned to find Mark standing, ready to leave.

"You know what this means?" he said to me.

"What?"

"We are both going to have to read Oliver Nott just in case there is any connection between his novels and his murder."

"We should read the new one, then," I said. "The one that is presently in manuscript form at the publisher's."

"Good idea. Do you like his work?"

"Not particularly. But I only read the first one."

Mark thought about it. "I like procedurals, but his have too much improbable action to be believable. I'll ask for that manuscript though and make you a copy."

"Ask for any maps or research material as well."

He agreed to do that, kissed me briefly and was gone. I heard a van pull up. The rest of the team, I supposed, ready to exam Patrick's home and garden.

I let Gulliver into my garden for a quick pee. I did not look over the fence into Patrick's yard. Then I wandered off to my study.

I called the librarian in Penzance. Two minor miracles occurred. She was working on Sunday and I was put through to her on the first try.

"The publisher of the Oliver Nott mysteries? Sure. My public here will be thrilled. They all think they can write just as well as Nott, and some of them who are self-published are quite sure they are going to gather pounds and pence by the truckloads. They'd love to talk to a publisher."

"What about an honorarium for him?" I've found people are more likely to fulfil commitments if they're getting paid, even a small amount. I didn't want to make all the arrangements and have Patrick neglect to show up.

"I have a National Arts Fund I can tap for a small one."

"Thanks, that would help. What day?"

We arranged the day and the time. I just had to be sure to get my group of tourists there. They should be delighted to partake of an authentic Cornwall experience that involved mysteries and the book business.

I disconnected as my doorbell crashed again. This time it was Patrick. I glanced behind him but didn't see any press cars or reporters. The police van and Mark's car were parked on the street.

"Come in."

"I've had the police at my place all morning," Patrick started complaining as he crossed the threshold and continued the complaints as he followed me into my kitchen.

"Coffee?" I would have to make more.

"No thanks. I'm coffeed up." He leaned on the door jam. "The morgue guys came and took Oliver away. That was a relief. I had Rita crying all morning, so no help from her."

I stared at him. Perhaps, Rita was the only one in that household who had any feelings. "That's too bad." I had a sudden tug of empathy for Rita. Someone should care about her.

"Well, yeah. She knew him best because she was his editor. I guess I should make allowances."

I studied him. Didn't he have any compassion? "Come on, Patrick."

"I might be more supportive?"

I nodded. "You might."

"I suppose." It wasn't much compassion and it didn't last long.

"Kyle and Alexandra are working—at least trying to amidst all the comings and goings. We have to organize a high-class promotional blitz. Kyle's on it. It'll make his career. Hanson was thinking of cutting back on sales staff and ad guys, but not now. Kyle will do a good job, too. We need him in the company. Hanson's getting too old to make decisions like this. "

Patrick paced in front of my kitchen window. I sat and waited for him to wind down.

"We've got press coming in about an hour. I thought I'd let you know in case you want to talk to them."

"No, Patrick I do not. I will be out. Thanks for the warning."

"No problem. We'll handle it all. We're going to go to Cornwall on the weekend. Maybe we can get some of those press guys to show up there. Kyle will have a videocam and good cameras for stills. We want to get something up on Facebook and on our website as soon as we can."

I worked hard at not letting my distaste show. It's not that I blamed Patrick for making the most of Oliver's death to sell Oliver's books, he just seemed to be doing it without any regard for anyone else. Relatives, for instance. The nephew Mark mentioned might not like all this promotion. Then again, he might. It wasn't my problem. My tour was.

"I've just spoken to the librarian in Penzance. She would be happy to have you speak to her library users on Saturday afternoon. Her honorarium is low, but it's National Arts Fund money, and that's always low."

Patrick shrugged. "That's fine. I'll be there. I can talk up the new book to the locals."

"My tourists will be there as well."

"Uh, good. They're international. Kyle, can take pictures."

"Not of my clients. Not without their permission." I wasn't having one of my clients sue me for transgression of privacy.

"Oh, okay. They'll be lots of other picture ops."

He paced another circuit of my kitchen and stopped near the hallway. I eased him toward the front door. He moved in that direction, down the hall, then stopped.

"Your garden gate is locked. I tried to come that way."

"And it's staying locked. Someone around here is a murderer."

"Oh yeah. Right. Makes sense."

I piled Gulliver into the van and drove to Basingstoke for a late and desperately needed lunch. I had a lovely crisp Viognier with it. Gulliver lay at my feet. Bless English pubs for their acceptance of dogs. I texted Mark. "Patrick is coming to Cornwall on Saturday with a film crew."

I got his reply quickly.

"I'll be there."

CHAPTER THREE

Ileft Gulliver home in the evening and attended a choir recital at the local church. It was peaceful, tranquil and just what I needed. The last rays of the sun lit the rose window, dappling soft primary colors over the congregation. The music was Vivaldi's *Gloria*. Lovely.

I went to bed determined to jiggle my life back to normal.

Monday morning brought Rose Jones, my weekly cleaner—right on schedule and normal for her.

"Such a to-do," Rose said as she arrived. "Hello, beautiful." She petted Gulliver, making it clear who was beautiful.

"A murder, right next door. That's a dreadful thing." She shut the door behind her and continued to speak. Her eyes sparkled, with excitement and curiosity. She could say it was 'dreadful,' but she acted as if it were entertainment

She was the mother of two and the hard-working wife of Frank Jones, local bricklayer. She saw the world as one huge soap opera. Deirdre had hired her as a housewarming present for me, which had annoyed me at the time, but Rose was so efficient at her job that I'd hate to be without her. She cleaned my house as if it were a hospital. Every bit of Gulliver's silky hair was hunted down and eliminated. The down-side was, she talked while she did it.

"An author, so my mother said."

Her mother would know. She was the postmistress. She paid attention to letters, parcels, purchases and gossip. There wasn't much she didn't know about the villagers and not much she kept private.

"Yes, that's right," I said. "Oliver Nott, the author."

"Did you hear anything when the murder happened? Shots in the night? Sirens?"

"Not a thing," I said, inaccurately. I had heard a car leave.

Rose hung her jacket in the closet, petted Gulliver again and marched toward the cupboard under the stairs. She hauled out the vacuum cleaner, incessantly talking.

"Drugs. I bet it's drugs. Those people party every time they're down here with artists, authors, those types. Drugs. I'm sure of it."

I wondered why she was sure of something she couldn't possibly prove.

"I don't think so, Rose. They use drugs, I grant you, but I don't think they sell them, deal them or are part of any gang."

"You wouldn't know. You don't do that stuff yourself."

Did she check my drawers? How did she know that?

She continued. "They're city types. Used to wheeling and dealing. Probably bring people down here to get them hooked. I've seen the stories on TV."

That was her last word on the subject as she disappeared up the stairs.

Peter Brown knocked on the kitchen door. He is my plumber and weekly gardener. In this village, I've discovered, many people had two jobs, or three.

"Morning," he said.

"Good morning."

"Got bulbs. Invoice." He shoved a paper in my face.

"Come in, Peter."

He came as far as the kitchen-door mat.

I glanced at the invoice. "Bulbs" I said, reaching for my purse and my check book. Peter bought what the garden required, paid for it and then billed me. At some point, I might want to take control of planning the garden myself, but I am such a new householder that I didn't trust myself with garden decisions—yet.

I wrote out the check for the bulbs as well as the check for the three hours he would spend putting them in my garden. "What kind of bulbs?"

"Daffs. Some tulips. Violets for that shady spot above the drains. Violet plants, not bulbs."

He had dug out my drains in September, replaced the tiles, then covered them up with soil. I expected the violets were going there.

"What colors?"

"The violets?" he asked.

"I assume the violets will be violet."

"White. The violets are white."

"Tulips?"

He just shrugged. Either he didn't remember, or he didn't want to discuss it. I'd find out in the spring when they bloomed. When I talked with Peter, I spoke in short sentences. I couldn't help it. It was as if I was compelled to match his speech patterns.

Rose walked into the kitchen, ostensibly to pick up a roll of paper towels. "You heard about the murder, Peter?"

"No one from here," Peter said.

"No, a city guy. An author, my mum says."

"No doubt true, then."

"Poisoned, then stabbed. Gory. Blood everywhere."

"No," Peter said before I could correct her. "You got that wrong. No blood. Nephew's the ambulance."

I knew his nephew was not the ambulance. He was likely an ambulance attendant, but Peter's parsimonious speech gave me some odd mental pictures. I kept out of the argument. If they knew I'd seen the body, they'd want to know all the details—and then they'd embellish them.

"Who do you think did it?" Rose asked.

Peter shrugged. "Probably that Patrick. Full of nerves, that one. Shaky."

I filled out Rose's check and stuffed it in the pottery vase on the table. She'd take it when she left. I inched toward the hall and my study, while Rose continued to speculate.

"It wasn't Rita. She's that upset."

That caught my attention.

Rose continued. "The only one who has an ounce of feeling in her. I hear she's been crying. Taking on all the sorrow in the house, no doubt."

I escaped into my study. I'd be safe there until Rose finished with the upstairs.

I answered fourteen emails and made the necessary small adjustments to the tour that a demand for 'a real cave' and at least 'one elaborate meal' required. The cave was already arranged, but I upgraded the reservations for one of the meals.

My mobile rang. Deirdre.

"Felled by a virus," Deirdre pronounced before I could even say 'hello.'

"You're sick?"

"No. I'm not."

"What are you talking about?" Were the kids sick?

"The judge of my murder trial is home with the 'flu. The trial has been postponed until March on next year's docket. I'll have to spend an extra week next spring updating my info. It throws everything out.

Judges are not allowed to get sick. The client is angry. My clerk here is biting his nails as it upsets his schedule. I'm just tired."

"Deirdre, I'm sorry." It must be like getting ready for a complicated tour and having Heathrow close down for a strike. "But, doesn't that mean you have some free time?"

"Yes. That's why I'm calling. How would you feel about Kala and me joining your tour to Cornwall?"

I wasn't sure how I felt about it. Kala is nine. Would she be interested in the tour?   Undoubtedly, as we were going to the seaside and that's endlessly fascinating to everyone, including nine-year-olds.

"Sure. I'd like that. What about accommodation? How long would you like to join the tour? The whole two weeks? Do you want me to send the itinerary?"

She answered the last question first. "Send me the itinerary. I'll bring my own vehicle and make my own hotel arrangements. I'll be bringing the dogs, too. We can take Gulliver with us when it's easier for you to leave him behind, and we can do independent excursions when there'd be too many people for what you have planned, but we could join some of the time. I'll have to suss out the B & Bs that take dogs."

"I can give you a list of those. I had to do that as well." Typically, Deirdre had thought out many details. "You've already planned this?"

"Someone has to." Her voice rose in pitch.

There it was again, a frisson of resentment. She and Michael were having problems. I was sure of it. I spoke calmly. "I'd love to have you and Kala."

"Good, I'm thinking we'll come on Thursday and leave on Sunday. That way Kala just misses two days of school. Josh has football. Michael can look after him. They won't be with us. It will be good for Kala to be the only one for a change. And good for Josh to have one-on-one with his father."

She sounded as if she had to strictly adhere to a plan or the world would spin out of control. If I said "No, don't come." Deirdre might shatter like one of those fragile Christmas ornaments that disintegrates into tiny pieces.

She could relax at the seaside and, perhaps, slow to the pace of normal people. But then, she lived a fast pace most of the time. She might not appreciate slow. I tried to remember what she had been like over the years I visited with her when I returned to England between my jobs. But we usually had only a few days, and she always tried to have time off her work then. She'd been relaxed. Now, she seemed a speed version of herself as if the fates had pressed her into "fast-forward" mode.

I had just slid the disconnect bar over when my mobile rang again. This time it was Patrick.

"You have to come over. Rita's crazy. Not herself. She won't stop...."

"Patrick, slow down. What's going on?"

"It's Rita. She's crying, and she won't stop. Like it's not normal." His usual fast speech was even faster, and I had to concentrate to understand him.

"Did you call a doctor?"

There was silence for a moment. "This is England. I can't get a doctor to even come to the phone."

"Or to the house, I take it."

"Of course not. And she won't go to the clinic. So come on over...."

There was silence while I let his peremptory command hang on the air. He was upset. I'd have to allow for that.

"Claire. I don't know what to do. Would you *please* come over and talk to her?"

I imagined Rita sitting alone and crying. She would need someone sympathetic. "Yes, I'll come."

I grabbed my jacket, Gulliver's leash and Gulliver and headed out the front door.

"I'll be gone for a while," I said to Rose. She didn't want Gulliver in the house without me when she was cleaning because he followed her around.

I saw a cleaning van parked on the street, labelled "Todd's Quick and Clean" on the side panel. Of course, the house had to be cleaned as soon as the police allowed. The Major Investigations Team's van had left about nine last night, but a police car was parked on the street this morning.

Patrick met me at the door, stooped to pat Gulliver and then ushered me in.

"Bring the dog. Rita will want to see him."

Todd's workers must have started in the hall. The floors shone. There were no piles of papers or debris. I could hear dishes clattering from the kitchen. Patrick ignored the activity in the back of the house.

He led me toward the stairs, talking as we went. "The police are searching everywhere, every bush, plant, and tree for Oliver's mobile."

I wondered if that sergeant Mark hoped to get from another district had set some constables on the job. Investigating murder was a complicated logistics problem, involving the Major Investigation Team, local bobbies, seconded officers, shift changes and overtime pay.

"I don't know why it matters. I expect they think the murderer took it and it might contain a phone number they want."

"Or a text," I said.

"I have Oliver's number, and they've been trying to phone his mobile. So far, no tree has started ringing."

"They think the murderer stabbed him and took his mobile?" I asked. "You'd think he wouldn't have taken the time to search for it. After all, someone might have come out and seen him at any minute."

"It was probably on the table in front of him. He hated fishing in his pockets for it and often had it out. Left it behind a lot, too. He might not even have had it with him."

"Was anything else missing?" I was curious.

We were walking along an upstairs hall now, carpet underfoot and lovely paintings on the wall. I would like to take more time to view them some day.

"Nothing. He wore a gold coin on a chain around his neck, and that was still there. He said it was from the nineteenth century smugglers' treasure, but ten to one, it wasn't even gold, just something anyone could buy in a souvenir shop in Cornwall. I didn't argue with him. You picked your fights with Oliver, and I didn't care about the coin. It might have been a promotional piece, and I wouldn't have discouraged that."

We stopped outside a door. Patrick knocked, and opened the door as he did so.

"Rita, I brought Claire." He stepped aside to let me enter the room then backed out into the hall. He shut the door and left me and Gulliver inside with Rita.

The room was elegant: pale green with white drapes, white carpet and splashes of coral in the lampshades and on an upholstered chair. A dressing room door stood wide, and I could see another room where Rita presumably dressed from the row of clothes hanging there and from whatever was in those many drawers. I expect Patrick slept in this room as well, as this house isn't any bigger than mine and the dressing room took up the space occupied by my second bedroom. I saw a pair of men's shoes by the door and a man's dressing gown hanging on a hook. Other than those signs, this was my lady's boudoir.

Rita was propped against some pillows, a box of tissues beside her and wadded tissues all over the bed.

Her long blonde hair looked dull; her eyes so red from crying that the blue looked dull as well. She was dressed in her usual leggings, tunic top, but with a warm hoodie over it.

"Hello," she said weakly.

I sat on the bed. "Gulliver's with me."

Rita brightened a little. "Hello, Gulliver. Can he come up on the bed?"

I nodded. Rita patted the bed, and Gulliver jumped up. He immediately snuggled up to Rita and licked her face.

She pressed her cheek to Gulliver's neck and petted him. "Hello sweetie. You're a good dog. That's a good boy."

Gulliver takes adulation as his due and wiggled even more to get closer to her.

"Do you want to tell me about it?" I wasn't sure she did want to talk, but I was here and I was ready to listen.

Rita glanced at the door.

I got up and tested that it was shut then returned to the bed.

Rita sat back and absently petted Gulliver.

"It's awful."

I nodded.

"He wasn't old, you know. Only fifty."

"Not old at all," I agreed.

"He had so much to live for. Who could *do* this?"

"I have no idea," I murmured. At least, it sounded as though *she* hadn't stabbed him. I relaxed a little.

She stroked Gulliver a few times and then looked straight at me.

"Oliver and I were lovers."

Oh, crikey. I hadn't seen that coming. There wasn't much I could say.

"I guess the tense is past perfect: *had been* lovers."

I nodded. They had been. They no longer were. Got it.

"We'd been close for about two years. I knew it wouldn't last. I'd been his editor for ten years. I knew what he was like: faithful while he was with his current lover but only for about a year, then he moved on to someone else—male or female. He was more comfortable with women, but he liked the excitement of a man. He had come off a homosexual relationship with a poet when he honed in on me. I was flattered."

I said nothing. This was what was behind her grief, unless she had killed him and this was remorse.

She took a deep breath and looked at me. "I *did* know it wouldn't last. Believe me. His history was against it. I wasn't exciting enough for him, although conducting an affair under Patrick's eyes aroused him. But to really make him stay involved, he wanted me to tell Patrick and keep on with the affair. It was a power thing, I guess, but that was nasty. Without that added stimulation, he said, the affair was boring and he was through with me. I couldn't do that to Patrick. I knew Oliver was going to leave and, yet, I wasn't prepared for it. It shouldn't be so hard when you're prepared for it."

"It would be hard any way it happened."

It would have been painful and messy, at least for Rita. Some relationships start with a "best-before" date as part of the plan. Rita wasn't seventeen. She knew most affairs were temporary. I wondered at her severe reaction. Perhaps it was more about finding his body than about his rejection of her. Teasing out her feelings was beyond me. In any case, I wasn't required to say anything.

She kept talking, as if once started, she couldn't stop herself.

"He broke it off. Just told me one day that it was over."

That would be harsh. "When was this?"

"September 16th. A month ago."

"I see." She remembered the date the way some people remember the date of a disaster or a death.

"And then he told Patrick that he was going to leave the company. I felt responsible, but I couldn't tell Patrick about our affair. I just couldn't. Oliver wanted to leave me and leave the company. He's a big seller with us. It would hurt us, maybe even bankrupt us. I was stupid and confused about what to do. I should never have put the company in jeopardy like that. But you know, he was charming sometimes, witty and interested in what I thought and ...." Her voice trailed away.

"Seductive," I prompted.

"Yes, very. He said I wasn't strong enough. He needed someone stronger."

Why would she believe him? He wasn't the least bit trustworthy. She knew that. "Rita, you said he usually went to someone else after a year."

"Yes."

"You were with him for two."

"Yes."

"He said he needed someone stronger? He might have said he wanted someone weaker, someone who relied on him more. I imagine he had a cupboard full of reasons to break off a relationship. You didn't have to believe him."

"Oh" she looked straight at me again, considering what I had said. "True."

She had stopped crying which was good sign. She petted Gulliver while we sat in silence.

Then she sighed. "I need advice, and you seem to be practical."

I hoped, I really hoped she wasn't going to confess to murdering Oliver or helping Patrick to murder Oliver.

"Oliver had told Patrick at the party that he was going to leave our company. Patrick was incensed but…. Don't think I suspect Patrick of killing Oliver. He just couldn't. But he was angry and left Oliver alone. There were a lot of people coming and going all night. I was busy. You know how it is. Is there enough ice? Did anyone leave anything burning: joints, matches, cigarettes? Should I refill the coffee urn? You know how it is?" she repeated.

I haven't given a party in years, but I could imagine it.

"I didn't go to bed, just dozed a little on the couch in the lounge, but in the morning, I made myself some fresh coffee and walked out into the garden to have it in the sunshine. Oliver was there. He was dead. I felt for a pulse. Nothing." She shuddered. "It was horrible. And his mobile was on the table." She blinked back tears. "I took it."

She took it. That's where the mobile was. She didn't kill him to get it. She took it after he was dead. Or so she said.

"Why?"

"It has my number on it and my texts. I couldn't have that. I deleted my texts, but the police are looking for the phone."

I didn't tell her that the police could reconstruct those texts if they got their tech department on the phone. However, they might not bother and just pay attention to the ones they could see.

"What should I do? I was thinking of throwing it into the garden. Or saying I found it in a couch in the lounge."

I stared at her for a moment. "Think about when you picked it up from the table."

Her eyes flicked up to the right and then back to me.

I continued. "Pretend this part of the bed is the table. The phone is right here." I put my own phone on the bed. "Just exactly how did you pick it up?"

Slowly, Rita moved Gulliver to the side and leaned forward. She put her left hand on the bed and picked up the phone with her right hand and then shoved the phone into her pocket.

I held out my hand, and she returned my phone.

"You are going to have to go to the police and tell the truth." I was definite about that.

"Why?"

"You leaned on the table. Your fingerprints will be there."

Her eyes rolled back. She was going to faint. Oh, dear heart! I had no idea what to do with someone who fainted. I frantically tried to review my first aid instructions.

"Rita!" I said sharply "Stay with me. Don't faint." The first aid instructions had disappeared from my memory. She *couldn't* faint.

She closed her eyes and gulped. "Okay. Okay. I'm okay." She grabbed Gulliver and hugged him. He squirmed and she released him. She took a few deep breaths, then said, "This is a mess. I'm going to be a suspect."

I agreed. "Bound to be, but there are many suspects." I was breathing a little more easily. She no longer looked as though she was going to escape into unconsciousness.

"What should I do?"

"Either call the police to come here or go to the station and give them the mobile. Tell them you were shocked and didn't realize how important the phone might be, but you realize it now. They will take your fingerprints then."

"Ugh."

"But they would want them at some point, simply because you were here last night. They will be collecting everyone's. Make virtue out of a necessity and give it to them."

"All right." She was calmer and swung her feet off the bed. Gulliver jumped down.

Rita moved to her bathroom, continuing to talk to me as she washed her face and put on some make up.

"Thanks for coming over. It's easier to figure out what to do when someone listens."

"Can you get away to the station?"

She brushed her hair and clipped it back with a barrette. "I'll tell Patrick we need groceries, and I'll get some. He's not the suspicious sort." She gave me a wry smile. "I should know."

"I'll talk to him for a few minutes and let you get away."

So, that's what we did.

"Thanks for coming Claire," Patrick said as I stood at the door. "I seem to be calling on you a little too often, but thanks."

"Rita was just shocked, I think. She was winding down by the time I got here. Gulliver seemed to help."

He looked at Gulliver and leaned down to pet him. He was good with Gulliver: calm and affectionate.

"Maybe we should get a dog."

Maybe he should think about giving Rita some of that affection. I didn't say that. He wasn't asking me for advice.

"Tell me about Oliver Nott, Patrick. What was he like?" I wondered what had been happening in his life that provoked someone to murder him.

"He was a bastard, really. But he could write. I think he saw himself as another Hemmingway. He wasn't that good, but he could rip out a book every six months, and it would sell. We had him for ten years and got him consistently on the best-sell list for thrillers and procedurals. He was meticulous, you know, in his background checks. Always got that right. No one wrote to point out an error of fact, and that happens all the time in most publishing houses. He'd even make us stop when a book was ready for printing while he checked a fact that might have changed since he researched it. Picky. Really picky."

"How did he keep track of all that research?" I imagined him recording bit of information on a small computer. I was wrong.

"Wrote it all down in a notebook. Snippets of information, but all the references accurately detailed. Drove editors crazy because they had to search through his notes to find the precise information. He was seldom wrong, but editors, like Rita, had to check. He was professionally reliable."

"And personally?"

"No family. Always had some lover around. Not the last year or so, but usually."

Rita might be right. Patrick hadn't known about her relationship with Oliver.

"He had a nephew. He inherits. Oliver told me about that. He left a copy of his will in our safe at work. Sad, really. No parents left. No siblings. His sister died last year, leaving just the nephew." He was quiet for a moment. "He worked hard and fast. We are going to miss him."

"He was going to go to another publisher?" Would Patrick have murdered him to prevent that?

"He threatened to go to Maxman and Brown. They were offering more money. We'd have matched it. We knew he was going to ask, so he was going to get his increase. He was just playing with Maxman & Brown."

He smiled a little sadly and looked older, a little thinner and tired. He sighed. "Now we have twenty books already published, one ready for release, and one in the proposal stage that we can get someone else to write." He brightened. "We'll hype this last book and that will increase the sales of all of them."

"You'll make money on his death."

He sent me a sharp look. "Not as much as we would have made if he continued writing for another twenty years."

I didn't go home but took Gulliver on a brisk walk around the village. We stopped at the small park near the village center. Gulliver stared intently at the ducks, swimming out of reach on the pond. I looked around for an empty bench. Rita was sitting on one, as immobile as one of those statues on the park benches in Norway. They startled me when I first saw them, as if someone left a body in the park to supervise the birds. Rita turned and watched me approach.

"Can we join you?"

She nodded.

"Hi, Gulliver." She petted him, glanced at me and smiled a little. "I did it. I handed the phone in and talked to the police."

She pulled her woolen shawl closer around her shoulders. "I'm glad I did, and I told them everything. About the affair and everything."

I was surprised. I'd thought she'd just admit to taking the mobile, not to anything else. I sat beside her.

"The officer was really nice. I thought I might as well get it all out." She smiled at me. She did look a little calmer.

"Who did you talk to?"

She looked at me. She was an editor, after all. I corrected my grammar. "To whom did you speak?"

"A Detective Inspector. Some Welsh name."

"Evans?"

"Yes, that's it, do you know him?"

I nodded.

"Oh," she said with recognition. "is he your....?"

"My friend, yes."

"Well he's nice. Kind. So that's over, and now I can mourn."

Not openly, she couldn't. Not unless she was going to tell Patrick all about it, and I didn't think she was cruel.

"That's good."

"No one will mourn him, you know."

"His nephew?"

"They never saw each other. He was his only relative, but they didn't meet." She pleated the edge of her shawl with nervous fingers.

"His fans will miss him." He was a celebrity, after all.

"Lots of people will miss him, but no one will think the world is less bright, less interesting, less loving because he isn't here. I will."

I reached over and took her hand. His death mattered to her. She was wounded. We sat there for a long time while she looked over the pond and bid her lover goodbye.

CHAPTER FOUR

I was up early, took Gulliver for a walk and was ready to drive to Heathrow when my doorbell clamoured.

Two women, one smartly dressed in a charcoal-gray, tweed pant suit with a crisp white blouse and the other in jeans, a hoodie with an adorable Yorkshire terrier in her arms like a furry muff.

"I'm Mrs. James Malkin," the suit said.

"Hello. I'm Tansey Finn-Smyth. And this is Poppet." The dog-clad woman held up the Yorkie.

"Hello, Tansey and Poppet." I smiled at her. It was hard not to. She exuded friendliness. I made myself turn back to the tall, imperious woman in tweed.

"Mrs. Malkin. Are you James' wife?"

"I am. I am Pamela Malkin. We drove down to talk to you about this ridiculous will of Paul's."

Uh. Oh. Paul had left me his money and James and Harold, his sons, had made an effort to divest me of it. Now, the wives had arrived. No doubt to try the same thing.

Gulliver chose that moment to peek around my legs and notice Poppet. He barked.

Tansey dropped to her knees on the doorstep and cooed at Gulliver. "Aren't you a lovey. Hello. What's your name?"

"Gulliver," I answered for him.

"Tansey," Pamela all but hissed. "Get up. We are here on business."

"Dogs are my business," Tansey insisted, and stayed kneeling in front of Gulliver.

I grinned at her. "Why don't you come in. I'm sorry. I am due at the airport shortly so I can't offer you refreshments or much of my time."

"We have driven quite a way to talk to you." Pamela was indignant.

I was unmoved. "Perhaps you could call ahead another time."

I ushered them into my parlor and sat. Poppet and Gulliver sniffed each other under the watchful eye of Tansey.

"Is it all right to give Gulliver a treat?" Tansey asked me.

"Absolutely," I said. I was a little overwhelmed by these two. Pamela was what I'd expected the wife of James right up to the diamonds on her fingers and her Alexander Wang boots with silver studs. Tansey was a surprise. She wore a plain wedding ring and trainers. I wondered what Harold was like. I might even like him.

Pamela launched into her pitch immediately. "James and I have two children as you well know. Both are in good schools and both will require a lot of financial support until they attain their degrees."

I assumed she thought I should support them. That didn't seem enough reason to do so.

"Do you have children, Tansey?" I switched my attention to her.

She looked up from the floor where she was playing with the dogs. "No, I have dogs."

"How many?"

"Five, right now. Three permanently, and two training for owners."

"What are you training for?" Tansey sounded a lot more interesting than Pamela, although I hadn't given any effort to getting to know James or his wife.

"I show dogs and ..."

"Tansey!" Pamela said, her voice as sharp as glass. "Forget your dogs for one minute. This is important!"

Tansey sent a smile my way and an apology to her sister-in-law. "Of course, Pamela."

Pamela turned back to me. "I am sure you know that Paul's will was immoral."

I stared at her. "It's legal." Immoral? What did she mean?

"Yes," she sounded exasperated. "Yes. I know. We have looked into that thoroughly. But it isn't *fair*!"

"To whom?"

"To James and his family."

Here we go again. I did not want to have this argument for years. "I think it is. Paul explained all that in the will. James had a good start and lots of money from Paul. He wanted me to have the rest—and I'm keeping it." I stood. "I have to leave for the airport now."

Tansey scrambled to her feet. "Do you need any help training Gulliver? He is such a beauty."

"I might." Tansey could be someone I'd like to be around.

"Here's my card," Tansey pressed a business car into my hand. "You call me and I can tell you a bit about socializing him and getting him started in basic obedience."

I escorted the two women to the front door. Pamela hovered beside Tansey and interrupted her.

"Claire, you must reconsider. James and I have many expenses and we need Paul's money. It is unconscionable for you to keep it all."

I thought of the section in Paul's letter sent to me after he died. He had written: Do not be tempted to share any of it with my sons. They have had more than their share of my wealth and they are not easy to deal with.

He was right about that. James was not easy to deal with. Nor was Pamela. But Tansey was another story. She didn't seem to be the least bit interested in the legacy.

"Goodbye, ladies," I said and shut the door on them. At first, I felt triumphant. I had bested Pamela. I wasn't afraid of her. She wasn't as threatening as her husband had been, but she left me feeling disturbed as if I wasn't quite measuring up in the compassionate category. Was I being selfish? Should I share? I hadn't listened to Pamela long enough to find out if she was in real financial need. I might get an opinion from Tansey about that. I still might not do anything about it, but I could inquire.

It took me a few moments to settle Gulliver but I finally got into my van and headed for Heathrow.

Odd, that. I hadn't expected James to send his wife to importune me. She was easier to get out of the house than James had been. I shuddered, remembering the petty violence of the man. Pamela, even with her arrogant attitude, was preferable to James.

I drove to Heathrow against the traffic as the commuters were leaving London. The overseas flight my clients had booked wouldn't arrive until the late afternoon. They were flying from Portland, Oregon, to Vancouver, Canada, and then over the pole to Heathrow. I was to meet them at 4:30 p.m. at the Arrival Pod in Terminal 3. If their British Airways flight from Vancouver was on time and there were no problems with security, I could whisk them away quickly. I am always prepared for snarled traffic, belligerent security guards, unexpected strikes by workers and flight delays. None of that happened today.

I pulled into my commercial standby parking allotment. I paid a yearly fee for the convenience of parking in a limo space. It was essential in keeping clients happy and my temper calm. Because I could park relatively close to the terminal, there were no long treks to the van and no lining up to pay at a toll booth. My new seven-passenger van gave me a possessive thrill with its leather-scented interior and its gleaming silver coat. I'd driven vans for years, but they had been owned or leased by my last employers. This one was mine, owned by *British Mystery Book Tours*, my company. I patted the wing as I left it in its privileged spot.

I had a few moments so I speed-dialed my sister Deirdre. With luck, she would be between clients. She was.

"The Malkin ladies visited me today," I said with preamble.

"Hi, Claire. Did they? James and Harold wives?"

"Yes."

"Were they threatening?"

"Pamela was, but Tansey was not. What happened with James' charge of vandalism?" James had slashed the tires of my rented van when I refused to give him money and Deirdre had used the might of her law office to encourage the police to charge him.

"The video evidence wasn't clear enough, so the charge was dismissed. It might have served to deter him, nevertheless. Are you all right?"

"Yes, surprisingly fine. I think Pamela could be nasty, but I felt a little sorry for her."

"Watch that," Deirdre said.

I laughed and clicked off.

I checked on the arrivals board as I entered Heathrow to find that the flight had landed on time—a good way to start the tour. Four of the women were arriving on this flight. The fifth, Professor J. L. Prior, would meet us here. She must have taken a different flight. She'd given me her home address as Seattle, Washington, and her occupation as a professor of English Literature. She hadn't told me what airline she was using.

The four women off this flight were easy to spot—all over 65, talking to each other and gazing around, no doubt looking for me. The tallest one, an impressive Black woman with grey hair shorn close to her head, caught my eye, nodded and spoke to the others. That must be Ellie Armstrong, a retired high school English teacher. Another, like Professor Prior, who might have knowledge for the rest of us.

"Welcome to England," I said as they approached, "and to the British Mystery Book Tours."

"Lovely to be here," said a slightly plump woman, with large brown eyes. She smiled. "I'm Holly Ormstead."

Holly Ormstead was a retired hairdresser from Portland, Oregon.

I reached for the luggage and started to pile it on the first of the two porter carts I'd managed to grab. One of the women, dressed in jeans, shirt and quilted jacket, reached for the other.

"Sharon," she said. She had grey hair, braided and wound in a cornet on her head. Sharp blue eyes inspected me.

"Claire," I responded. This must be the rancher from the southern interior of Oregon.

"I'm Grace," a white-haired woman moved up beside Sharon and smiled at me. She wasn't tall, but imposing, as if she had an inner authority.

My impressions were often lightning fast and could be wrong. My goal was to distinguish them one from another as quickly as I could.

Introductions were dropped in favor of getting all the luggage piled onto the carts. A fifth woman came up to me as I bent over the luggage. "Claire Barclay?" She inquired.

I straightened. "Professor Prior. How nice to see you." She was much younger than the Oregonians, nearer my age, and dressed flamboyantly in a multicolored jacket with a purple scarf floating around her shoulders. She had her own porter's cart and fell in line, nodding to the others. I led the way out of the terminal but stopped in front of the cloakroom and gestured.

"Ladies," I said.

"Bless you," Ellie said and four disappeared through the archway. Professor Prior stayed with me.

"Thanks for finding me," I said. "I know I have your mobile number, but you saved a lot of time by showing up quickly."

"It wasn't hard. You gave me the BA flight numbers."

We smiled at one another. She recognized I had to be careful of time, and I appreciated that she knew how to accommodate others. She might fit in well on this trip.

"Have you been here long?" I asked.

"I've been in England a week, but I wanted to meet you at the airport. The trains to the airport are convenient, and it saves a lot of trouble."

I hadn't realized she'd come to England early. "To quote our new friend, Ellie, Bless you. It can be difficult trying to meet in the city. Have you been to London before?"

"Several times. This time I had work to do there. I have a three-month sabbatical from the University of Washington to research my book on Mary Wesley. I still need to do some work in the National Library, although I expect to find more in the library in Penzance."

"I don't remember much about her. She lived in Cornwall, didn't she?"

"For quite a bit of her life, yes, but she was in and out of London during the war and survived the blitz. She worked for M16." M16 was the intelligence service. Mary Wesley sounded as if she'd been quite a character. I'd heard of her but couldn't remember any information.

"Did she? And she was a writer?" I asked.

"Yes, she started writing in earnest at age 71."

I was intrigued. I'd have to hear more about this author.

The ladies returned, and we hustled out the doors to my van. This time, I'd left Gulliver at home. Rita promised to take him for a walk and feed him his supper. If I had a chance, I'd introduce the ladies to him tonight on the way to the B & B and trust no one would mind him accompanying us to Cornwall.

Once everyone was inside, the luggage stowed and seat belts buckled, I introduced Professor Prior to the others.

"Lena," she said. "I'm Lena."

Her name didn't suit her. I thought of swans and ballet, for some reason. That was Leda. Lena was not particularly graceful, but strong-looking with luxurious, wavy brown hair, brown eyes and an athletic body. Not a Lena in my mind.

I addressed everyone in the van.

"Would you like to go to your B & B to freshen up before we go to dinner, or would you like to go straight to dinner? I've picked a comfortable restaurant near Basingstoke—which isn't far."

I started the van and moved out into light traffic.

The ladies murmured among themselves.

"We'll go to dinner," Sharon said. "We might not want to leave our B & B once we see a bed."

I understood that. These four had been en route for about fourteen hours.

"That's what we will do, then. I hope you like the Hoddington Arms. It's in the village of Upton Grey and has a fabulous menu."

"I, for one," Holly Ormstead said, "am looking forward to making decisions about food and drink and nothing else for two weeks." I suppose she had worked hard all her life, and, as a hairdresser, on her feet. She might enjoy being pampered in her retirement. I remembered the information on her booking form. She was interested in the way the characters in Carola Dunn's mysteries are intricately part of the landscape they inhabit. I'd have to be sure to point out the similarities of Port Isaac where we were going and the Port Mabyn of Dunn's novels.

The women talked among themselves, politely including Professor Prior, and seemed relaxed by the time I pulled up to the Hoddington Arms where I had reserved a table.

We settled like chickens roosting, fluffing out our bags, scarves, coats, and various papers. The waiter passed out menus, and everyone gave serious consideration to the choices.

"One of the reasons I chose this restaurant," I told the women, "is that it has quite a few Cornish dishes."

"I see that," Ellie said. "Some of them I've never heard of. What's a Cornish cod goujons?"

I thought back to my life in Seattle, looking for a comparison. "Fish nuggets," I finally said. "Strips of cod, deep fried."

"Ah."

"And what is 'crushed pink fur heritage potatoes?'" Sharon asked. "It sounds like it was once some kind of animal before it was crushed."

Ellie's eyebrows rose, and she looked more closely at the menu.

"'Pink fur' is a type of potato. As you might expect, it is much like a red potato in the States, but I think it has more flavor. There are many types of potatoes here in England. One close relative is the pink apple potato. My favorite is Mr. Little's Yethom Gypsy."

They stared at me as they absorbed the information.

"Do they taste different?" Grace asked.

"They do," I affirmed.

"I'll have to try as many as I can," Sharon said. "Potatoes are one of my favorite foods."

"'What I say is that, if a fellow really likes potatoes, he must be a pretty decent sort of fellow.'" Grace intoned.

Sharon laughed. "Who said that? Dickens?"

"A.A. Milne."

Grace had retired from owning a bookstore, she knew about books and remembered them.

"'Seared venison loin,'" Holly murmured as if chanting a prayer, "'with slow braised mini pie, salt baked celeriac, celeriac puree, red cabbage, toasted hazelnuts and venison jus.' It's poetry." She beamed at us.

"Go for it, Holly," Ellie encouraged her. "I'll be just as decadent with the 'honey roasted Creddy Carver duck breast with lentils, smoked bacon, mixed wild mushrooms, cep sauce and crisp mushroom croquette.'" She put her menu down and looked at me. "I'm going to order it anyway, but what is Creddy Carver duck?"

"It's the name of the farm where the duck was raised. It has a good reputation." I studied the menus before I brought my clients to a restaurant. There were usually items they hadn't encountered before, even bangers and mash which is common in England.

"Got that. What's cep sauce?" Ellie asked.

"Mushroom sauce."

"Thanks. You're as good as Google"

I laughed. The ladies placed their orders for drinks and food and, once the drinks were served, sat back and chatted. I noticed Holly had ordered tonic water. Perhaps she didn't drink alcohol.

"I have an itinerary for each of you, but I thought I'd pass it out when we get to the coffee stage. We are going, as you know, north to the Tintagel area, then south to Penzance and then on to Fowey, then back to Penzance where you will catch the train to Heathrow."

They nodded. I had sent them a tentative itinerary by email.

"We'll have one more person on the trip. George Baker is a last-minute addition. He is from London. You might find it interesting to talk to someone here who reads mysteries as well. I have booked you all into the B & B. That means Holly and Grace share a room, and Sharon and Ellie share a room. Lena you have your own room, and George will have his. I realize that often on a tour those who register as singles are thrown together whether they want to be or not, but I hope that this group will see that everyone mixes."

Ellie looked amused. "I'm happy to mix."

I looked at her brown skin, thought about some areas of America, and suspected irony. I smiled with appreciation. She was going to be interesting.

Sharon grunted. "We're grownups," she said.

I was embarrassed. "I'm sorry, Sharon. I didn't mean to imply that you wouldn't be gracious."

"That *is* what you implied, so what *did* you mean?"

There was silence as they stared at me, waiting for an answer. Had I treated them as children? Was she right?

"I meant I didn't want Lena to be always partnered with George." I hoped that explanation would satisfy here. I hadn't meant to offend.

"Unless I want to be," Lena said with a wicked smile.

"I guess you'll let me know if that is a problem."

"I will."

"Is everyone okay with this?"

"Sure. We didn't hire an exclusive tour. We're democratic. He can come." Grace made the pronouncement.

Whew! These women were powerful. I might as well get all my requests over with at once.

"I have another small change." I said.

They watched me.

"My sister Deirdre would like to join us at Port Isaac for a few days."

"And she will add to the tour in what way?" Grace asked.

"My sister is a barrister. You might like to ask her about the British judicial system. She is, of course, very knowledgeable. She just had a murder trial postponed, so she has some time."

"Ah, she's right in the thick of it then," Holly said.

"She's looking for some time off and thought she'd like to see some of the places we're going. She'll be bringing my niece with her. They have their own accommodation, and I can use her vehicle when we get to Port Isaac. We can walk the trail from Port Isaac to Tintagel along the coast and, because Deirdre can drive her car, we only have to walk one way."

"Already she has benefits," Ellie said.

"Yeah. No problem," Sharon spoke for the group.

I was relieved. I'd ask about Gulliver accompanying us later.

The waiter passed out another round of drinks for the women. I joined Holly in a glass of tonic water. I was driving.

The food arrived and was as delicious as I'd hoped. I had the twice-baked Keens Cheddar soufflé. Wonderful. I passed on dessert, but Holly and Ellie shared a sticky toffee pudding, and Sharon had her own Rhubarb and Custard Crumble with ice cream.

"I've never had rhubarb ripple ice cream before. I wonder if I can make it?" she said.

We had coffee, decaf all around, and I passed out the itineraries. There were comments.

"It looks," Grace said, 'like we are going to be walking from Port Isaac to Tintagel with a stop at Port Gavone for lunch."

I nodded.

"This is Eleanor Trewynn country. Particularly that novel where her niece jumps into the sea to rescue the kid," Sharon said.

Ellie pulled her tablet from her bag and scrolled down a list. "*The Valley of the Shadow*," she announced.

"I liked that one," Sharon said.

"If the landscape is as she described it," Grace offered, "it should be spectacular, although I'd prefer it to be sunny, and the ocean to be calm."

"The forecast looks good," I said.

"I see we are going to Fowey," Grace continued. "I don't know anything about it. Who set their novels there?"

"L. A. Kent is a thriller writer from Fowey and that is the setting Daphne du Maurier used," I said.

"Oh, yes. I should have remembered her," she said. "You pronounced it Foy."

I nodded.

"Interesting. I'm really looking forward to the Port Isaac section of the tour," Grace said. "I can stretch my legs, enjoy the scenery and remember the intrepid Eleanor Trewynn."

I paid the bill and assured the host that I would be back with more clients. He nodded and subtracted ten percent. I would definitely be back.

It was a twenty-minute drive from the restaurant to Aston-on-Tinch. As we approached the village, I thought it a good time to orientate the women to where I would be. I didn't live far from their B & B.

"Would you like to drive by my house? It's only a block out of the way."

"Sure," Grace said, "but then I'm ready for my bed."

I turned down my street and slowed down in front of the house.

"That's mine," I said with certain pride. Even in the dark, the garden light showed the charming brick and flint with paned windows. "It's a semi-detached which you might describe as a duplex"

"Who lives next door," Lena said from behind me.

"The Stonnings. They've had a…" I hesitated. "A spot of bother."

"What kind of bother?" Lena was insistent.

"Someone died there on Sunday."

"Who?" Holly asked.

"Oliver Nott," I admitted.

"That's been all over the Internet. Murder, wasn't it? And next door to you? Well, that's fascinating. Do you think we can find out more about it?" Holly was a mystery fan, after all.

"Perhaps," I equivocated. Mark would be furious if I brought five or six interested onlookers to his investigation.

"Do you live alone?" Ellie asked politely.

"With my dog, Gulliver," I said. "I will bring him with us, if no one objects. He travels in his own crate and sleeps while I'm driving. Dogs can go everywhere in Cornwall. Is that okay?"

"I think so," Holly said. "If he isn't big and slobbery. Can we meet him?"

"Sure." I pulled over behind Mark's car. "If you'd like to wait, I'll bring him out to meet you. I'll be quick."

Gulliver was panting at the door. He had, no doubt, recognized my footsteps. I grabbed the leash which hung on the hook at hand, snapped it on and trotted him out to the car. I was proud of him. The white part of his coat gleamed and the sable colors just added striking accents. He tossed his head, stopped to mark a particularly fine piece of brick beside the walk, then approached the car.

"This is Gulliver," I said.

Holly opened her door and invited Gulliver in. He hopped into the van and almost pranced between the seats, accepting adulation from all the ladies.

"He's adorable," Holly said. "What is he?"

"A Cavalier King Charles Spaniel."

"You even have an English dog," Ellie said. "This is part of the British tour experience?"

"I hope so."

"I'm fine with having him with us," Lena said.

"Me too," echoed through the van.

"He can accompany us on the short drive to your B & B. I'll put him in the crate when we get there."

"I'll hold him," Holly offered.

I was about to pull away when someone knocked on my window. Mark. I buzzed my window down.

"Hello, Mark."

"Hi." he leaned in to kiss me and then realized I had a van full of women.

"Uh, hello, ladies."

Various "hellos" came from behind me and from Lena who was sitting beside me.

"This is Detective Inspector Mark Evans," I said.

"Welcome to England," Mark said.

There were muted "Thank yous".

"Claire," Mark said. "Where are you staying in Penzance?"

I told him.

"All right. See you there."

I pulled away and immediately felt a reserve, a kind of coldness coming from beside me and oozing up from the back of the van.

"What the matter?" I asked.

"The police," Ellie said. "Why did he stop you?"

I glanced in the rear-view mirror. I wondered if Ellie expected racism from the police here.

"He's investigating the murder next door. That's why he is here at this time." I waited a beat. "He is also my current significant other."

"Oh." There was a soft sigh from someone and a noticeable relaxation of the tension.

"So, he just wanted to see you," Lena asked.

"I think so. He might have been on his way home and spotted my van. He and his team have been here most of the day."

"Investigating a murder," Lena said.

"That's right."

"The murder of Oliver Nott." Lena, like many professors I have met, wanted her facts clear.

"That's right. They will solve it, I'm sure. They usually do. The case is getting some notoriety because Olive Nott was such a popular writer."

"Yes," Grace agreed. "Very popular, even in the States."

"You might be interested then, Grace, in the fact that Oliver had written a new mystery. It should be out soon. It's set in Cornwall, as his others have been. I thought I'd include some of that setting."

"That *would* be interesting," Grace said. "He's sells very well in my shop. Or did when I had it."

"When did you retire, Grace?" I asked.

"Two weeks ago."

I laughed. "You'll be very current then on authors and books."

"That's true."

I heard Lena take in a deep breath, but her tone was relaxed when she spoke.

"I'm interested in your detective," she said. "Is he local?"

"He's stationed in Alton, but he has been assigned to this case. He is a member of the Major Investigation Team."

"Is that CID?" Grace asked.

"The MIT is part of the Criminal Investigation Department, but they are the same officers."

"So, he's an interesting man?" Lena asked.

"He is," I admitted. "He sings," I said, and then I was embarrassed by my impulsive praise.

"Well, that confirms his eligibility," Lena teased. "I'm working through the writings of Mary Wesley and she had a pretty free attitude to sex. I think she had orgies at her place in Cornwall. You could give me some hints of modern attitudes to sex. What's yours?"

Six women in the car, full of good food and wine. Sex was bound to come up.

"Pretty cautious," I said. Compared to these women, I was beginning to think that what romantic activity I'd seen as sensible would look downright timid to them.

CHAPTER FIVE

I met George Baker at the Alton Railway Station the following morning. He had left London early, transferred at Woking, and arrived promptly at eight. Alton Station was a depressing place. The creamy stone walls plastered with notices and posters looked like a tattered poor relation of the bright, glass and steel stations of Europe. I knew the track-side opened up to a bigger, more open space, and the operational side of the station was efficient and useful. It just gave the over-all appearance of neglect. I couldn't park for long. I hoped he would be on time. If George Baker needed coffee, we'd stop on the way to Aston-on-Tinch.

I spotted him easily. There were five or six people disembarking, and he had to be the man, about fifty, over six-foot, heavy build, long leather jacket, jeans, trainers, no hat and trailing a small case. Everyone else had briefcases or shopping bags.

"Mr. Baker," I said as I approached him.

He stopped and nodded.

"I'm Claire Barclay. Can I help you with your bag?"

He thrust out his hand. We shook.

"No, I'm fine with it. Thanks for meeting me."

His voice was low and pleasing. He probably sang baritone if he sang. Mark had a beautiful voice, but then Mark was Welsh; it's in the genes. Listening to Mark made me more aware of the possibility of song in people's voices. Mr. Baker was definitely a baritone.

I introduced him to Gulliver who was in his crate at the back of the van.

George smiled. "Will he be coming with us?"

"Yes. Do you have any objection?"

"Not me. I like dogs."

That was a relief. One day, I'm going to find a tourist who hates dogs. It would be challenge but I could find a dog sitter for Gulliver for that trip.

"Have you been to Cornwall before, George?"

"I have," he said. "I spent a summer there with my parents when I was about twelve. It was magic."

I smiled. "It *is* magic. But you never returned?"

"No, life gets in the way, I married and we had a boy, and then my Eseld got very sick. We stayed home while she was dying."

"I'm sorry." Many people had tragedies in their lives.

"It was a long time ago. My boy and I, we went on trips, but mainly to the Lake district. We were both good fishermen."

I noted the past tense. "Your boy?"

"He died last month."

I felt a frisson of cold up my arms. I must be tuning into his grief. There was overwhelming sorrow in his voice.

"I'm so sorry," I said again.

"Yes. My Jason was a great reader, and he loved those books of Oliver Nott's. He wanted to come to Cornwall and see all those caves and the places where Nott said there were drug smugglers. Jason followed Notts research on his blog."

I was quiet for a moment. "He knew Nott wrote fiction. I mean he made up his plot lines."

"Yes, Jason knew that, but he thought Nott based it on fact."

"Kids always like caves and smugglers. They think it's romantic."

George looked out the window and didn't answer me.

"Would you like me to stop for coffee?"

"Please."

I spotted *The French Horn*, pulled into the parking lot, took George's order for one large with two sugars and no cream and returned quickly with his drink and my own.

Gulliver woofed, but settled quietly as soon as the van was in motion. We were close to the B & B where I had left the ladies last night when I spoke again.

"George, do you read mysteries?" I was beginning to wonder if this trip was an odyssey to Jason, a kind of testament to his son's interests.

"No, I don't. But Jason did."

I thought about that.

"George, the ladies on the tour are mystery readers. They will be talking about authors and books that take place in the settings and villages that we are going too. They might want to engage you on your knowledge of the authors they are referring too. You might want to let them know that this trip was planned with you and your son who just passed away. You are going ahead with the trip, as your son would want you to."

"Do you think so?" He looked thoughtful.

"It's up to you."

"Okay. We'll see."

I felt sorry for George Baker. I sympathized with his loss, but I wasn't sure how the group would respond to him or how his grief would affect the group.

He surprised me and was charming when he was introduced to the ladies at the B & B. Holly was at the table finishing her breakfast. I made the introductions. George had his French Horn coffee in hand and sat with Holly.

"Ellie and Grace have gone for a walk," Holly reported. "Sharon is catching up on her emails."

Sharon arrived just then and joined us.

"I came on this tour to get away from business but even now my husband has to email me to discuss business."

"What kind of business?" George asked. "I'm George, by the way."

"Sharon," They shook hands. "The wine business. I live in southern Oregon in the interior, near Ashland. Ever hear of it?"

George shook his head.

I'd heard of it, though. "There's a Shakespeare festival there."

"That's right. We're a sophisticated bunch," Sharon grinned, no doubt aware she did not present as sophisticated.

"Have you always been in the wine business?" George appeared interested.

"No, just the last fifteen years. Before that it was cattle. It's easier to prune vines than it is to castrate calves, but I miss the animals. We have a few horses around, and I ride every day to check out the vines. I still miss the excitement of chasing cows over the open fields."

"Is that the biggest difference?" I asked trying to imagine Sharon racing across the fields on a horse. It was surprisingly easy to see her doing that.

"No, the biggest difference is the hobnobbing I have to do with buyers. Can you imagine me in fancy dresses, making nice to restaurant owners and rich velophiles? When we were cattle ranchers, no one expected me to dress like something out of a magazine."

We stared at her.

"How do you do it?" I couldn't imagine her weighing the merits of sequins over appliques.

Sharon finished the last of her coffee and slapped the cup down. I feared for the china.

"I have a friend who owns a high-end dress shop. I tell her where I have to appear, and she gets the dress, the shoes, the bag, the scarf or coat. The works. I just go in and buy it."

Good for Sharon. That was sensible. She had to dress in haute couture to promote the business, so she did, but with minimum effort on her part.

"Did you bring any of those clothes?" I had an urgent desire to see Sharon, all stocky, five-foot-nine of her, in regal wear. She'd be magnificent.

"No fear. This holiday is for the real me."

She was wearing jeans, a long T-shirt, a hoodie and carried her quilted down jacket which was practical as it stuffed into a small package.

Ellie and Grace bustled through and promised to be with us in moments. I heard the wheels of a suitcase rattling on the tile floors of the foyer as Lena arrived.

"I'm not late?"

"No," I said. "We're just getting organized. This is George."

I watched Lena flutter her eyelashes at George. They were of an age, George perhaps five or six years older. Lena, no doubt, fluttered her eyelashes at every male she met, a kind of automatic response. Maybe, I could learn how to flirt. Maybe, I wouldn't bother. I'd just embarrass myself.

George nodded at her but did not seem unduly impressed. Ellie and Grace joined us and we headed out to the van.

"If everyone is agreeable, we'll start with Ellie in the front seat and the rest of you choosing any other place you'd like. After that, we will change every day so that you simply move one seat over as everyone rotates through the positions in the van."

"That will work."

"Suits me."

"You get better pictures in the front seat," Lena complained. "What if we want to take pictures, and we're stuck in the back?"

"Let me know, and I'll stop the van. You can get out to get the pictures." Lena may demand more attention than the others. I'd watch for that.

"Oh, all right," she acquiesced.

The group loaded the back of the van while I paid the proprietor for their stay. Everything but alcohol, tips and some meals were included in this tour.

I let Gulliver out for a short walk around the van and onto the grass nearby, and then we were off.

I'd put a small bag of goodies in each of their places containing a bottle of water, a key chain with the Hampshire flower, the dog rose, depicted on it, a packet of tissues and a small diary and pen. A murmur of "Thank yous" fluttered through the van and they settled down to watch the countryside.

I wanted to avoid the traffic around Winchester so headed north and joined the 303 motorway to Salisbury. It was about an hour-and-a-half drive. I let them talk to each other and enjoy the countryside for the first twenty minutes. I could see George in the back seat, leaning against the window. He was asleep. The ladies, in deference, kept their voices down. I had a lively, interested group. Even Lena Prior, who had an edge to her tongue and a critical eye, was lively. George's grief over his son was visible to us all. It might be hard to be respectful yet enjoy what was ahead. Only time would tell how it would work out. I would have to think how I would approach this with future group tours.

I was sorry to wake him, but we were not going to travel in silence. I put on my speaker and began an information session about forty minutes from Salisbury.

"Salisbury, as you know, is an ancient town. It started as the Iron Fort from, yes, the Iron Age, at Old Sarum. It became a Roman garrison and then a Medieval fortified city. The Medieval cathedral was built on the same promontory, but lower than the garrison. In time, it crowded the garrison and the monks moved it to the present site of Salisbury and built the iconic cathedral there. The town followed the monks and Old Sarum, eventually, became only an historic site."

"Isn't the Magna Carta there?" Ellie asked.

"In Salisbury Cathedral? Yes, it is."

"The basis of freedom and the rights of the people," she said.

"Yes, that's right." Democracy owed a great deal to the Magna Carta.

"We need another." Her voice was flat as if she had looked at the world and seen chaos.

"And the Doomsday book? I've been doing some reading," Holly said.

"Yes. King William commissioned an inventory of the lands and resources of his vast kingdom. Basically, he wanted a tally of his assets and that's the Doomsday book."

"In the eleventh century?" Lena said.

"Right," I said. "1086."

"He came from Normandy and conquered England in 1066. After twenty years he wanted to know what he had." Lena said. "Probably so he knew what to charge in taxes, right?"

"So I understand," I said.

"Such a fascinating city," Ellie said.

"And beautiful," Grace added.

George was awake now and leaned forward listening.

"Who are the mystery writers who use Salisbury as a setting?" Grace asked.

"Mary Wesley set *Harnessing Peacocks* in Salisbury. I know that's not a mystery but it's of interest to me." Lena said.

"Did she?" I was intrigued. "Do you have any places that are of particular interest?"

I caught Lena's shrug in the rear-view mirror. I expected she was miffed at not being able to sit in the front seat.

"I read John Creasey," George said almost apologetically. "He set *The Theft of the Magna Carta* there and another one. *The Missing* something."

"*Masters*," Grace said. "*The Missing Masters*."

"Yes, that's it. How do you remember all that?" George asked.

"I owned a bookstore." She was only two weeks retired. She likely had her inventory in her head.

"I see. Professional talent." George was showing interest. Good.

"Possibly." Grace beamed at him. "Ellis Peters set Brother Cadfael's *The Price of Light* right in the cathedral."

"Hah! Caught you!" Holly said. "That was the Shrewsbury Cathedral."

I interjected. "I think Jeanne Dams used Salisbury as the setting for her Dorothy Martin series although she called it Sherebury. It has similarities, and we could imagine her there in *The Body in the Transept* and *Trouble in Town Hall*." I wasn't sure of that fact, but I suspected Salisbury was her setting.

"I loved those," Holly said. "I'm going to check out the cathedral."

I pulled into Brown's Open-Air Carpark on the east side of the city center. Everyone disembarked. I let Gulliver out of his crate and snapped on his leash.

"We will meet in an hour-and-a-half at The New Inn. It's north of the cathedral." I pointed in the correct direction. Everyone stared at the cathedral. I stopped talking and let them enjoy the sight and gave myself a few moments to appreciate its beauty.

The spirals reached to heaven. There was really no other way to think about the grandeur of those spires. The smaller arches directed your eyes up to the lower spires and then up to the tallest one. It was as if the Medieval god of the architect had constructed a stairway to the heavens. The green verge, the close, was wide and substantial giving the impression that the cathedral was isolated from commerce.

I pointed out The King's House which housed the museum, the park, and, again, the restaurant where we would meet for lunch. Everyone left to explore the cathedral and the town on their own. They all had my mobile number. If they got lost, they could text me. It's happened. But I thought this group would manage to be at the restaurant on time.

Gulliver and I wandered through the streets of Salisbury. I loved the way the centuries had melded in the architecture with Tudor houses overhanging the street beside 1960s flat-faced, square apartment buildings. Jumbled together it all worked as a lively and tolerant overgrown village. The food market was central and there were many buyers picking out tonight's dinner. The stalls were protected by white awning high above them, and the tables were stacked with colorful carrots, red and green peppers, Brussel sprouts, deep purple aubergines, and green bunches of parsley. I bought some apples, red, fresh, and likely from Somerset and stored them in my rucksack.

Gulliver and I took the path to Queen Elizabeth Park. It's not far from the cathedral and gorgeous with its green lawns, water ways and woodlands. There were few people there, but I kept Gulliver on leash. I did not want to spend an hour looking for him if he decided there was a path than required investigation or a squirrel that demanded his attention.

We were back at The New Inn and Gulliver served with a bowl of water under the table in time to meet the others. I hoped they would appreciate the Tudor look of the pub: old beams with axe marks gouged in them, brick walls and wood-paneled bar. I had taken menus from the bar and passed them out as the group arrived.

"You have to order from the bar. This is one of the meals that I have not prepaid." The itinerary is clearly marked with the meals that I had prepaid and the ones I had not, but I reminded them.

"That cathedral is impressive," Grace said. "I can see why Ellis Peters wanted to use it in her books."

"Oh, look at this," Holly said enthusiastically," 'smoked salmon and crab fishcakes, tartar sauce, and skinny fries.' Are they guaranteed to make you skinny?" She looked at me, smiling.

"We can hope," I said.

She laughed. "What are they?"

"I think you'd call them 'shoestring fries.'"

"What does onion marmalade taste like?" Sharon leaned forward, curious.

George responded. "It sounds odd, but it's really good. They have it here on pork sausages. I'm going to have that. Should be great."

"Another time, perhaps." Sharon was polite. "I'll have the tartlet of tomato, feta, basil, spinach, roast squash puree and new potatoes—which I think is quiche."

"It is," I agreed.

They picked up their food and drinks and brought them to the table. With a minimum of fuss, they settled into eating and chatting.

The sun was shining, the pub was not full—October is off season for Salisbury. The group was talking among themselves and seemed reasonably content. George and Lena appeared to be equally fascinated by the architecture of the cathedral and Grace and Ellie by the people who might have worshiped there over the years. Once we had moved through the repast to the coffee stage, the talk turned to mysteries.

"I can see," Grace said, "why you think this is the prototype for the Dorothy Martin series. Although I think the cathedral in her stories is closer to the town's building, shoved right into the town. Here the cathedral is set apart."

"True." Trust Grace to know the details of Jeanne Dams' setting.

"How ethical is it for a writer to change the place?" George asked.

Grace cocked her head. "What do you mean 'ethical?"

"I know its fiction, but shouldn't a writer keep the city as it is?"

"If," Sharon said, "the writer is setting the story in Salisbury, for instance, I agree then he or she should keep the Cathedral where it is, the shops where they are, and the restaurants where they are. But, if the writer changes the name and only generally sets the characters in a city *like* Salisbury, then she can move the restaurants around as she likes."

"I'd agree," Ellie said, "but George has an interesting point. Do authors change things in their settings and do we resent it.?"

"We do," Holly said. "I do anyway. I resent it if the building they say is in the center of Portland is not there or if they say, there is a lake beside a hospital in Seattle and there isn't. It seems to be cheating, and I don't think it's necessary."

"Does that mean," George asked, "that when a writer sets a story in a place, and that place actually exists, say Penzance, then you expect that what he describes is real."

The women stopped to consider the question.

"I'd say so," Sharon stated.

"For most authors," Grace said.

I was relieved that George was making an attempt to fit into the interests of the group.

"Sometimes," Lena said. "truth is a matter of fiction."

George stared at her.

"I mean, sometimes fiction can reveal truth, particularly emotional truth."

"Like the way the author reveals her belief in justice because she makes the villain pay and the heroine triumph?" Ellie suggested.

George was truly interested. "Don't writers have a responsibility to support justice, and truth and decency? Supposing the writer thought it was interesting and exciting to use drugs. Would he have a responsibility to the readers, particularly young readers to make sure they knew it was dangerous."

There was silence for a moment while the women thought about it. I began to wonder if his son, Jason, had taken drugs.

"I don't think so," Ellie said. "He would have to assume that the readers could find out information about that from other sources. Writers of mysteries don't set out murder plot lines for readers to follow, like instructions."

"I think that's happened," Gracie said.

"But it wouldn't be the responsibility of the writer to avoid writing about murder in case some wingnut decided to copy his plan," Sharon asked.

"No," Ellie said.

"Or we would be back in the days when the only books that got published were the ones the dictator, the controlling government, or the pope decided the populace could read." Lena was emphatic.

"I have a librarian friend," Ellie said, "who says 'Every book in my library offends someone.' If you start controlling what's written, then you prevent creativity, innovation and revolution—and sometimes we need a revolution."

"But making drug use seem like a normal and easy thing to do is dangerous to kids." George was insistent.

"It is," Ellie said soothingly. "It is a big danger, yes. But censoring books is worse."

"It can't be worse."

"We'll have to agree to differ then," Ellie said. She turned to Lena and deliberately torqued the subject matter. "Would you say that an author who objects to multiple partners would make her villains unfaithful? Is that the way she reveals the truth about her own feelings, or would she just be revealing the truth the character sees?"

"That's hard to say," Lena said. "Mary Wesley's characters, for example, did not value fidelity. But then neither did Mary. She thought sexual experience was natural, normal and not restricted to one relationship."

"She had a lot of partners?"

"She had a lot." Lena smiled as if in approval of Wesley's life style.

"So, you would say her truth was that sexual freedom was valuable, and her heroines could indulge in it."

"As she did herself," Lena said.

"Uh," George said to me. "Would it be okay if I took Gulliver for a for walk."

I smiled at him. The women would discuss sex a lot more frankly without George at the table.

"Sure. We'll meet back here in twenty minutes."

"Right."

The women hardly noticed he was gone.

"Do you believe in it yourself Lena?" Holly asked.

"I believe in it more in the abstract than the particular," Lena, said a bit ruefully. "I've discovered that I like the idea of sexual license, but it's a bit messy. Even serial monogamy is difficult to handle emotionally. Somebody's going to get hurt."

"People get hurt in marriages too," Sharon said. "Nothing's perfect."

"But I have to say," Lena interjected, "Even Mary Wesley seems to have believed in romantic love, a magic meeting of minds and bodies."

I wondered where Lena's own belief in romantic love had led her.

"In some ways Mary Wesley used her own life and her own morality as a background to her novels. In research and non-fiction, we call that autobiographical research. You research your own life."

The women nodded. Lena gave us the plot lines to two of Mary Wesley's books. The women discussed them and said, all in all, they preferred mysteries.

CHAPTER SIX

We met Gulliver and George at the van and headed out to Old Sarum. It was two miles from Salisbury. I guided them through Old Sarum, an Iron Age hill fort and the original Salisbury settlement, in record time, and we were off to Lyme Regis. I took the A354 and turned south on the A35.

"It isn't possible," I said as I drove down to the waterfront at Lyme Regis, "to come to this part of the country without running into Jane Austen. This is the setting for *Persuasion* and that," I pointed to a stone breakwater that jutted out into the sea., "is the Cobb where Louisa fell."

George look supremely disinterested, but the women said they would walk out there.

"I'll take Gulliver," George said.

I nodded. "Yes, fine. A half-hour?"

They agreed to meet me in a half-hour which would give them time for a cloakroom break and a walk of some literary interest. I walked over to the Cobb Inn and picked up my pre-order of cheese, biscuits and some small cartons of juice. With the apples I'd bought at the Salisbury market, that should satisfy the group during the next section of driving. They were back in time and we started on the three-hour journey to Port Isaac. Most of the group were older. They might be tired and jet-lagged. The snack would help with fatigue. I was going to join the A30 which was a much bigger motorway and smoother than the roads we had been traveling on and with fewer turns. The van was comfortable. I didn't give any information along this stretch, and eventually, most of the group dozed. Grace was awake and paying attention to the road signs.

"I've never heard of a St. Clether," she said as we passed a directional sign.

"There are a lot of saints particular to Cornwall." I had never heard of most of them either. Certainly, not outside Cornwall.

She stayed alert and called them out to me softly so as not to wake the others. "St Breward? St Breock. Breock?'

I nodded. Before we reached our destination, she had collected St Issey, St Tudy and St Columb.

The others woke as the van slowed near the car park for Port Isaac. I'd texted from Lyme Regis and a small electric cart with driver was waiting for us. I'd booked us into the Slipway B & B which was right on the harbor. The streets of Port Isaac are too narrow and winding for me to navigate the van through them. The hotel had recently changed hands, and the proprietor had promised great service in an interesting location. It was an historic building, once used, of course, by smugglers and said to contain a ghost or two.

I shook hands with Zoe, the manager who looked to be about twenty-four, dark hair spiked in prongs, large round glasses, metal in her ears and bands on her teeth. She had a huge smile. She had arrived at the car park in a golf cart and bounced out of it to shake my hand.

"Welcome."

"Thanks. I'm Claire."

"Zoe. This is my cat, Alphonse." It was a shaggy, grey Persian-type that was in possession of the front seat and looked decidedly unfriendly. Possibly, he didn't like dogs.

"My dog," I said. "Gulliver."

"Welcome," she said again this time to the group who crowded in behind me.

"Isn't this where the Doc Martin series is set?" Grace stared down at the town.

"In and around here," I agreed.

"This is a bonus," Sharon said. "I like that show."

Zoe took out luggage on the cart and we walked down the winding lanes to the B & B. The cat, Alphonse, followed us, keeping about ten yards behind us. It was like having an escort.

There were eight rooms in this B & B, and we occupied seven of them. Deirdre and Kala would take the eighth. I'd reserved dinner for eight o'clock. Everyone had time to unload their luggage, freshen up, and even take a walk. That would likely be Ellie and Grace, perhaps Lena. Sharon would get into her email, and Holly might nap.

Holly surprised me. She came to me while I was talking to Zoe in the lobby.

"I'm off to explore the town," she said, "at least this small section of it."

"The whole town is small," Zoe, said." Be sure to check out the harbor and the Squeezy Belly Alley. Dinner is at eight," she reminded her.

"I'll take Gulliver for a walk," I said looking down at my patient dog.

Zoe raised her eyebrows, a feat that jiggled various pieces of metal. "There are towels in your room for the dog," she said. "The green ones. If you take him on the beach, he's going to get muddy and wet. No sand here. Just mud and pebbles."

No doubt, I would take him to the beach, even if there was mud. He loved the smells of the seaside.

"Your other guests are due soon?" she asked me.

I checked my mobile. Deirdre had texted from Salisbury.

"Yes, soon. They have two dogs."

"No problem."

Deirdre would be tired when she arrived. She'd sounded tired when I talked to her last night.

"Could you put a bottle of wine in her room—red, dry?"

"Sure, French?"

"Yes, or Chilean. She likes that too. Put it on my bill."

"And a soft drink for the child?"

"Good idea and perhaps some nuts or some kind of nibblies."

"I'll do that. Thanks for choosing to bring your group here."

I imagined it wasn't easy to make a living in such a small town, but it would be packed in the summer. They would have to make enough then to last the winter.

Gulliver and I walked out the front door of the Slipway, across the street and down to the quay. The tide was out. The smell of ozone and decaying matter reminded me of the rare childhood jaunts to the sea that my mother used to arrange with one of my aunts. As always, it was magical.

This shore was not inviting, as Zoe had said. There was too much mud. I kept Gulliver at the edge and walked through the town. I caught up with Holly who was peering in a window reading something.

"Did you know that the pier was built in the reign of Henry VIII?"

"No, I did not. What else does it say?" I asked her.

"That the name Port Isaac is taken from the Cornish words that mean Corn port. Imagine that. Here I thought I might be looking for signs of some historic hero I'd never heard of."

We walked slowly while Holly looked around her. She seemed a contented woman, just turned seventy according to her passport, and interested in people and new sights. She nodded across the street.

"Looks like Lena and George have something to talk about."

I followed her gaze and saw them leaning on a stone wall looking out of the harbor but talking. At least George was talking.

"Do you think she'll eat him alive?" Holly asked.

I considered it. "Maybe."

"Maybe not. Something's wrong with both of them. They might comfort each other."

"Do you think there's something wrong with Lena?" I knew George was mourning his son. Lena didn't seem to me to be upset about anything. But then, I didn't know her, and I hadn't spent fifty years listening to women tell me their emotional worries and joys the way Holly had. Hairdressing is a subset of psychology.

"Something's eating her, but George might help. They are the same generation."

"My generation too, but I'll leave them to it."

She glanced at me from the corner of her eye. "Burned once or twice?"

I nodded.

"Very foolish to let one asshole dictate your love life forever."

I felt my shoulders set and my neck go rigid. I took a deep breath. "I'm working on it."

"Good. Let that nice detective turf up your life a little. There's a fair chance he could do it."

I laughed. It was hard to be angry with Holly. She looked like everyone's favorite grandmother but didn't act the stereotype.

"Did you fall in love, Holly?"

"Oh, yes," she said, "many times."

Grace and Ellie strode down the street toward us and joined us in our walk back to the B & B.

"There is a marvelous view from the top of the hill there." Ellie pointed back the way they had come.

"It's the start of a trail. Is that the one we are taking tomorrow?" Grace asked.

"No, we are going north. There are many trails around here." I gestured to the hills around us.

Port Isaac was popular in the summer with hikers and walkers, and the National Trust kept the trails in good repair. This time of year, there were few braving the wind, sudden temperature drops and mist from the sea. Today was sunny, but sunshine was rare.

"Will we be two nights in Port Isaac?" Ellie asked.

"Yes, I'll go over the itinerary at dinner tonight".

"Good. I hope we get a long walk tomorrow. I'm looking forward to stretching my legs."

By the time we returned to the B & B, Deirdre had arrived and joined us for dinner.

"How was your trip?"

She looked tired, but not exhausted. Her dark curls were wet and plastered against her forehead. She must have taken a quick shower.

"Quiet and fast. Just the way I like it."

"Where's Kala?"

"She took the dogs for a quick run up to the car park and back. She'll be here in a jiffy."

Kala slipped into her chair just as Zoe passed out the menus. Zoe stopped behind Kala, leaned down, and whispered.

Kala looked up and smiled. She made my heart turn over. She looked exactly like Deirdre when she was nine: short dark hair, curling around her face, huge brown eyes and freckles over her nose.

Deirdre and Kala could leave behind their everyday lives and have a holiday, and I could pretend murder had not disrupted my life.

I smiled at Kala, then turned to the group. "The menu offers a lot of fresh fish, but Zoe is willing to get us hamburgers or steak if anyone would like that."

"Fish should be good here," Grace said.

"It looks delicious. I never get fish like this in Oregon." That was Sharon. She lived in the interior of the state. Those who lived in Portland certainly got fresh fish.

These women knew how to enjoy traveling. Take what the local people offer and see if you like it.

The women devastated the local fresh crab, mussels, and salmon. George devoured the Cornish Beef and Ale Pie. Kala steadily plowed through deep fried fish, chips and mushy peas. We faced dessert. I had eaten every bit of my fish pie and couldn't stuff in another bite, but Grace, Ellie, and Holly found room. When everyone had coffee in front of them, I brought out the itinerary.

"Tomorrow is a little complicated," I said. "It promises to be a fine day, if a little windy, so good walking shoes, a windbreaker and hat would be in order. We will walk to Port Gaverne, which is not far. It is a quaint little town, and we can take a little time to explore it. The beach is sandy, so the dogs will, no doubt, stay there for play time."

"Is there anything to buy in Port Gaverne?" Holly asked. "I have some friends I need to buy souvenirs for."

"No, there isn't," I said "unless the gift shop is open. They usually close in October for the season, but we can look. The beach is controlled by the National Trust, so it is pristine. We can walk the whole way to Tintagel, but it is over nine miles and some of it is very strenuous."

Even Ellie, who looked the most fit, was a little dismayed.

"I propose that we walk to Port Gaverne. From there, we will drive in two cars to Trebarwith Strand. It's a much easier walk from there to Tintagel. We'll see the beautiful sandy beach of Trebarwith Strand, the remains of Tintagel Castle which some think was King Arthurs's Castle and the tunnel that goes under the sea to the castle—if you want to include that. We'll end up at Tintagel where we will have supper at Ye Olde Malthouse Inn which is a pub with excellent food. While you are ordering your meal, Deirdre will drive me back to Trebarwith to get the van, and I can take everyone back to Port Isaac. Does that suit?"

"Very well," Grace said. There were nods all around.

The conversation became full of King Arthur, magic and the place of fantasy in literature. No doubt due to Kala's nine-year-old presence, Lena didn't hold forth on Mary Wesley's views on sexuality and a fantasy involving Lancelot.

Deirdre collected her two dogs, Pike and Duff, and joined me when I took Gulliver out for his nightly pee. We left Kala playing games on her tablet and walked across the street to the edge of the harbor. The tide was in now, and the ocean here was calm.

"What's the matter, Deirdre?" She had been upset on the phone a few days ago, and she sounded subdued now.

"I'm at a kind of a crisis, Claire. I think Michael's having an affair." She leaned on the wall and stared at the water.

I had wondered. She'd made many small comments. I knew she'd been worried. "What makes you think so?"

"The usual: late nights, inattention, doesn't hear me when I say something, walks out when I'm in the middle of talking."

"What's going on in bed?"

"Not a lot."

"Have you asked him?" I wasn't an expert on relationships.

"No, I'm not sure I can face it."

I was quiet. I had no advice to give. I was sorry for them all: Deirdre, Michael, Josh and Kala.

"I don't know what to do." She let out a deep sigh. "But I'm going to enjoy this trip. Kala and I are looking forward to it. The dogs will love the beach, and I'm going to get into conversations about Oregon with this group and blast myself out of this funk."

I reached over and hugged her. She felt like a cushion, soft, a little plump and cuddly. She was my little sister, and I loved her. I didn't like to see her this unhappy. It was as if her inner, sustaining light had dimmed. We stood like that for a few minutes.

Deirdre slipped her arm around my waist and hugged me. "Thanks, Claire. You are just what I need."

I hadn't said anything at all useful, but perhaps she just needed a little comfort.

We brought the dogs back and said goodnight.

I was glad someone needed me. If you love someone and they love you, you need each other. That's pretty simple.

I opened my emails. There was one from Pamela Malkin. She must have found my email address on my website. I read it. Nothing new here. She still wanted money. I wasn't going to answer her.

There was another from Mark. "I'll call you tonight."

I checked my mobile. He had called, but I had turned off the sound when we were eating and forgotten to reactivate it. I called back.

"Where have you been?"

"Running a business and neglecting my mobile. Sorry."

Silence. Then, "Sorry, too. I miss you."

That was better. "What's going on in your world?"

"Not enough. I've got David Pemberthy seconded to me for two weeks. David thinks the murder might be connected to the research Nott was doing on smuggling in Cornwall. It's possible, but more likely it's a local problem. Nevertheless, I'll have to look into that."

"Where would those research records be?"

"Not sure. Perhaps in his flat. We're checking."

"If it's not there, the publishing company might have it."

"I'll check. Thanks."

"Rita was his editor. You could ask her."

"Good idea."

"Is the investigation interjurisdictional now? Hampshire and Cornwall?"

"That's right. But with the new team I can go across boundaries. At least, before they change their minds and put us back in silos." Mark's police department amalgamated with other jurisdictions and then just when they were learning how to cooperate, broke away into smaller units. It was as if every time there was a new Chief Constable, he or she changed the organization. I had a mental image of the National Council of Chief Constables meeting around a table and dividing up the country, moving constabularies together and then breaking them apart, trying to fit them into a giant puzzle. Mark was in one of those puzzle pieces that moved around.

"You have David Pemberthy for two weeks? Does that mean you have two weeks to solve this murder?"

"Pretty much. After that I get so few resources that solving anything is unlikely."

"Better get the little grey cells working."

He laughed. He'd read Agatha Christie.

"I'm thinking, all right. I have a list of suspects and no way to absolutely rule out any of them. I've interviewed everyone who attended the party, and I haven't come any closer to finding the perp. I couldn't find the woman, Jane, who left, probably in that car you heard at three in the morning."

"Did you get a description of her?"

"Sure." He read it to me. "About 45, well spoken, more educated—than most of the others I think that person meant, American or Canadian, beautiful hair someone said but couldn't remember the color. Great clothes but couldn't describe them."

I thought about that description. It reminded me of someone. "Mark, I'll call you back. I want to check something."

"Right."

I disconnected, shoved my mobile into my pocket and walked down to the lobby. I was lucky. Zoe was just finishing her work and heading for her apartment.

"A moment, if you can spare it, Zoe?"

"Right you are. What is it?"

"You have all the passports?"

"Of course. I keep them in a locked drawer." Most hotels now just photocopy the passports, but some smaller places still keep them.

"Can I see them?"

She looked at me for a long moment and then said. "No prob."

I took them from her and pulled out Lena's passport. I opened it to the picture page. "Jane Lena Prior".

I handed it back. "Thanks." Her name wasn't a secret. I could tell Mark. Back in the room, I phoned him. "You might be looking for Dr. Jane Lena Prior. She's going by Lena Prior. She's on my tour."

"What? Did she tell you she was at the party?"

"She hasn't admitted to even knowing Oliver Nott, but she answers your description, and she was in England for a week before she joined my tour."

He said nothing for a full minute.

"I'll be in Penzance on Saturday."

"And?"

"I'll talk to her then. Don't tell her I'm looking for her."

"Of course not! What do you think is in my head, cotton wool?" I was annoyed.

"No, I don't think you're stupid. I've never thought you were stupid. Irritating, so sensitive I get rebound burns, inventive to the point of driving me crazy, but not stupid."

I felt a welling of love for him. I'm sure it had something to do with his acceptance of my faults, but I'd analyze it later. Now, I just enjoyed it.

"Mark, you are good for me." I said on an impulse.

"Like medicine." He sounded a bit rueful.

"No, like sunshine—warmth and light." I wanted him to know that he mattered to me.

He was silent again; this time only for a moment, then he sighed. "I'm getting so close to loving you, Claire. It's scary."

"Yeah. I know." It *was* a little scary. It was easier when it was just fun.

"See you Saturday."

I was about to disconnect when he said, "There's something else."

"What?"

"The Drug Abuse Prevention Society is holding an auction on Saturday night in Penzance. My Superintendent wants me to attend. Would you come with me?"

"As an unofficial couple or as an official couple, uniform and all." Was this a public appearance?

"No uniform, but official."

Appearing at an official function as a couple seemed even a greater declaration of commitment than either of us had yet given.

"I don't know, Mark. I have my tourists to look after."

"They aren't children."

I thought about Grace's determination to go her own way and Holly's sensitivity. "You'd be surprised."

"Deirdre's there to help you out, isn't she?"

"I'll think about it."

I'd let that invitation worry around in my head overnight. I could support the drug prevention cause by donating some of my money toward it, but Mark wasn't expecting me to do that. I was sure he had no idea I was wealthy.

I slipped into bed, patted the place beside me and waited until Gulliver had settled in a tight ball. Then I stretched out and enjoyed the feelings that flowed through me. At first, I felt warm toward Mark with only a slight worry about the auction. Then I felt cold. Had Jane Lena Prior been at the party? Did she know Oliver, intimately enough to be so angry she thrust a knife into him? It was possible. Lena impressed me as someone who made her own morality, not someone who abided by society's rules. What a tour. Four ladies from Oregon who were delightful, one morose man who had an agenda I hadn't quite figured out and one possible murderer.

CHAPTER SEVEN

Today, I had to coordinate meals, driving time and the tides. The result had to give us smooth progress through the day. We were heading for Trebarwith Strand which was only accessible when the tide was ebbing. I hoped this was a group that respected my timetable, because the tide certainly wouldn't accommodate them. Zoe had announced breakfast would be served at eight.

Everyone but Jane-Lena was seated with some kind of meal in front of them. Zoe produced a hot breakfast in steamers along the wall and coffee carafes on the tables. I joined Sharon and Holly and poured my first cup of coffee of the day.

"How are the beds?" I asked.

"Mine has a memory foam," Holly said. "Pure luxury."

"Mine too," Sharon said. "No complaints. Fancy soap in the shower too."

I was interested in what travelers appreciated. Sometimes, they liked the books at the bedside, sometimes, the lamp on the desk. I noticed what they didn't like as well: outside lights that shone into their rooms or shower heads that were too high or too low. The complaint list was often endless.

"Does everyone in England eat fish for breakfast?" Holly sniffed the air.

I smelled something from the sea.

I glanced over at the serving table. "Kippers?"

"Is that what they are?"

"Sure," Sharon said. "You read about them all the time in the mysteries."

"True enough, but it's a different experience to face them up close and intimate." Holly wrinkled her nose. Fish smell is distinctive.

I shared Holly's aversion to fish for breakfast. I loved it for dinner, but I avoided it before noon. "It might be pilchards, which are large sardines. We can ask Zoe."

"Do they taste different?" Sharon asked.

"I don't think so."

Deirdre was enjoying hers. Kala had a boiled egg in an egg cup. The egg had a face drawn on its shell and a warming cap. Cute.

"Kippers?" I asked Deirdre.

"Pilchards."

I shuddered. I really couldn't face fish in the morning. She and Kala shared a table with George and Grace. Everyone was eating and talking.

Lena arrived. "I'm not late, am I?"

She was dressed in casual clothes: jeans, shirt, sweater and walking boots, but she managed to look stylish. It might be that scarf artistically draped around her shoulders. I wondered if she had been the woman at Oliver Nott's fatal party.

"You have time for breakfast," I said. "But I'd like everyone to meet me in the lobby in a half-hour. I'll explain the rather tricky logistics for the day."

"I hope we get in some good hikes," Lena said. "I need my exercise."

Sharon paused with her coffee cup held in front of her and glanced up and down Lena's figure. "It's either exercise or less food," she agreed.

Lena blinked. She had expected admiration.

"More coffee, Sharon?" I held up the carafe, repressing a smile. Lena moved off to the serving table.

Sharon held out her cup. "Sorry about that. It's just tempting to take her down a peg or two."

"I'd appreciate your restraint," I said. It *was* tempting to yank Lena back to the world of the ordinary where she was not the diva at the center, but neither of us had been ordained from above to correct Lena's character faults, and she was entitled to an enjoyable holiday. She wasn't necessarily guilty of anything but lack of sensitivity. I didn't want Sharon to act as the arbitrator of manners. I didn't say all that, though. Sharon was sharp. She got it.

"I'll keep it down," she promised.

"Thanks."

I met my group in the lobby and stood while the others sat on sofas and chairs.

"I propose that you walk to Port Gaverne which isn't far," I said.

"How far," Holly asked. I was beginning to suspect that Holly was not inclined to walk more than shopping required.

"About a mile along the gorgeous cliff paths to a beautiful cove."

She nodded as if she could manage that.

"Deirdre and I will drive the vehicles to Port Gaverne because we need to travel inland and the come back out to the sea. There is no direct vehicle route. Then we will walk back up the path to meet you. Kala, would you like to walk or ride to Port Gaverne?"

"I'll walk," she said. "And take the dogs."

"I'll take Gulliver," George offered. He was dressed for the walk with a weatherproof anorak and boots.

"Wonderful. Would anyone else like to ride to Port Gaverne?"

No one wanted to miss the cliff walk. I hated to miss it myself. Today, with the October sun shining on the sea, it would be spectacular.

It was part of my routine to discuss what we doing, where we were traveling and what to expect. "From Port Gaverne, we'll drive in two cars to Trebarwith Strand, that beautiful sandy beach I told you about." I repeated the itinerary I'd discussed earlier. "We have a few sights to see in Tintagel, and I plan to be back to Port Isaac in time for dinner here. The Fishermen Friends' chorus concert begins at 8 pm. Agreed?"

"I'd rather walk the whole way to Tintagel," Lena said.

I looked at her sharply. She seemed to be holding herself rigid. Had Sharon upset her? Maybe, she had other problems she wanted to sort out on a long walk. Murder, for instance.

"It is nine miles, and it would take more hours than we have time for today. I'm sorry about that, but I'll try to give you as much opportunity to walk as possible."

"Oh, all right," she gave in with obvious reluctance.

"If you would like to start off to Port Gaverne now," I said, determined to see my tour sorted. "I'll get the van and join you there shortly. It is a beautiful cove and we have glorious weather." They trailed me outside.

Was I overdoing the cheerful patter? Americans usually liked a lot of talking, at least northern and western Americans. Canadians wanted my speeches to be a little slower and leave room for more silence. Italians wanted discussion. In spite of knowing that, I had to be sensitive to individuals. I couldn't assume a national preference. Deirdre would likely tell me if I was speaking too much or too quickly.

Sunlight bounced off the ocean, lit the bright white of the houses along the quay and brightened the scarlet and cobalt blue of the boats floating in the bay—a true Cornish postcard scene. The tide was on its way out. We needed a low tide when we got to Trebarwith Strand or we wouldn't have a beach. I pointed out the path to Port Gaverne. I had printed the directions and now passed a copy to each person, including Kala.

"You start at the car park at the end of the beach and follow the path to the top of the cliff. There are stairs. It is not too difficult. From there, the path is well signed. You have my mobile number. If you have any questions, just call me. In any case, I will meet you on the trail."

"There should be good pictures from up there," Holly said.

"Yes. I guarantee it," I agreed.

"Coffee at Port Gaverne?" Grace wanted reassurance on that.

"Absolutely," I said.

"Then we're off." She led the way.

I handed Gulliver's leash to George. Kala joined George with Pike and Duff prancing beside her. I counted them as they moved off toward the beach. I had once left a tourist behind. I never wanted to do that again.

"All there?" Diedre asked.

"Yes. Let's go."

Deirdre and I drove in tandem to the beach and parked in front of the pub. In the summer, it's impossible to park there, but October thins out the tourists to a trickle and parking is allowed. I popped my head into the pub and asked the barkeep if my van and Deirdre's car would be safe from tickets and towing there.

"As houses," he said, barely looking up.

"I'll bring tourists back for a drink or coffee in about an hour."

"No problem." He didn't seem at all grateful for the business, but at least, the pub was open.

Deirdre had already started up the cliff path to meet the others. I hurried after her. A fringe benefit of my life as a tour guide was the amount of time I spent walking. The stairs to the cliff top presented no problem for me, and I was barely puffing when I joined Deirdre.

We walked for about a half-mile before we saw our group. They had stopped at the cliff edge to view the ocean. It can be cold and miserable here, but not today. I scanned the sky, noticing wispy clouds far out. I didn't know enough about weather to interpret them. I hoped they were not a harbinger of rain.

I could see Holly well back from the edge of the cliff, observing the world through her viewfinder. George and Kala were near her. Gulliver spotted me and bounded straight at me, tearing the leash from George's hand.

"Whoa," he said and started after Gulliver.

"It's okay," I called. It was more than okay. It was heart-warming to have Gulliver sprint toward me as if I were his dearest love.

"I love you too, sweetie," I said as he wiggled and flopped around my feet, delighted to be reunited.

Deirdre's dogs greeted her as she joined Kala to view the impressive cliffs and shores. With the ebbing tide, we could see snatches of the shoreline.

"Amazing," Sharon said, coming up to me. "What a great idea to come on this path. Beautiful."

"Stunning," Grace agreed. "I understand why Eleanor Trewynn had to come up to the cliff tops to attain peace and tranquility."

"And to practice her Aikido," Sharon said.

"That too." I expected that the women from Oregon had reread Carola Dunn's mysteries as they were familiar with the setting.

The others seem to have enjoyed the walk as well. Neither Lena nor George was stomping ahead in high dungeon.

Kala bounced in the same way Gulliver had, with energy and delight in the day.

"Auntie Claire, we're *so* high, and we can see *so* far." Her dark curls bounced around her head. Her enthusiasm was infectious. She threw out her arms as if to encompass the world.

"And the sea is *immense*." I had played this word game with her since she was about seven.

"And vast,"

"And colossal,"

"And…and gigantic."

I grinned at her. She smiled, turned in a quick pirouette and followed the others down the path toward Port Gaverne.

From the cliff top, Port Gaverne looked like a magical harbor from one of the Cornish legends. Surely, raiders, smugglers, kings and fairies sailed into this bay. It was hard to believe these calm waters held the remains of many shipwrecks, sunk there after storms threw the boats onto the rocks, some of them even enticed there by the false lights of the greedy wreckers. None of that violence showed today.

Gulliver and I caught up with Ellie who had stopped to appreciate the view of the village, nestling at the bottom of the cliffs. I admired her beautiful profile, brown skin and white, close cropped hair. She looked almost regal, even in her jeans and jacket.

"Amazing the countryside remains so…so country." She waved her hand at the grasslands above the village.

"At first, the will of the lords and kings prevailed," I said. "They wanted to preserve the agricultural land in order to either take the produce or garner taxes on it."

"At some point, it must have become the will of the people."

"Yes," I agreed. "It is amazing that the people have preserved the land."

"Likely for the some of the same reasons," Ellie said thoughtfully. "England is an island, after all. The people of England want to feed themselves."

We joined the others on the beach. The tide was on its way out, leaving an expanse of beach to explore. Ellie looked around. "They lived from the food in the sea as well, and the goods they could trade. It makes sense to have a village on the sea where people and goods arrived and departed."

Ellie had taught English literature in high school and was now retired, but she maintained her teacher's curiosity about people and places. I imagine she'd read about Cornwall. I've found my tourists who studied English literature felt an affinity to the country, almost as if they had been born here or lived here at some time.

Gulliver was nose deep in the empty shell of a crab. I didn't want him to eat it. Shells can be sharp.

"Come away," I said and, while he looked at me, he didn't move from the crab shell.

"Gulliver." I pulled on the leash. He came, with a few reluctant looks back at his treasure.

Holly had found a bench overlooking the beach and claimed it. Sharon was far out along the shore, studying the barnacles and kelp on the rocks. Everyone seemed to be enjoying Port Gaverne in their own way. Deirdre had her two dogs at the water's edge and was throwing a stick into the waves. The dogs, both black Labradors, were getting very wet and very dirty. I'm glad they were going to travel in Deirdre's car.

Kala had picked up a handful of shells and was examining them with the help of an older man I hadn't seen before. It was daylight; a small village in Cornwall, not downtown London, but I moved over to supervise.

He was about sixty, perhaps older, burly, wearing a fisherman's hand-knit sweater containing years of ground-in dirt, jeans, and work boots. A jacket with big sagging pockets hung loose from his shoulders. He wore a navy, small knitted cap, the kind sailors on fishboats wear. You can almost identify a fisherman by that cap. When I got closer, I could see he had brown eyes, dark hair and the dark Spanish skin of some of the Cornish population.

"Myttin da," the man said as I approached. I think that was Cornish for good morning.

"Hou." The word for "hello" was my only Cornish word.

"Falla genes?"

"Sorry," I said. "That's it for me in Cornish."

"I see your little daughter has an eye for beauty." He gestured to the shells Kala held.

I smiled. "My niece. Yes, she does."

Kala smiled as well. "See, Auntie Claire. This one has an animal inside." She pointed to a dull greyish looking shell.

"That's a common periwinkle, and you must put it back and gently," the man said. "It will die away from its home—and it will come addled and smell as it dies."

"Oh," Kala wrinkled her nose. "I'll put it back."

I enjoyed her expressions. When she is older, she'll adopt the mask protecting emotions we English seem to think is essential for survival, but right now, her thoughts flitted across her face, and I appreciated the show.

"What's this one?" she asked.

"That's a pointed top shell. Lovely thing." He gave the shell serious consideration. It was small, light pink with lines swirling to a point.

"There's nothing in it," Kala said hopefully.

"I see that. You can take that one with a free conscience."

"And this?" She showed him another.

"That's a Dog Whelk. You don't see that bright yellow color very often. That's a find."

Kala looked pleased and hurried back toward the ocean to return her live periwinkle to its home.

"I'm Claire Barclay," I said.

"Bert Wynn." We shook hands.

"You live here, Mr. Wynn?"

"Bert. Not so as to live here. I'm from Fowey, but my wheal is the coast. I travel it in the in between. My sister's girl is Zoe at the hotel."

I nodded. "I see."

"I mostly go where I feel I need to on that day. Penzance is usually best, and they have meetings there."

"Meetings?"

"AA meetings. I get to as many as I can."

"That's a good thing," I wish my dad had found Alcoholics Anonymous. He went to his death a raging alcoholic when I was seventeen. My stepfather came into my mother's life soon after, giving my mother and my sister a better life. It was all in the past. I couldn't give my dad a second chance now.

"Each day has everything I need," he said.

"You're a philosopher, then."

"Everyone is a philosopher. I don't give advice. If that's what you're angling for. I'm a carver and a fisherman."

I felt as if I had somehow insulted him. I switched the conversation to business.

"You carve? Do you sell your art to tourists?"

"When I can. Not much this time of year. My Zoe lets me know tourists are coming. I have some carvings for sale." He put his hand in his pocket.

"May I see?"

He took out a small carving of a shell. It was a replica of the pointed top shell Kala had shown him.

"That's lovely."

He smiled. "I have quite a few. Do you think your visitors would like them?"

"I'm sure they would. Why don't you meet us at the café? They will head there for coffee in about twenty minutes. We have to wait for the tide before going to Trebarwith."

Bert was sitting at one of the two tables outside the Pilchards Café when I finally left the beach. In the summer, the area in front of the hotel was jammed with tables, but now there were just two. It was quiet here and almost warm, with the sun beating down on us.

I fetched a coffee from the bar and joined Bert. I could see my tourists from there and they could see me.

He had set up a collection of small carvings on the table. There were shells such as the one he had shown me on the beach and small birds, including the inevitable puffins. They would be a popular memento of Cornwall. My father used to teach me about birds, and I could identify most of what I saw here.

"That's a kingfisher." I pointed.

Bert nodded. "And a kestrel and an oystercatcher."

"No sandpiper?" I asked.

"Beaks are too long. The wood would snap."

I nodded. He carved compact birds that would fit into a traveler's luggage and remind them of the wild coast of Cornwall.

Holly joined us and brightened as she saw something to buy. She pulled out her purse and set it on the table. That was a signal. Like seagulls who spot a stranded fish, my tourists moved toward us. I slipped away to let Bert make his sales. I'd like to buy the carving of the pointed top shell if it remained after my group had bought what they wanted.

The barkeeper roused himself enough to top up my coffee. I took it to an inside table. Deirdre joined me there.

"Kala's having a good time," she stated as she arrived.

"Were you worried about that?"

"You never know. Nine years old is the new thirteen. They're contrary."

"Not that you ever were that," I said, I must admit, with some sarcasm.

She grunted. "That's a point."

We sipped our coffee in silence for a few moments. Silence is rare around Deirdre.

She seemed to relax, sitting back in her chair and lifting her face to the sun. "Those carvings are special. I got a kingfisher for Kala. I'll give it to her later. I was thinking of getting a shell, but she is going to keep the one she found on the beach, and I didn't want her to think the carved one was better."

"Parenting is a series of constant moral decisions," I intoned.

She smiled. "Seems to be."

"Are you calming down at all?"

"What do you mean?" She glanced at me.

"You arrived full of angst, nervous energy and constant movement. Bert out there says he takes one day at a time and enjoys it."

"Giving advice, is he?"

"No, he's not. He says that's just what *he* does. Want to try it?"

She was quiet for a moment, the said, "I might as well. At least for this holiday. It is beautiful, and the group is interesting."

We sipped our coffee and sat quietly, enjoying the peace. I thought about asking Deirdre's advice about what to do about Jane Lena Prior, but Professor Prior's passport was privileged information and I couldn't pass it on, at least not to Dierdre who was a barrister. The police were another matter. Professor Prior might not be guilty of any part of the murder. Perhaps she hadn't been at the Stonning's party. As Dierdre finally appeared relaxed, I wouldn't tell her.

"Since you are in such a tranquil mood," I ventured, "would you like to do me a favor?"

"Depends on what it is."

"Mark has invited me to a charity function, an official one with his department, on Saturday night. It's in Penzance, and we will be there overnight. Can you manage the tour for me while I go with Mark?"

She was quiet for a moment, no doubt considering all that might occur without me. "Sure. I have your mobile number if any great emergency arises. Is this a progression of your relationship? Official and public recognition of you two as a couple?"

"Maybe. Maybe it's just a charity auction." I wasn't going to overthink this.

"Humph. An auction. Are you going to bid?" Deirdre finished her coffee, moved the cup aside and leaned forward her.

"I guess so. It's for drug prevention. I'm all for that."

The only constraint my accountant put on me was to get a tax receipt for any money I gave away. I would like to help prevent drug addiction in kids. After all, I had a niece and a nephew. You never know who is going to find drugs attractive.

"Does Mark know how wealthy you are?" Deirdre looked at me and waited for an answer.

"He knows I have some savings," I said slowly. "I'm pretty sure he doesn't know how much that is."

"You haven't talked about it?"

"No. I'm a bit afraid of talking about it. I don't want him to see me as someone with pots of money, someone who doesn't have to stay in the area or be reliable. I have a slight bias against wealth myself. I can understand if others also have that prejudice."

"Bidding at the auction is going to make your wealth very clear."

I was afraid of that.

CHAPTER EIGHT

H olly shared her delight in her purchases with us as we drove north to Tintagel. She'd bought the shell I had my eye on, the pointed swirl Bert had carved so delicately it seemed it would float away, and several others as well. She passed them around. Ellie had bought a gull and Sharon a puffin. I glanced at the tiny wren Grace held—it was her turn for the front seat—but then turned my eyes back to the road. Bert had, no doubt, sold out.

We joined the B3314 just past Port Gaverne and drove the short, fifteen-minute route through the grasslands and down the steep road to Trebarwith Strand.

"There are," I said through the microphone, "at least 385 varieties of flowers, 30 kinds of grasses and 16 of ferns in this area. There are fields full of cultivated daffodils in the spring as this is the warm part of the British Isles, but there is still some beautiful flora at this time of year."

"What are those pink flowers on the edge of the sea?" George asked.

"That's thrift," I told him. "It's everywhere."

I managed to find a parking space near the beach in front of the Port William Inn and passed out the menus I had printed off their inn's website, along with some pencils.

"Could you mark what you'd like in the sandwich section? I have water, fruit and biscuits for you as well, and there is another café at the end of the trail."

I opened the back of the van, freed Gulliver from his crate, stepping on the leash so he wouldn't wander, and pulled the insulated bag forward. When each person came up to me to give me their sandwich selection, I gave them a bottle of water, their choice of an apple, banana or orange and a package of biscuits.

"I'll bring the sandwiches when I catch up with you on the cliff path."

When everyone was supplied with a snack, I handed out the booklets I'd prepared which gave an explanation of the birds and sea life as well as the history of the area and a guide to the sights along the Cliff Path to Tintagel. I had other reference books in the van and a Wi-Fi connection at the Slipway if I had to add information.

"This is wonderful, Claire." I knew Grace would appreciate a book. "Can I keep it?"

"Yes, of course."

Kala decanted from Deirdre's car and let out the dogs. She bounced up to me. "Can I have one of those, Auntie Claire?" Deirdre thought she was sulky but she looked enthusiastic to me. Perhaps the friction between them was normal for her age. I had no children of my own, so they could teach me how relationships of mother and daughter worked these days compared to when Deidre and I were growing up. I gave her a brochure. "You'll have to share with your mom."

She rolled her eyes but nodded.

The women each had a small rucksack where they stowed their provisions. The pack allowed them to carry a little weight, well-distributed on their backs, leaving their hands free to deal with their cameras, grasp hand-holds, or break a fall. George did not. There was always one who was not prepared. I rummaged through my extra supplies and found a fanny pack, a small pack on a belt.

"Try this, George. It should take a water bottle and a bit more."

He took it and dangled it from his fingers. His face contorted a little in puzzlement.

I demonstrated how to snap it around my waist and handed it back.

"Ah. Thanks." He clicked it on and then held out his hand for Gulliver's leash. I passed it to him.

"You can explore the beach and start up the trail to the cliff path while I order the sandwiches from the café. Deirdre and I will drive to Tintagel, leave her car there, return and catch you up on the beach of cliff path—wherever you are. We will walk together on to Tintagel."

I glanced over the sea. Those wispy clouds were far off on the horizon. "It looks as if you will have excellent viewing."

I took a moment to show Holly in her guide book where there were benches and where there were good viewing spots for pictures.

"Most of the cliff path is an easy walk, but there are a few places where you must climb stiles and, when we get to Tintagel Castle, the stairs are very steep—but most of it is a stroll."

"What is a stile?" Holly asked.

"It's steps built over a fence. You use it to get to the other side instead of going through a gate. They are usually easy to climb."

The others nodded.

"I told Holly it would be an easy hike," Lena said. She may have told Holly that, but Holly would be unlikely to believe her. Lena's idea of an easy hike and Holly's were sure to be chalk and cheese.

I turned to Lena. "You'll find Tintagel Castle a good work-out if you traverse the island and investigate all the areas. You can do it at any speed you like; you can even run some of it."

She brightened "Thanks. I might do that."

She stood for a moment looking at the others as they made their way to the beach.

"Do you suppose Olive Nott explored this area?"

I froze. Was she admitting to knowing Nott?

"Why do you ask?"

"I'm thinking of writing a paper on him. An academic paper about his research and his efforts for self-aggrandization."

"You knew him?"

"I knew his work. I'd like to get hold of his research. This would be a great time for me to put out a paper on him. Even academics would be interested in him. It could help my career."

I was struck dumb, staring at her.

"It would *not* be flattering." She smiled at me and turned to follow the others.

I didn't know what to do with this information. Perhaps she had only an academic interest in Oliver Nott.

I hurried to the Port William Inn and placed the sandwich orders. Deirdre gave hers and Kala's. We paid, and I promised to be back in forty minutes to collect them.

The tide was far out now and the sands were truly as golden as the brochures promised. I think the group would spend a lot of the time on the beach before they started up the path.

Deirdre left her car in the Tintagel Visitor's Centre parking lot, and we hustled back to Trebarwith Strand. It was exactly on forty minutes when we returned, and I picked up the sandwiches, packing them carefully into my rucksack. I made sure both Deirdre and I had water, an apple each and some biscuits. The walk to Tintagel was only two miles, but some of it was steep. I had a small collapsible bowl for Gulliver. Deirdre had the same for her dogs.

The group had remained on the beach. Trebarwith Strand catches the warm sun, and the rocks trap the receding tide which supports sea life in the tidal pools. That makes it a beautiful and interesting site. Kala hunched over a rock pool on the right side of the beach. Her dogs sat on their haunches staring into the pool beside her like black statues of Egyptian gods, still as stone. There must be something fascinating them in the pool.

"Come look, Auntie Claire," she called.

I came up behind her and looked.

"Blennies. See?" She pointed.

I stared for a moment then saw a small gray fish, hovering under a rock ledge.

"Well done. They're hard to spot."

"I know. They change color to match where they're hiding like lizards."

"What are the dogs looking at?"

"Crabs," she said and pointed to one as it scurried for a moment, then sat motionless, then scurried again. The dogs started and leaned forward, their eyes following the crab, then sat back, waiting for the crab to move again.

She opened her hand. "I found some Legos."

"You did? You know the *Tokio Express* lost some containers of Lego in 1997 and they have been washing up ever since. People try to find dragons, cutlasses and octopus Lego pieces. Did you find one of those?"

"No." Her brow wrinkled. "Just a round yellow piece." She held it out for me to examine.

"That's a good find," I said, paying respectful homage to a treasure.

She smiled then and returned to staring at the rock pool.

Gulliver was lying beside George who sat on a flat rock, looking out over the ocean. The rest were walking along the sand. Elle spotted me and said something to the others, and they gravitated slowly my way. I moved out onto the sand. We could start our walk by following the beach to Lil's Cove. I poured some water in the collapsible bowl for Gulliver. He lapped it up. I must remember to do this every hour or so.

I don't know if my group knew how lucky they were with the weather. Cornwall can be beautiful, but it can also be foggy, misty, rainy and cold. Today, the sands glowed, the ocean beamed a postcard blue and the breeze touched us gently.

We turned to admire the mile-long golden beach as we left it and headed up the beach from Lil's Cove to join the cliff path. A few pieces of slate left over from the mining days spilled onto the beach. They had escaped the fate of most of the loose slate which ended up on roofs or as part of a stone fence. When I was half-way up, I turned to look over the sea. Gull Rock jutted out of the blue water, a timeless home for the birds. Hundreds of them rose in a swirl high into the air. Gulls, likely. Puffins fly straight down into the water and, despite the association of Cornwall with puffins, I have yet to see one.

The path was steep, but everyone found it possible. Holly occupied a bench at the top. I had Gulliver with me now as I didn't want to risk him tripping George on the ascent. I realized with a little jolt that I was a jealous of George and wanted *my* dog with *me*.

"Ignore the sign to Treknow and bear left," I called up the line.

Obediently, Lena, who was in front, turned left and onto the dirt and gravel cliff path— dry today. She bothered me. She might just be interested in Nott as an academic challenge. She was ambitious. She didn't get to be a PhD and a professor without being ambitious. Had she been at Patrick's party? I found that in spite of her sharp and sometimes aggressive personality, I didn't *want* her to be guilty of murder. I'd talk to Mark about her.

The grasslands on either side stretched to the horizon. Gorse and bracken were turning bright orange. There were some flowers lingering in the October sunshine: pink thrift, yellow daisies, and Cornwall heath, the pink heather unique to this area. It wasn't long before the group stopped to look at the remains of a slate quarry: stone stacked in purposeful patterns.

"How did they transport the slate?" George asked me. Grace studied her booklet for information.

"I believe here they slid it over the cliff onto the ship." I'd read about a lot of different aspects of the area I intended to visit, but I wasn't an expert in history. I knew that different mines had different ways of getting their slate to the sea.

"They must have had some kind of a chute." George gazed over the crumbling stone huts, the remains of walls.

"They constructed timber scaffolding on the sides of the cliffs and lowered the slate in buckets and baskets to the boats hobbled below." It would have been dangerous. The weather wasn't always this sunny, and I imagined men working on the cliff face in slashing rain or biting wind.

George must have been thinking about it as well. "When was this?"

"From about 1650 to 1937."

"No shit?" He was clearly fascinated and stared at the holes and pits in front of him then walked closer to the cliff edge to peer down to the water.

"What are those steps going over the wall here?" Sharon pointed behind me.

The steps, placed in the stone wall, were stone, worn to a round depression in the center.

"Those are the steps built by the miners who worked these quarries along the cliff," I said. "They wanted a way over the wall to their homes. A shortcut to work, as it were."

Sharon nodded. "Clever. I've never seen walls built in a stone pattern like that."

"The chevron pattern?"

"Yes." We stared at the pieces of slate placed on end and angled one way along one layer and the opposite way on the next layer above. Sharon took a picture.

"That's typical of Cornwall," I said.

"A laborious way to build a wall. It would take months." We followed the wall with our eyes over the fields almost as far as we could see. "I use my tractor and string wire between posts. A mile done in a day."

"But not standing after four hundred years." I tried to say that politely.

"Not a chance." Sharon agreed. Cornwall stone walls had survived the test of centuries of use.

Lena led us onward past more quarries and then to a stone stile. It was high, the steps up were placed far apart. It is the most difficult stile to climb along the path.

"Would you like me to take a picture of you climbing it?" I asked Holly.

She took a deep breath, nodded and handed me her camera.

"As long as you don't make me appear ridiculous."

"I won't," I promised.

She clamped her mouth shut and looked determined. I expect Holly's determination overcame many physical challenges. She was short and unused to exercise. The wall, at least this part of it, wasn't designed for her. She tried hard, and I hoped that she knew her limits so she would not end in the hospital.

The stile had two stone steps that were manageable but climbing over the top required skill and strength. Holly turned on the top step, placed her bottom squarely on the stone top and swung her feet over. That was clever. I hadn't thought of that.

I captured that maneuver on her camera.

The path was close to the cliff edge and I was occupied with keeping Gulliver near me and not allowing him to dart under the wire and over the precipice. Deirdre had Pike and Kala had Duff. If I stared at them, I could tell the dogs apart: Duff was black with white on his chest and

Pike was pure black. Deidre and Kala were also being careful not to let the dogs loose, because they could roam for miles before they decided to return, they could fall over the cliff, and they could knock one of my tourists over the edge.

Lena waited for us at the next stile. She seemed more relaxed. She wasn't bouncing with impatience, just standing quietly. Trips into small villages with picturesque scenery could calm most people.

"This is the remains of Bagalow quarry." I scanned the area and gestured. The group disbursed through the field to examine the rocks and remaining walls. "Try to imagine it as a working site," I called to them.

"Slate again?" George asked. He'd stayed with me.

"Slate," I agreed. "The whole cliff face was quarry from the sea to this path. There are the remains of a powder magazine here somewhere."

George looked around. Neither he nor I could tell which crumbling rocks the powder magazine had been. "My boy would have loved this," he said.

I was quiet and let him talk.

"He was always into finding out how things worked. He'd have liked to know how these mines worked. At least," he turned and looked at me, 'before the drugs got him."

"I'm sorry."

"They rob a boy of his humanity, you know."

"Yes, I know." Adam, long in my past, didn't use the drugs of today, but he lost his humanity to alcohol. My dad, as well.

George looked over the sea as he spoke. "He was apprenticed to a friend of mine. He was going to be a plumber. He was doing good. Then he missed work, stopped coming home and then he died. It was fast."

I felt the warmth of the sun on my face, felt the breeze on my arms. George stood in his anguish and stared at the sea. I felt totally inadequate. There was nothing I could think of to say.

"I miss him so much." He gripped the edge of a crumbling wall.

I reached out and stroked his hand. "I'm so sorry."

A gull keened a lonely cry from far out on the sea. Gulliver barked. We had stood long enough as far as he was concerned.

George smiled. "Okay, little one. We're moving now."

Lena, following the instructions in her booklet, bore left and was clambering over a wooden stile when George and I caught up to them.

"That Lena," George commented to me. "She's pretty lively." I looked at Lena who had hopped over the stile with ease and disappeared up the trail. True enough. She was lively.

Holly managed to navigate the stile, even though the stiles appeared to have been made for tall men and not for short women who had to stretch or climb to get over them.

Sharon waited on the other side and took Gulliver's leash as I passed it between the rails. Not many people would think about the problem a small dog would have climbing a tall stile. I lifted him through the gap in the lower fence rails at the side of the stile.

Once I had successfully climbed over the stile myself, Sharon passed me Gulliver's leash with one hand and held up her booklet with the other. "What is a kissing gate? It says here that we will meet several kissing gates?"

George gave Sharon a sharp look as he passed.

"They are gates that require you do an acute angle turn, letting the gate swing behind you. Sheep can't figure it out, so they don't go through them. The gate isn't latched, it just "kisses" the post. Or if you'd rather a different explanation, you have to stop and give your companion a chance to kiss you."

Sharon smiled. "I like that one." She turned to the sun, letting the wrinkles mapping her face absorb more rays. "Feels good."

There were several kissing gates, which are much easier to traverse than stiles, and we walked single file at the edge of the world. It was glorious—grasslands beside us, fall colors in the bracken, some flowers remaining at the cliff edge and in the fields—and no other tourists. I joined Holly on the beach at Penhallic Point. Lena and her followers went ahead. They wouldn't get lost. They each had a map, and there were way markers everywhere.

I pulled out Gulliver's bowl and poured water for him. He lapped all of it. I poured a little more. That was a sign that I also needed water. I sipped from my bottle and admired the view.

"Amazing," Holly said and snapped another picture.

"One of my favorite places." I breathed in the salty ocean air that carried with it the hint of cooler air to come. I checked those clouds. For now, on the horizon, but a little closer.

We caught up to the others at St. Materiana Church.

"That's another saint I've never heard of," Grace said.

There seem to be many odd sounding names around here," Ellie agreed.

"The church is old," I heard Grace say, reading from the booklet. "First started in the fourth century by the Romans, not as a church likely. There's an inscribed Roman stone inside. Then in the sixth century a

Christian church was built and then this modern church was built in the eleventh or twelfth century."

Ellie laughed. "Modern?"

Grace grinned at her. "Well, relatively modern."

"The tower is Medieval," Lena said staring at it.

"That's right," Grace agreed, checking her booklet. "There is a list of vicars since 1249."

"The oldest church in my town was built in 1894," Sharon offered. "And I thought that was remarkable."

"It's just the sort of place Oliver Nott would have put in his books," Lena said, half to herself.

"Are you a fan?" Grace asked her.

"Not really. But I know that he did write about this area."

She said she wasn't a fan, but she spoke with some authority about what he might write. How did she know so much?

They spent a half-hour prowling in the church and in the graveyard around it.

"What's that flat wall in the middle of the walk for?" Kala asked me.

"It's a coffin rest."

"Cool," she said. "Ghosts sitting out in open air. Totally cool."

It's my favorite church, partly because it's made mostly of stone and partly because it has a tiny chapel with a beautiful stained-glass window.

Keeping one eye on the time, I gathered everyone and we headed toward Tintagel Castle, the legendary King Arthur's Castle.

We congregated at the entrance to the castle where there were a few picnic tables. Tourists dotted the pathway to the castle, but far fewer than in high summer. I handed around the sandwiches, labelled by the Port William Inn staff, thank goodness, so I didn't have to peer into each one to see what it was.

Sharon had a tiny camera and recorded the scenery. Lena used her tablet to take pictures of the castle. George used his mobile. Kala had a point-and-shoot and Deirdre also used her phone. When the cameras are clicking, pinging and chiming, I know my tourists are impressed with the scenery.

The lunch was excellent, made even better by the fresh air and exercise that preceded it. I passed out the tickets for entry to the castle and arranged to meet them all at this spot in an hour-and-a-half.

"I might want to stay longer," Lena said.

"That's fine. You have a map? You know how to get to Tintagel?" I was telling her, in a polite code that, if she stayed late, she could make her own way to Tintagel.

"Certainly," Lena said.

"We'll look for you at the Ye Olde Malthouse Inn where we will have coffee."

I hoped she wouldn't hold us up. We had to get back to Port Isaac and to the concert tonight.

"Is this King Arthur's Castle?" Kala asked, turning to look at the steep stairs down the cliff face, the bridge across the water and and the island beyond with its ruins. There were walls and crumbling rock everywhere on the island and explanatory plaques, so she could read about the sites.

"That's what they say. A least, there is some evidence that it was owned by a Celtic king and that king might have been Arthur."

"If he existed," Deidre murmured.

"Built in the thirteenth century by Richard Earl of Cornwall," Grace read from the booklet. "And on a Roman site."

Sharon snorted. "Those Romans, they got everywhere."

After lunch, everyone scattered to explore the castle. I made my way to the Ye Olde Malthouse Inn and waited, sipping my coffee in the cobblestone courtyard and enjoying the sunshine.

Deirdre arrived first, as was the plan. She had both dogs and loaded them into my car. I had already loaded Gulliver into his crate where he curled up and let out a long breath of fatigue. He was only a puppy and the walk must have been exhausting. He slept as I drove back to Trebarwith to deposit Deirdre at her car and returned to the café before the others arrived. I watched my tourists come in couples and, occasionally, alone, staring around the village, apparently interested. Sharon stopped at the old Post Office; I saw her enter. It was built in the fourteenth century as a residence for a yeoman farmer. The roof, called "undulating thatch," is fascinating, a giant wave of thatch on the top of the building.

We were loading into the cars when Lena arrived. I was happy to see that she looked hot and a little tired. I hoped she'd stay with the group after this.

I made a stop at the hotel on the top of the hill above Tintagel about six p.m. It was not yet dusk and the sun had that glow that infuses the land in the long twilight of Cornwall. I hopped out of the van and slid the side door opened. Grace climbed out and joined Sharon who was staring at the hotel.

"For God's sake, it's a frigging castle!" She sounded as if she'd just discovered that there really were magic carpets.

The rest lined up beside her and stared. The sun lit the walls as if light had been infused into the very bricks. Ellie gaped at it and then stared out at the sea, the perfect backdrop behind it.

"Grace," she turned to stare at the hotel again. "It's the hotel in *Buried in the Country*."

"It is," Grace agreed. She turned to me. "Does it have marble columns in the lobby?"

"It does."

"Got to be it, then."

They might be right. I'd reread that Dunn novel to see if I could match it with the Castle Hotel. "I had to let you see it, but I didn't want you to stay here. The owners decorated it in high style, a little overdone, I think, but it is sumptuous, and I thought you'd appreciate it."

"Odd, are they?" Sharon looked intrigued.

"Rich of course," Ellie said.

"Of course," I agreed.

"Did they build it here on this promontory?"

"No, another eccentric built it in 1894. This couple bought it in 1999 and have endowed it with their particular opulent taste—which isn't everyone's."

"Slipway suits me," George said.

We were home at the Slipway in a half-hour. They disappeared into their rooms. Dinner was at seven; everyone was on time. My schedule was maintained. I sometimes feel a little OCD about the schedule, but if a tour gets off by even a half-hour, problems ensue and can become challenging to overcome for me and my tour.

"Are there smuggler's caves around here?" Sharon asked. "Seems to me Eleanor found some in *Buried in the Country* or was it *Valley of the Shadow?*"

"In one of those," I agreed, keeping one eye on the time. The concert would start soon.

"Didn't Oliver Nott set a story in this area?" George asked.

I was glad he was joining the conversation about books. It would make him feel more part of the group.

"Not here," Lena said abruptly. "That was near Fowey".

"East, then." George nodded and went back to his haddock and chips.

"There are caves around here though, aren't there?" Sharon repeated.

I answered her. "There are, and some of the them would have been used by smugglers, but the waters are treacherous and the storms vicious, so there was more activity in the Fowey, Falmouth, and Looe area. You can ask Patrick Stonning about it, Oliver Nott's publisher. He will be speaking at the library in Penzance tomorrow and will know exactly where the stories were set."

I reminded everyone that the Fishermen's Friends' concert started at eight, and we just made it. It was a rousing concert, and everyone sang sea shanties as I drove them home, even Ellie who I thought had too much dignity. They had a bottle of something to share and they congregated in Sharon and Ellie's room for more sea shanties. Holly joined them. She wasn't a teetotaler; she just didn't drink very much. I didn't think Zoe would mind. We were the only ones in the hotel.

"I left Kala in the room with her headphones on," Deirdre said as she arrived at my door, a bottle of Drambuie in hand. She poured us each a small shot.

"Have a seat." I gestured to the spare bed. She started for it when my mobile rang. I glanced at the ID. Mark.

Deirdre took her drink and stood looking out the window, ostensibly to give me privacy, but she could hear every word I said.

"Hi Mark." I took a deep breath and relaxed.

"Any more information on Dr. Prior? I need to take a closer look at her."

"No. She concerns me as well. But I hope she didn't know him intimately. She's showing quite a bit of interest in Nott, but she's an academic. They can be interested in almost anything. She wants to write an article."

"On Nott?"

"So she says. Do you think that's suspicious?"

"Everything is suspicious at this point. It might be a cover for her ferreting around for information about him." He spoke slowly, as if thinking aloud.

"She seems to be doing that. She wants his research papers."

He snorted. "She won't get them. I haven't got them myself yet and when I do, I'm holding onto them. There might be something in them that could point me in the right direction. I left a message for Rita Stonning to get them to me."

He changed the subject. "How was your day with the tour?" He seemed fascinated by my tourists, what they saw and what they were like. He often saw the dregs of society, while, for the most part, I saw the interesting, accomplished and curious people. I could see how they might intrigue him.

"Lovely. We walked some of the Coastal Path."

"That's a treat. We should take some time off and do that."

"Maybe in the summer?" I warmed a little, thinking that this relationship might last until the summer.

"Sounds good." He hesitated. "About the auction."

I sat up straight and said with some timbre of resolution in my voice. "I've been thinking. Deirdre promised to tour-sit, so I can get away. Is it formal dress? Because I didn't bring anything fancy."

"No, just dress up."

That wasn't helpful. What did "dress up" mean? "Will you be in uniform?"

"I don't wear a uniform."

I was learning right now that Mark was not fashion conscious. At least, not for himself.

"Don't worry about the dress code. I'm wearing jeans and a sports coat, shirt with a collar."

"So, dressy casual?"

"That sounds right."

I wanted to know what to wear as this was our first official engagement. I realized that he didn't see the dress code as important. That could be a positive attribute. I wouldn't have to try to dress to any standard he held, only my own. My mood lightened. If I didn't have something appropriate, I'd buy something in Penzance.

"The important thing is you're coming. I'll pick you up at 7:30. Where are you staying?"

I gave him the address of the hotel. "What kinds of things are they auctioning?"

"Not sure, just a minute." I could hear paper rustling. "Jewelry, books, some furniture, gift certificates to various places, a romantic weekend at the Secluded B & B."

"I might, bid on that," I said.

"No. No. Let me get it. We can go together, I hope." He paused for a moment and then said. "My insecurity is showing."

"No need," I answered. "I'll pick you for a romantic weekend anytime."

"Well, that's a fine thing." He was quiet for a moment. "Listen, your tourist Dr. Jane Lena Prior."

"Yes?"

"She was Oliver's lover."

"You're having a laugh." I was incredulous.

"No."

"She hasn't mentioned a word about it to me or the group."

"I was in contact with an old lover of his. The guy was really jealous of Dr. Prior. Apparently, Oliver turfed him for her. Is she with you? She hasn't left, has she?"

"She's here."

"Don't let her know I'll be in Penzance tomorrow. I will want to talk to her."

"I won't tell her." I thought for a moment. "Mark, do you know how Rita is doing?"

"Rita Stonning?"

"Yes. You met her. She's Patrick's wife and she brought you the mobile."

"As far as I know she's doing all right. She's back at work. I'm keeping tabs on her, but I don't find her high on my suspect list."

That was a relief.

"I've asked her for Nott's notes," Mark said, "but she hasn't delivered them yet."

I thought she would give up the notes. She was anxious to be clear with the police.

When I hung up, Deirdre sank onto the second bed in my room, stretched out, and sipped her liquor.

"Who is he talking about?" she asked.

I reached into my purse, hauled out a two-pound coin and handed it over. "I'm your client. You have to keep your mouth buttoned."

She took the coin and shoved it into her pocket.

"Spill it."

She heard my brief precis and then looked away. I could almost *see* her thinking.

"Oliver Nott," she said, "a man who was essentially self-centered, who stirred up jealously and hate with impunity. He might have been a murder magnet. A lot of people could have wanted him dead. Who benefits? Who makes money if he dies?"

"The publishing house will make some money, but Patrick said they would have made more if he lived because he would have kept on writing."

"The publishing house could hire another writer to use Oliver Nott's name and write any number of books. They would have to check it out with his estate lawyer."

She was right. "Like Heron Carvic and the Miss Seeton series. There must have been at least three different authors for that series."

"If Nott had lived, would he have been writing for them? Do you think Patrick was sufficiently miffed that he saw a dead Oliver better for business than a live Oliver at another company?"

"I really can't see it," I said.

"That's irrelevant."

And before I could even think of being affronted by that she went on. "And then did Dr. Jane Lena Prior daintily thrust a sharp knife into the heart of the old reprobate and speed off into the night? She appears capable enough."

I had to admit to both possibilities. "According to my schedule, they'll be together at the library tomorrow. You can watch them."

CHAPTER NINE

The clouds I'd been worried about yesterday developed into a mist—not quite rain, not thick enough to be fog, but a trailing film that obscured the view. I took the A39 highway to join the A30 and piloted the van through the gray morning until Penzance. There, we finally broke through into sunshine. A tall palm tree at the side of the highway proclaimed that, truly, this was the warmest spot in the British Isles.

"Hah!" Holly said from her place in the front seat. "A tropical paradise."

"If the rain holds off," Lena said. "Jane" suited her much better than "Lena", but Lena was how I first knew her and how I thought about her.

"Should do," Sharon said, "if it's going to live up to its hype."

I had opted for speed rather than scenery, so we didn't see much of the ocean until we were approaching Penzance. The A30 puts us directly onto the shore of Mount's Bay.

"Look," Holly was the first to see the impressive sight. "That's St. Michael's Mount."

Rising like a mythical castle from the sea, St. Michael's Mount combined history and magic. It looked like an illustration in a book of fairy tales. There was even a thin wisp of mist at its base to enhance the ethereal atmosphere.

"There's a causeway, isn't there?" Grace asked. "We can walk to it."

"At low tide. I'll get the tide table, and we can talk about the best time to see it. I scheduled that for tomorrow." Everyone should explore St. Michael's Mount. It was an experience not to be missed. But once seen, I didn't find it interesting enough for a repeat visit. I usually sent my tourists unaccompanied.

"I've read about it," Holly said, "and I'm anxious to see it, but I'm shopping today."

"You're all on your own today," I agreed. "There's lots to do and many good shops here."

"And galleries," Ellie said.

"And a smuggler's museum," George said.

"All that is here in Penzance. I have another booklet that lists the points of interest."

"Of course, you do," Lena said.

I noticed she took a booklet as I passed them out. She glanced at it and tucked it into her rucksack.

"I plan to shop along Chapel Street," she informed us. "They have a vintage clothing store there I saw on the Internet."

"Yes, it's good." I'd been in there once and enjoyed the experience. I'd buy something later this afternoon. I wanted to look my best tonight.

Lena continued. "I'll be gone for the day."

I briefly thought that small mercies were greatly appreciated. I suppressed that thought for fear it would show on my face. I didn't want to cause her any discomfort. Lena was going to get as much pleasure and enjoyment as I could manage as her tour guide.

After a few blocks, I pulled onto Morrab Road and then into the Queens Hotel parking lot.

Deirdre arrived as we were unloading our luggage.

"Where's Kala?" I asked her.

"On the beach. With the dogs. She's fine."

I felt a little guilty at leaving Gulliver in his crate, but I had to make sure all my guests had their room keys before I could take him to the beach.

The receptionist had other ideas. "Where are your dogs," she asked me. "Ms. Barclay, you have registered a dog, Gulliver. Mrs. Spencer, you have Pike and Duff."

"Mine are on the beach with my daughter," Deirdre said. She was Deirdre Barclay, but she sometimes used her husband's name.

"Mine is in the car," I said, feeling like a neglectful parent.

"He's welcome here." The receptionist was firm.

I know British hotels are often dog friendly, but this receptionist was so determined to register Gulliver, I felt as if she had been expecting my dog and I was only accompanying him. I handed Deirdre my van keys and sent her off to collect Gulliver.

The hotel was on the promenade. The rooms had ocean views and were beautiful. Deirdre had booked the family room which had a king-sized and a single bed. I passed out the room keys to my tourists.

"Please remember we have our lecture at the library at three pm. Patrick Stonning, Oliver Nott's publisher, will talk about the latest in the mystery series by that author. It's eight blocks away, but the hotel will provide a shuttle if you need a ride. It's at the end of Morrab Road at Alverton. St. John's Hall and Library."

"Don't worry, I'll shop my way up to it," Holly said.

"I'm looking forward to it," Sharon said.

"I'll be there," George said.

Lena said nothing, so we might be spared her company. Mark would want to see her, though. I assumed she would return to the hotel in the evening.

"There is a map in your booklet, and you all have my mobile number. Call if you need anything." I hoped I sounded relaxed, but I was beginning to worry about Lena. In spite of her breezy announcement that she would be shopping, I sensed a restlessness in her as if she was unhappy. If she had been Oliver's lover, she would be upset, even if she had walked away from him in a temper. I hoped she'd left him alive. I was uneasy about George as well, but I understood him better now. He had to grieve and he had to do it in his own time and in his own way. It had taken me over a year after my mother's death before I could think of her without crying. I would leave them both to handle their problems in their own ways, but stay aware that they had troubles.

I had a morning without tourists and, after I had taken my van to the petrol station, filled the tank, wiped the dust from the inside and hosed off the exterior, I enjoyed the beach with Deirdre, Kala, and the dogs.

We were near the far end of the beach when Kala stopped to read a poster in the park. "Look, Auntie Claire. There's a dog show on."

I read over her shoulder. "At the Penzance Leisure Centre. That's not far. Want to go?"

"Absolutely. Can we take the dogs?"

"No. That might cause trouble." I imagined Gulliver barking at every moving animal.

Deirdre came up behind us. "I can keep the dogs if you two want to catch that show. Do you want to meet me for lunch?"

We agreed to be back then, thanked her and ran for the van. I could leave Gulliver. There was no one more reliable than my sister.

I paid for the day-passes and we walked into a world of dogs. We toured the aisles gaping at the strange and wonderful breeds we'd never seen before and impressed at the time and attention the handlers were giving those dogs. I don't think I'd want to spend that much time grooming Gulliver—as much as I love him.

We slipped into the seats where we could see the judging competition. The class was Agility for Yorkshire Terriers—and there was Tansey with Poppet. Her business card had said she showed dogs, so I supposed she went where there was competition.

We watched fascinated as Poppet tore around the course like a speeding ball of fluff. She ran through a tunnel, up a ramp, over a see-saw and down the other side and wove in an out of pylons—all with Tansey at her side. Tansey must have been giving her commands or encouragement, but we couldn't hear them, so Poppet looked as though she'd memorized the route and was racing through it on her own. Both Tansey and Poppet beamed at the end of the course. Kala and I clapped.

"Who is that, Auntie Claire.? Do you know her?"

"She's your mother's step-brother's wife." It sounded complicated, and it was.

"I don't think mum likes her step-brothers."

"I think she might like Tansey."

We hurried around to the competitors' grooming section after the class and found Tansey putting Poppet into her crate.

She smiled at me.

"I thought you didn't have any children?" she said, looking at Kala.

"My niece, Kala. My sister, Deirdre's girl. This is Tansey."

Kala said hello. "Can I pet your dog?"

"Sure." Tansey opened the crate, hauled out Poppet, instructed Kala to sit on ground and plopped the little dog onto her lap. Kala was entranced.

"You did well?" I asked.

She nodded at the blue ribbon attached to the crate. "Very well."

"I will have to consult you about training Gulliver."

"Do that. Claire," she began just as I said. "Tansey."

We laughed.

She waited and I spoke. "Tansey, how dire is Pamela's position? Do I need to give her some money?"

"No," Tansey said. "You don't. Her position isn't dire at all. She just wants more."

We looked at each other for a moment. Kala was concentrating on Poppet but we kept our voices low.

"I have quite a bit of inherited money," Tansey said. "Harold and I are comfortable. I grew up with it. I almost take it for granted."

I nodded.

"Pamela grew up with ambitions and little money. She is constantly looking for more. James is greedy, so he makes her worse. I wouldn't give her money if I were you. I don't."

"Is she vindictive when you refuse?"

"Sometimes. I just pretend she's normal and ignore it."

"Thanks," I said and impulsively hugged her.

We rushed back to the hotel and left the van in the car park. We met Deirdre, reported on the dogs show and headed for the Wheelhouse Restaurant.

"Cool dogs," Kala said. "The Yorkies had long hair like silky scarves. But they can run. We saw Tansey."

Deirdre cocked an eyebrow at me.

"Harold Malkin's wife."

"And you lived?"

"She's the nice one," I said.

Once we had our lunch, we sat at the picnic tables with the dogs secured to the legs of the table by their leads. The restaurant staff provided a bowl of water for them. The dogs were happy to rest, keeping one eye on our food, every ready to snatch a dropped crumb.

Kala had taken her paper of chips to the stone steps leading to the beach and sat there watching the waves. Deirdre and I had a rare moment of privacy.

"I thought I'd come on this trip to sort out what I'm going to do about Michael, but I don't seem to be any further along," Deirdre said.

I crunched on my deep-fried crab cakes. "Mmm." I swallowed. "What's the biggest problem?"

"I just feel more or less invisible to him. He doesn't seem to know I'm around, and he rarely talks. I loved his conversations. I loved all the things we talked about and argued about. Now he seems off in another world. There must be another woman."

"Deirdre, you can't just assume that." But she might be right. Michael was kind, funny and attractive. Other women might pursue him.

"I'm afraid to ask him," she said glumly. Then she slapped her hand down on the table. "I hate being helpless. I'm *never* helpless. He just ignores me, and I hate it!"

I'd seen Kala approaching and tried to warn Deirdre, but she was in the throes of frustration and didn't heed my waving hands.

"I want more!"

Kala spoke from behind Deirdre. "You aren't the center of the universe, you know, mum. Everything doesn't revolve around you." Her voice was tight with anger.

Deirdre closed her eyes and took a deep breath. "I'm sorry, Kala. This doesn't concern you."

"Yeah, right. Josh and I are in the middle. You're blaming Dad because he's isn't paying enough attention to you. Maybe you should pay some attention to him."

"What do you mean? And don't you take that tone with me."

Kala glared at her mother, reached down and unleashed her dogs. She sniffed and refused to speak.

Deirdre passed her hand over her face and breathed deeply. "Sorry, Kala," she said. "Yes, you are in the middle."

Kala was not mollified and headed to the beach.

"Don't forget the library," I called after her.

"What time?" She turned and walked backwards for a few steps.

"Be at the hotel at 2:30."

"Okay."

Deirdre stared after her, biting her lip.

"I didn't handle that well." Then she turned to me, with an accusation in her eyes. "And you pretty much gave her permission to be gone for a couple of hours."

"Yes, I did, didn't I?" Deirdre wasn't the only one who could be high-handed and manipulative on occasion.

Deirdre held motionless for a few seconds, shrugged and then smiled. "Oh, well".

"Want a beer?"

"Good idea."

We sat in the sunshine, absorbing the peace and tranquility of Mount's Bay and talked about very little.

Kala had exhausted her dogs and Gulliver had enough exercise. We left all the dogs in our rooms when we drove to the library. I wanted to be a half-hour early to meet the librarian and Patrick. Deirdre and Kala would have no trouble entertaining themselves in the library as they were both readers.

It took me some time to find the librarian. She had a small desk in a small room, one of the many small rooms that comprised this odd library. She stood to meet me.

"Aria Rowe," she said. "Head librarian."

"Claire Barclay, tour guide." I looked around me. "This is an unusual library." There was no central desk or foyer, just a maze of small rooms with books in every available space.

"We used to have a perfectly good library. Solid, spacious. Built in the nineteenth century—fairly modern and still useful." She paused.

"But?" I encouraged her.

"But the town council decided it was too costly and they jammed us into basement of the town hall."

She obviously wasn't happy with the change and I didn't blame her. It was crowded. I hoped that wasn't going to happen all over England. I loved our libraries.

"That's a shame." I smiled in sympathy. "Thanks so much for putting this on. Do you have room?"

"Oh, yes. We use the hall."

"Good. My guests are very interested in mysteries."

Aria was about my age, perhaps a little younger, with short red curls that tumbled over her head. She had vivid blue eyes and freckles on her nose.

"I like mysteries too, although not Oliver Nott's. He's too gritty—a good writer, even though he romanticizes smuggling and creates wild drama. I have two preteen kids who create plenty of drama in my house. I look for escape from it, so I read the cozies. Competent writing there, usually, some gripping scenes and a sense that justice will be done. Satisfying."

I nodded, trying to keep up with her flow of ideas.

"Where are your emmets?" she asked.

Stranger or tourists. I remembered that Cornish word.

"They'll be straggling up one at a time. They had a free day here in Penzance."

She nodded. "Good. I like to see tourists mingle with the locals. I opened the lecture to the public because first, the Arts Council will pay for it that way, and, second, because Oliver Nott's books do well here and, of course, there's the added enticement of his murder. We should get a crowd."

When we moved from her cramped cubicle, we discovered Patrick in the lobby of the hall adjoining the library.

"Claire," he said." Where is this gig?"

I introduced him to Aria. Patrick doesn't have charm, at least I hadn't seen any, but he does have manners.

"Thank you for having me. Where will I be and how long do I have?"

"An hour, and I'll show you where you will be."

Aria headed toward a door and Patrick and I followed her.

"Kyle's with me." Patrick said to me. "At least, he's following me. I was trying to get away from him. He's touchy and I'm tired of him, but he came. He's going to do a video. He's got the marketing for Oliver's next book well underway. Got to hand him that. He's good at his job. He's unloading the camera and checking out stuff on his mobile. Something about tweeting right away.

He's never still. He has his mind on spreading tweets, instagrams or blogs. He doesn't have any personal substance, you know. It's all superficial, instant, gone in a moment. He's like a bouncing ball that's everywhere and never contributes anything."

I stared at him. This was quite an indictment of Kyle. Patrick's voice flowed over me like a torrent.

"He wants Oliver's notes. Rita found them and gave them to me because she wanted me to get them to the police. They asked her for them. It's not like we have a choice. I'll do it. I will do it. I just haven't done that yet, but I'm not giving them to Kyle. I'm in enough trouble with the police. I'm not keeping anything they want."

"D. I. Evans will be in town this afternoon. Perhaps you can give them to him today."

"I'll try. If I can keep them from Kyle."

He shrugged his shoulders and hunched over a little, looking guilty. "I shouldn't put Kyle down. He does his job well. Very well. This is a new age. We need promoters like him. The company has to have a presence on the Internet, and he's it. I just long, truly long, for the days when publishing books was about literature."

I wanted to say "There, there." But refrained. "I agree, Patrick. But there *are* avid readers, like my group. They pay attention to words, to ideas, to characters."

He smiled. It changed him completely. His brown eyes lit, and he nodded. "Yes, Yes. There are a few appreciative readers. I'll try to give them a good lecture."

And he did. There were about fifty people in the lecture hall. All my tourists made it except Lena. Mark was not going to be happy if she'd skipped off. That would cause me a lot of trouble as well as I would have to report her missing. Then, I'd worry about her. I hoped she'd return at some point.

Patrick *was* charming. That was a surprise. He talked about Oliver Nott as if he'd liked him and about the setting of his books as if he'd been born in Cornwall. I should have suspected that a successful publisher was talented, but I hadn't realized Patrick could be so personable.

He answered a few questions from the podium but kept his eye on the time and stopped at precisely one hour. Aria thanked him most sincerely. I think she was surprised as well. Kyle had taken a few pictures.

"Not much doing here," he'd said to me as he passed me at the door of the hall, the crisp businessman in his tailored sports coat and jeans. "Talking heads don't play too good."

I had an odd mental vision of disassociated heads refusing to play with each other. Then I translated that to mean people who stand and talk don't make good film.

George hurried up to Patrick as he was leaving. I heard him ask Patrick if the caves where Oliver set his last mystery were nearby.

I didn't hear the answer because Sharon took my attention.

"Good lecture. Clear speaker. Nice to hear about all the work that goes into publishing a book, even one of Nott's."

"Not a fan?"

"What's that?"

It was noisy as people discussed the lecture as they passed us. I guided her to a quieter spot.

"You're not a fan of Oliver Nott."

"No, but I am interested in the setting. This is where Jeanne Dams set *To Perish in Penzance*."

Dams is another cozy mystery writer.

"Yes, it is."

Sharon looked satisfied. The others drifted over to us, and I soon had them all around me.

"I have the van. I can take you all if you'd like a ride back."

"Not me," George said. "It's a little after four. I'm going to walk through the town some more."

The others agreed with George that the town was small enough to walk through, and they weren't ready to return to the hotel yet.

"Just a reminder that I am not available tonight, but Deirdre is." Deirdre stood on the outside of the group and waved. "If you need anything while I am out, just ask Deidre."

"Can you take my parcels?" Holly asked. "I stashed them at the front desk."

She came with me as I collected her parcels and loaded them into my van. It was easy to make Holly happy—just find some shops.

Kala stood in front of Deirdre, almost as tall as her mother with the same dark curly hair and dark eyes. I even remember that same look of haughty defiance Deirdre had at nine. "Can I go with Sharon and Ellie? They're going to the Lighthouse Gallery."

Deirdre looked hurt. I expect she had wanted to take Kala there. She swallowed whatever she was going to say and substituted, "Yes. Fine. Remember you can't take pictures in there. "

"I *know* that," Kala said impatiently.

Deirdre's smile at Sharon was a little strained, but she managed it. "Thanks."

Sharon waved.

We watched them leave, then I turned to Deirdre. "Now! To the shops. I need a dress."

Deirdre brightened. There was nothing she liked better than to instruct her older sister on how to be fashionable.

We found the dress, deep blue with a flare on the hemline and a neckline that revealed more cleavage than I usually exposed. I stood entranced at the vision in the mirror and felt overwhelmingly feminine. I slapped down my credit card and committed to the dress.

We dumped the parcels on my bed at the hotel and collected the dogs. We kept them on leash in the harbor because the road was too close to let them run loose. They trotted happily beside us. We tried to increase the pace, especially at first, to give ourselves some exercise and let the dogs work out their naptime kinks. About a quarter of a mile from the hotel, I spotted Bert Wynn sitting on the embankment.

He got to his feet slowly when he saw us.

"Dydha da, Claire, Deirdre."

"Hello. Nice to see you," I said. "My tourists appreciated your carvings."

"Yes. I bought one as well," Deirdre said. "A chough with its feathers splayed. Lovely thing."

Bert smiled. "That one be 'ansum."

"You sold out with my group," I complained.

"I know," he said. "I made another pointed shell. Here it be." He reached into one of his capricious pockets and pulled out a shell about the size of the palm of his hand. It was exquisite.

"Lovely, Bert. Thank you." I reached for my wallet.

"You told my Zoe you'd be here a day or two. I thought I might catch you up."

"Do you live nearby?" I asked as I paid him.

"No. No. I live in near Fowey, but I travel up and down the coast some. Not many tourists this time of year, so I come this far. I'll stop home come the end of the month, dreckly."

"And stay home and carve?" Deirdre asked.

"That's right, miss. That's right. I work a little. Sell a bit. Carve a bit. I take each day as it comes. You can't see the future, so just live now—one day at a time. Today is a bit of a blessing."

We looked over the sea. There were patches of sunlight picking up the blue of the ocean, but most of it was grey, reflecting the increasingly thick clouds. I shivered.

"I'm an alcoholic, you see," Bert continued in his slow deep voice. "who's not drinking. Haven't been drinking for twenty years. Still an alcoholic." He spoke slowly, drawing out the word 'alcoholic', giving full value to each syllable. "We take one day at a time."

I remember reading from the Alcoholic Anonymous Blue Book when I was a teenager, trying to deal with my dad and his drinking. Bits of the advice from that book returned to me when Bert spoke. I wondered what my dad would have been like if he had stopped drinking before he died of it. I couldn't imagine him taking Bert's philosophical view of daily living. He would have raged at it.

I caressed my lovely shell. "We're scheduled here for two days, but we are going to visit the caves around Fowey."

Bert was quiet for a moment. "That 'ansum young lady, a professor I think."

I waited.

"She wanted to know about the caves. And about that writer who was here backalong."

Lena. Why was she asking? "Did you know Oliver Nott, the writer?":

"We talked a time or two."

And then Bert was silent.

"Dr. Prior wanted to know about the writer?"

"She did."

That was all Bert was going to say about it. Why was Lena asking? Was this research for her book? She had said she admired autobiographical writing. Was she going to write about her involvement with Oliver? What did Bert know about Nott? I doubt he'd tell me any more.

"I hope to see you again, Bert."

"There's a rehab meeting in Fowey on Saturday night so I will stop at home."

"We might see you in Fowey then. Look for us. I'm sure my group would like to see you."

"I'll get some treasures ready for them."

We said our goodbyes and returned to the hotel.

I stowed my beautiful carving in my back pack, wrapped in a sock. I wasn't going to risk getting any scratches on it.

I wondered if Lena was trying to trace Oliver Nott's path through Cornwall. I might do that as well.

I had an omelet sent to my room. Deirdre ordered the same. I bolted mine, but she took her time and drank her tea like a lady on holiday.

I showered and pulled out my silk and lace underwear.

Deirdre raised her eyebrows. "Do you have plans for those?"

"I like to feel feminine from the skin out some of the time." I felt a little defensive. I wasn't sure what my plans were and I didn't want to talk about them.

"The dress looks wonderful and worth every pound you spent on it."

I'm more athletic than voluptuous, but the cleavage made the most of my figure and I loved the way the skirt swished around my legs. In the mirror, I looked almost pretty.

"Smashing," Deirdre said.

I grinned. "Better, anyway."

I took out my small arsenal of cream, foundation, cheek bronze, eye shadow, and mascara. I could not bring myself to stick false eyelashes on my lids. I tried it once, and it felt as though I had bats flicking about my face.

"Where's Kala?" I asked Deirdre.

"Having dinner with Sharon, Grace and Ellie."

"What happened to Holly?"

"Surprisingly, she's having dinner with George."

"Hmm. And Lena?"

"Haven't seen her."

I turned back to the mirror and carefully outlined my lips. I'd better ask the receptionist to let me know when Lena returned. Mark would want to know.

"Claire," Deirdre said, somewhat pensively.

"Hmm?"

"What am I going to do about Michael?"

"What do you want to do about Michael?" I expected her to say that she wanted to have him followed, collect a dossier on his movements, gather information and whack him with a divorce.

"I want Michael in my life as my best friend and lover, and I miss him," she wailed.

I dropped my lipstick and dashed over to sit beside her. She looked lost and unhappy. I remembered the nine-year-old who had wailed in my arms. I hugged her.

"Deidre. That's important. Hold onto that. Whatever you see, whatever you think, hold onto that." I felt helpless. She was usually bright, competent in control of her life. "Hey, little sister. Think positive thoughts."

She wiped her eyes and sniffed. "Okay. I'll do that."

"You could phone him. Just to talk about the trip. Nothing too much. Just stay in touch." I was giving advice. I shouldn't give her advice. What did I know about marriage?

"I'll do that." She sniffed again.

The hotel phone rang. "Mark," I said.

It was Mark. He was in the lobby.

"Come on up." I told him.

Deirdre took one more sip of tea and rose. "I'll leave now. Have fun."

I hugged her again. I hated seeing her desolate. She really loved Michael and a break with him might devastate her. At the moment, she felt abandoned by Michael, Kala and probably Josh as well. She'd go back to her room and pet the dogs, listen to Kala and, I hoped, call Michael.

CHAPTER TEN

Gulliver greeted Mark with an excited yip and a welcome dance of twirls and jumps.

Mark squatted down and spent some moments in dog play. It gave me a chance to appreciate his thick, curly hair, damp from the shower and his strong arms. He moved easily and had that solid, stocky build of many Welshmen. I imagined his ancestors stumping over the hills, chasing sheep or shoving railcars of coal through the mines.

"Hello," he said as he stood and leaned over to kiss me briefly.

I returned from my fantasies. "Hello."

His eyes travelled down, taking in my new dress and my Aquatalia boots.

He let out a heavy breath. "You look amazing."

I grinned. "Let's go."

He looked around the room, taking in the huge bed. "We'd better."

I grabbed a light raincoat, checked that Gulliver had water, petted him and abandoned him to the comfort of the Queens Hotel.

We drove to St. John's Hall which is part of the library and town hall complex. Mark parked in the reserved area. He pulled out a small sign and placed it in the window. "Police."

"That's handy."

"It can be," he said.

I shut the door and joined him on the walkway. "Who will I be meeting at this auction?"

"Superintendent Tregere who is in charge of this district, for one."

Mark put his arm around my shoulders and propelled me toward the library.

"Is he in charge of you?" I deliberately slowed my pace. My boots were made for walking, not running. Mark adjusted to me.

"Temporarily. While I'm in his district."

"Who else?" We made our way past the shrubs which blurred in the mist and past a few trees, equally indistinct.

"One of his staff. I haven't met her yet. She's organizing the drug prevention program."

"Which this auction supports?"

"That's right."

The rain began almost tentatively, lightly drifting around us. I didn't trust it. It would be pouring soon.

Mark turned up the collar of his jacket and hunched a little against the cold and damp.

"There will be outreach counselors, treatment center staff, and some district nurses, trying to get the public to support centers and programs that can help addicts."

"Many people think addiction is self-inflicted."

Mark grunted. "Do they think an addict likes the life?"

"Some people do think that."

He snorted. "That's ignorance. No one would choose the life of an addict."

I didn't know much about addiction. Mark did, and he seemed passionate about it. He must have a reason.

I stopped and turned to look at him. "What happened?"

He stopped and faced me. "My sister," he said.

"What happened?" I repeated.

"Death from an overdose."

No wonder he cared. I met his eyes. "I'm sorry. When?"

"Two years ago,"

"Fentanyl?"

"No, a bad combination of opioids and cocaine. My brother-in-law thinks I could have done something."

"Like arrest her or something?"

He turned toward the hall and started walking. I tucked my arm in his and walked with him. We were nearing the entrance now.

"I don't know what he thinks. I didn't know she was in trouble. She lived in northern Wales, and I didn't see her much. I just didn't know she was having trouble. It's hard to tell, sometimes. All addicts aren't on the street. Some of them are your doctors and dentists."

"Your sister?"

"She was a teacher."

I tugged on his arm and stopped him. "I'm so sorry, Mark."

He pulled me toward him and hugged me, for comfort, I think. Then he ran a hand down my hair and touched my face. We stood like that for a moment. "It still hurts...especially that I couldn't do anything." He started toward the door of the hall. "So now I'm trying."

I nodded. "Okay. I'll help. I'll buy some things. Maybe we can make a difference."

"I'll get the romantic getaway. Don't bid against me." He lightened the mood.

I laughed. "Go for it."

The hall was set up with long tables with reserved signs on some of them. Mark checked his tickets and headed for a table near the stage.

"Just a minute, Mark. We need to register."

I nodded toward the side table laden with numbered paddles and staffed by an impressive looking young woman with metal in every visible orifice. She had shaved her head and used enough eye makeup to rival a racoon. She made a statement. No one was going to ignore her.

"Good evening," I said to her.

"Hello. Do you want to register?"

"I do."

"Sign here. Credit Card info on this card. "

"You too, sir?" She narrowed her eyes. "Cop, yes?"

Mark smiled. "Yes. I'll take a card, as well."

"Spend lots," she said, "and we can keep the sick out of the prisons."

"That's the idea," he agreed.

"Is this a registered charity," I asked her. "Do I get a tax receipt?"

"You do. So, spend more."

"That's the idea," I parroted.

Mark looked thoughtful. "I suppose we can get some tax relief from this."

"My accountant insists I get that receipt." I said.

"You have an accountant?"

"I do. I have a lot of money." I might as well let him know that.

"You do?" He looked sideways at me. We were going to have a conversation about my money at some time. Perhaps soon.

A uniformed, tall, wide-shouldered man stood as we approached the reserved table.

Mark gestured. "Claire, this is Detective Superintendent Edward Tregere of the Cornwall Criminal Investigations Department. Superintendent, this is my friend Claire Barclay."

The superintendent was about Mark's height. His uniform jacket was tight across his stomach, the material pulling as if he had grown wider since it was issued to him. Detectives didn't usually wear uniforms. I expected this one hung in his closet most of the time. He had bushy eyebrows and sharp, dark eyes. He stuck out his hand, and I shook it. He turned and waved to the tiny woman sitting beside him.

"My wife, Chesten. This is Detective Inspector Mark Evans from Hampshire and his friend Claire Barclay."

Mrs. Tregere and I nodded to each other. She was about sixty, around the same age as her husband and delicate looking, all creamy skin and wavy, white hair. She smiled.

"Are you part of the police, my lover?"

I blinked a little. No one in Seattle or even Hampshire would have addressed me that way, but this was Cornwall.

"No, I'm a tour guide. I bring tourists to different areas of England, and sometimes other parts of the British Isles."

"And to Cornwall," she said.

That was a reminder that the Cornish consider Cornwall a different country. They have their own flag and have never dissolved their parliament. As far as the Cornish are concerned, they are part of England only because they are temporarily aligned and momentarily congenial.

"And Cornwall," I agreed.

"Evans," the superintendent said. "You take my wife around with you, and I'll take Ms. Barclay. We'll circulate. Chesten knows everyone."

Mark raised his eyebrows at me. I looked at Edward Tregere.

"That would be very kind of you, Superintendent." I said, making a courtesy out of an order.

"This is an official event. We do our duty," he said.

"I assume I am seconded for the evening."

He looked at me quickly. "As you like."

"I like." I might as well. The evening would go more smoothly if I left the superintendent in charge of it. He steered me purposefully toward a small group of three men.

"Amos, me 'ansom," he said.

Amos was a little taller than me, stocky like many men in this area, with dark hair peppered with grey, dark eyes, a quick smile, and a nod.

"Ms. Barclay," the superintendent continued, "I'd like you to meet Amos Gwavas and his wife Emblyn."

A fair-haired, tall woman with similar dark eyes, smiled at me. "Em," she said.

"Claire," I said.

"Amos is one of our successful fishermen in this area," the superintend announced in his loud, gruff voice. "Good to see you here supporting the cause."

"Of course. Of course," Amos said.

"Are you going to bid," Em asked me, flicking her finger toward the paddle I carried in my hand.

I half-turned to exclude the superintendent from our conversation. I had the notion that he wanted to talk to Amos.

"I am. I have my eye on that scholarship. I thought I could bid that up a bit."

"That would be a good choice."

We wandered over to the goods table and looked at the items. The be-metaled receptionist had given me a catalogue and I opened it to the last page.

"This scholarship goes to a worthy student. It would give them something to look forward to and perhaps keep them off drugs," I said to Em.

"Just be careful you don't get stuck with it. Last year it went for a thousand pounds."

"I see." I wasn't sure if Em was giving me some kind of direction, but if she was, I missed the meaning.

I must have been mistaken about the superintendent's need to talk to Amos because he hustled me back to the table quickly— I noticed he limped slightly—and we were seated when the auction started.

Mark bid on the romantic weekend. He got it, too.

Em raised her eyes to me. "I trust, my dearie, that it's you he's thinking of taking."

I laughed. "He'd better be."

"Well, enjoy it. Our men don't get much time to themselves and even less with us."

I wondered if she was trying to warn me. I looked straight at her. "I like being alone a lot of the time. It might suit me."

"Oh, then. That's good. Not one of those clinging types be you then."

I shook my head. "I don't think so."

I raised my paddle for a couple of items but got serious when the scholarship came up for bidding. The auctioneer got it up to six hundred pounds where only Amos Gwavas and I were bidding. Em might have been trying to tell me that her husband was going to bid. Too bad. I bid one thousand pounds, and he dropped out.

"Sold to the lady in the blue dress!" I realized that Amos probably wanted local publicity for his generosity. Publicity didn't matter to me. No one here was going to book into one of my tours. I walked over to the registration desk, handed over my credit card, stopped to have a word with Amos, and walked back to the table.

"That's a whack of money," Mark said.

"I told you," I whispered. "I have money."

"So much you can give it away like that?"

"Yes."

"And now," the auctioneer said. "The lady who bought the scholarships has kindly donated it back. So, Amos, me lover, you can get into the game again." I had won the bid and paid for it and then I had donated it back to the organization so they could sell it again.

"Can you do that?" Chesten asked me.

"Yes. I just agree not to have my name associated with it. The person who gets the bid this time has their name on it."

This time the scholarship went for seven hundred pounds. The rehab program got my thousand pounds and Amos's seven hundred.

A young man in jeans and a hoodie came up with a tray of pins. He consulted a list on the tray and offered Mark a pin and then me.

"If you wear them," he said. "Other people will want to bid. Like competition, see?"

Mark and I looked at each other and smiled. The pin identified those who had successfully bought something. Without a pin, you identified yourself as *not* having donated. Clever.

"Sure," I said.

"Ta," he said and left us.

"Now, me bird." The superintendent leaned closer to me. I had thought he always spoke in a loud voice, but I found he was capable of a whisper. "That Amos. I suspect he gets his money from smuggling. I haven't caught him yet, but I'm watching him. Where do you get your money?"

Mark was quick to defend me. "She's not running a drug cartel, sir."

Tregere lifted his head and stared at Mark.

It flashed through my mind that no one had stood up for me in years, except Deirdre. It felt a little strange. I wanted to tell Tregere: It's none of your business. But I thought about how hard he must work to keep Cornwall safe and how much information he had to gather to do that.

"I inherited it. And just recently."

"Did you now?"

"I did." I said that firmly.

"Well, that was a generous thing you did. Some youngster will do well with that scholarship."

"I hope so."

I still glowed a little from Mark's quick defense of me. I could get used to someone caring for me. We said our good nights. Mark collected his coupon for the romantic weekend away, and we walked to the car.

Mark started the car. We should be heading for a loving night, but somehow the magic had dissipated.

"What's the matter?"

He drove toward the Queens Hotel and pulled into a parking lot near the harbor.

He turned to me. "You have a lot of money."

"I do."

"That makes me uncomfortable."

I thought about that. Before I inherited Paul's fortune, I too would have felt a vague irritation that someone with money wasn't of my class, that they could do things I couldn't, that somehow, they had more worth. It had something to do with how we had been raised.

"Tell me about your family."

"Middleclass upbringing, I guess. My dad was a teacher; my mum a nurse. It was a work hard, have fun, but you can't have everything you want sort of household."

I nodded, understanding him a little better. "I grew up poor. Before my dad died and Paul came along, my mom, my sister and I lived in poverty. I had to give up my place at the university and go to work."

He looked at me but said nothing.

"Then Paul met my mother and everything changed. Deirdre got a chance to university. I had left home by then. I worked for over twenty years, living on my pay check, taking the occasional gift from Paul, but managing on my own. Then Paul died and left me quite a bit of money. I have had so many years of frugal living that I have to remind myself that now I can afford different things. I live, though, as if I didn't have that money. I use it for big items, like my house and my business." It was hard to explain how I felt about having all that money. Secure. Supported. But I didn't use it every day. I would have to convey that to Mark somehow. I was just getting used to having money.

"My romantic weekend is pin money to you," he said.

I wasn't having that. "It's not the money. It's the weekend, romance and you that's important. Are you saying I only value it because it cost money?"

"Ow. I guess I sound a little sulky. Let me get my mind around it. How do you feel about having a lot of money?"

"I haven't had it long. My values in life haven't changed."

This wasn't going to be a night of romance. The money was bothering him, and I doubted he would put it aside and make love to me. I felt the smooth material of my dress. I'd had a good time at the auction, but I was disappointed it was going to end so soon. "I guess you need to think about it."

We sat in silence for a few moments. We were parked by the ocean, but we hadn't gotten any romantic inspiration from it. Besides the rain was teeming down now. We weren't going for a beautiful walk along the shore.

Paul would never have wanted the money to prevent happiness, but the money was part of me now. It had to factor into any relationship "How much is this going to affect us?"

He shook his head." I can't really know."

I truly hoped this wasn't going wedge us apart. It was growing into more than I anticipated. I made another attempt to talk this out.

"What do you want to know?"

He turned to me, his back against the car door and studied me for a moment. "Why do you work?"

I shrugged. "I've always worked. I like working."

"Why don't you splash it around more?"

"Why would I? I spend it where I want to. Like on drug prevention."

He smiled. "And Gulliver."

"Well, yes, I go overboard a little there," I said, thinking of the padded collars and designer rain coats.

"But you don't spend a lot on clothes."

"No…well. I'm not in the habit of shopping. I live the way I've always lived, but without the worry that I might be a bag lady when I'm old and I do spend more than I used to on clothes. These Aquatalia boots for instance." I felt a little desperate for a moment, that having this money was going to put a kybosh on this relationship and perhaps on any relationship. "I'm the same person I was when you picked me up for the auction, Mark".

"I know. I know. I just have to get used to it like you're trying to do."

He walked beside me toward the hotel lobby. At least he didn't just dump me at the door.

"Claire, to business. I have to interview Dr. Prior tomorrow. Is she here?"

I was happy to change the subject.

"I haven't seen her since we arrived."

"Can you find out if she's here? I don't want to alert the hotel clerk the police are looking for her."

"Do you think she might have taken off? Is she a suspect?"

"You know I have a long list of suspects and none of them have any supporting evidence." He said that a little bitterly.

I left Mark sitting on one of the sofa chairs in the lobby and walked over to the receptionist.

"Hello. I'm just checking that all my people make it back from their various activities and that I don't have to go looking for stray tourists."

"Ah, Ms. Barclay. Let me check."

She did. I waited. "Everyone's is back," she said.

"Including Dr. Prior?"

She checked again. "Yes, she came in about ten."

"Oh, thanks. That's a relief."

"Ever lost one?"

"Once," I told her, "in York. It took me hours to find her."

"Where was she?"

"At a rugby game and then at the pub in celebration afterwards, having a wonderful time."

She laughed.

Mark stood as I approached him and walked me to my room. I told him that Lena was safely in bed.

"Good. I'll see her tomorrow. She had the opportunity to knife Oliver Nott, and she left the scene. She knows he's been murdered, doesn't she?"

I nodded.

"And she hasn't called the police. Not the action of the blameless."

I thought about that. "On the other hand, she's a foreigner and may not want to get mixed up with foreign police. She could be innocent."

"She could."

"She's been asking about Nott as we travel around."

"She has?"

"She told me she wants to write an article about him. She's an academic. They write books and articles."

"Interesting." He stopped outside my door.

The magic had disappeared so I might as well talk about his investigations. "I forgot to tell you. Patrick has the research notes that Nott made."

"Patrick does?"

"So he says. Rita found them and gave them to him before he left."

"At least they are finally getting to me." He didn't sound enthusiastic. Wasn't he interested in the research notes? They might contain something useful.

"I think they could be important," I insisted.

"There probably isn't much in them that would help, but I need every piece of information I can get."

"Just ask him. I'm sure he'll give them to you."

He smiled at me. "Thanks, and thanks for coming tonight."

"I enjoyed it."

"You sure impressed Superintendent Tregere."

"I did?"

"He says you're a 'bleddy lovely lady' and probably too good for me."

I laughed. "And what do you think?"

He pulled me into his arms. "You surprised me. Really surprised me".

"Maybe I can keep you off balance."

"Maybe you can."

CHAPTER ELEVEN

I took Gulliver for a quick walk before breakfast. He trotted along the promenade and gratefully bounded onto the grass at the Alexandra Grounds. Few people were about so early on this Sunday morning, but seagulls whirled above an old man, diving for the bread he tossed into the air. Their wings whirred; beaks snapped as they complained harshly. The ducks who had waddled toward him were outnumbered and out-maneuvered by the aggressive gulls and sat patiently waiting for crumbs. Gulliver tugged toward them—- bread and birds were irresistible, but I kept a firm hold on the leash.

Back at the hotel, I fed him, abandoned him to the comforts of the bed and hurried to meet the others in the dining room. Deirdre and Kala were sitting at a table for two, but the others were seated at a round table. I sat beside Sharon with my full plate of eggs, rashers and scones.

"Coffee?" George reached past Sharon, poising the pot above my cup.

"Thanks." I accepted the nectar of the gods and sipped it appreciatively.

"I found a great pair of shoes in a small shop on Chapel Street," Lena was telling Ellie. "Really exquisite."

Ellie was listening politely, but I expect with little attention. I observed my group while I slowly indulged in my ritual coffee. Lena seemed relaxed, her gestures were slower, her eyes didn't move constantly the way they had yesterday. Her shopping excursion to Chapel Street must have agreed with her. She wasn't going to be so relaxed after Mark called.

"I can't seem to get into shopping when I'm on holiday," Ellie said. "It's such a chore."

"Unless you're buying books?" Lena suggested.

Ellie smiled. "That's true."

"I enjoy shopping," Holly said. "If I can sit down every so often. It's the domain of women. Everything is set up to entice us and cater to us. Lovely."

George was expounding on bird life to Sharon who was on his immediate left.

"I want to catch sight of a puffin. I know they're not exactly rare, but people haven't seen any in some time. What do you think?" He peered around Sharon and directed the question to me.

"You might be lucky." No one had seen one in this area for five years, but it was my job to encourage the guests, not discourage them.

"Grace," Sharon called across the table. "Isn't Penzance where P.D. James set a mystery?"

"Certainly," Grace wiped her mouth with her napkin and sat up very straight as if good posture contributed to accurate recall. "*The Lighthouse.* I liked that one. Veronica Black set her Sister Joan series here as well."

"I'm not a fan of them," Sharon said. "Too tepid."

"They seem a little too cozy," Grace agreed, "as if the author was creating an ideal world, not setting it in the one we live in."

"That could be said of many," Ellie chimed in. "Take Carola Dunn's Eleanor Trewynn. She is definitely a Miss Marple in modern dress or relatively modern dress."

Grace thought about that for a moment. "But the characters in Dunn's work seem more real. Eleanor seems like someone you could meet; Sister Joan does not."

"You might have to be Catholic to appreciate Sister Joan." Lena suggested.

"Perhaps," Grace said.

Holly disagreed. "I was brought up Catholic and I don't really like Sister Joan either."

That disposed of that literary series. They had finished their meal and were at the coffee stage. I was ready to put forth the plan for the day when Ellie brought out her mobile and passed around a picture of her granddaughter who was in first year at Reed College, a prestigious and exacting university in Portland.

"I'm impressed," I said as I passed the picture of a grinning, very young woman to Sharon. "Not everyone can get into Reed."

Ellie smiled. "She is a gem. Smart and sensible. My husband will miss her as she always spent such a lot of time with us. Well, he'll just have to deal. He will hop a flight to Palm Springs for a week while I'm away and golf with his retired dentist buddies. It will keep him occupied." She received the mobile from Lena and dropped it into her purse.

Ellie's report of her family reminded me that the people who came on my tours were usually wealthy. Even George was probably well off. Plumbers made money in this country. I was lucky they wanted to spend their money on a tour.

I told the group about our upcoming excursion to the Prussia Cove Cave. Deirdre and Kala moved their chairs closer so they could hear everything and receive their daily bulletin. I had just finished speaking when Mark loomed at the door.

"Dr. Prior?" he said.

Lena looked up. "Who's asking?"

"Detective Inspector Mark Evans of the Major Investigations Team. Could I have a word?"

Lena sat immobile for a second. I assumed she was processing Mark's title. "Major Investigations" usually means murder. No one spoke.

Lena took a deep breath, grabbed her purse and stood. George reached over and patted her arm.

"You'll be fine," he said.

She walked over to Mark. He stood aside and gestured her toward the manager's office. He never looked at me once. Either he didn't want to mix duty with off-duty, Lena being duty and me being off-duty, or he'd thought over my financial situation and decided it was intimidating. Damn. But surely, he'd talk to me about it and not simply flounce off? I smiled a little thinking of the solid detective inspector "flouncing".

"Mark, I mean Detective Inspector," I called after him.

He turned.

"Could you deliver Dr. Prior to the Prussia Cove Cave when she's finished her interview. We need to get moving, and I would appreciate it."

He hesitated, then nodded.

The cave was only twenty minutes away, but I didn't want to leave my group to come back for Lena.

Everyone retired to get what they required for the day. Kala dashed off to take her dogs for a quick outing, and Deirdre and I had another cup of coffee.

"I think Mark is cooling off," I said to Deirdre.

"Why?"

"Paul's money."

"Then he's a fool."

I thought about that. "He's not a fool."

"Perhaps he isn't cooling off. He has a murder investigation on his hands. It takes concentration."

Patrick joined us then, coffee in one hand and a scone in the other. He looked harried as usual, but he was clean, his hair wet from a shower and he had shaved.

"What's up with the tour today?" he said. "Where is everyone?"

"Getting ready to go to the Prussia Cove Cave," I told him.

"What for?"

"Because the cave is typically Cornish," I said. "And they are on holiday."

"That's where Kyle wants to go today. 'Get atmosphere for a promo video.'" He shrugged. "He's annoying, you know, all energy and angles and looking for a way to get our 'brand out there,' but he's right."

"What would you rather be doing?" Deirdre was curious.

"I'd rather be publishing autobiographies of notable people or biographies—something inspirational. Mysteries," he lowered his voice and looked over his shoulder. I was impressed that he remembered that my paying guests were mystery fans. "Most mysteries," he corrected, "are really frivolous."

I stared at him for a moment. They weren't frivolous, at least not all. Sometimes they were profound.

"In my opinion that is," he qualified. "I'd rather not publish them, although there's no question that Nott's death is increasing our sales, and we badly need that." He downed the last of his coffee. "I might see you at the cave. It depends on when Kyle gets moving."

Kyle moved into the dining room at that moment. He cruised the buffet, loading his plate with eggs, bacon, blood pudding and boiled eggs. I saw him put two boiled eggs into his coat pocket. That was not classy. Even Kala, young as she was, knew better than to pilfer from the breakfast bar. I headed for my room and Gulliver, after making sure Deirdre knew the way to the cave.

I didn't think there wasn't much smuggling in this part of the Cornish Coast any more. Most of it took place to the east near Devon, but there might be some. One of the most interesting endeavors of the past had been a smuggling business run by the Carter brothers out of Prussia Cove. I told my group about them as we drove the short distance to the cave.

"Three brothers, John, Harry and Charles ran a smuggling family business around the end of the eighteenth century. The boss was John who considered himself a businessman and from all reports, including his own, ran an unusual smuggling racket. Unusual in that they had ethics and sound business practices. They once broke into a revenue storage house to retrieve seized goods because they had promised delivery and they didn't want to break their promise. They didn't steal any of the other cache but took only their own goods. They had their own standards. They used Prussia Cove and operated from there. You'll be able to see the slipway they built to load and unload goods. They apparently prospered, evading the English tax."

"Walt Disney smugglers," Sharon said. "I mean," she said as I looked at her with some puzzlement. "Everything is prettied up and only the righteous prosper."

"Yes," I agreed. "Most smugglers weren't like that."

"Lots of brutality among smugglers then and now," George said. "From what I've read."

"Is this one of those ancient caves?" Grace asked, "used by Neolithic peoples for sacred ceremonies?"

"Not this one," I said. "There is a hand-dug cave near Helston where ancient peoples created shelters and sacred spaces. There are also caves left after the tin miners excavated. This one we are going to see today is on the beach and was formed by the action of the waves and perhaps improved on a bit by men."

"Are we going to get wet?" Ellie asked.

"Not today," I reassured her." The tide is out and the sea is calm. You'll be fine."

I parked above the cove and we walked down the trail to the beach where we met our guide. I'd hired a local guide for this cave because the hotel had recommended him and because his thick Cornish accent gave my tourists an authentic experience. They crowded around him, listening to him extoll the virtues of the Carter brothers. I could hear his voice roll over the beach, but I couldn't see him. Because he was short, he was hidden by the others. Deirdre and Kala hurried and joined them.

I sat at a picnic table a little distance away. Lena should be here soon. I didn't have long to wait as she came steaming down the trail. I held out my hand, guided her to a seat and poured her a cup of coffee from my thermos. My panacea for all ills.

"How was it?"

"Officious pigs!"

"Officious?"

"Officious, pompous even, but they aren't thugs like some cops at home. They seem to be intimidating while they are polite. How do they do that? It doesn't give you any grounds for slapping them with a lawsuit."

"Do you think they were satisfied with your answers?"

"No. I don't. I wouldn't care, but this is serious. There is no point in fooling myself. A murder is serious."

The sunlight lit red highlights in her thick brown hair. She was what my mother would have called a handsome woman, rather than a beautiful one. She was upset now and frowning, but even with that disadvantage she would attract attention.

I could hear the guide's voice tripping through his story, his tone rising and falling with the drama.

Lena gulped the coffee and thumped the empty cup on the table. "I did have an affair with Oliver last year. There's no denying that. We met at a writers' conference in Portland, and I enjoyed him. I often meet men at conferences. That's where the intelligent and interesting men are." She shrugged her shoulders as if trying to get rid of feelings.

"I wrote him and told him I was coming over and expected to pick up where we left off last year."

"You thought he'd want that?"

"It wasn't an unreasonable expectation. That rat had been emailing me for months, letting me think he was just waiting for me to arrive."

"When did you find out he wasn't interested?"

"At the party. Rita, his editor, told me *they* had been having an affair. I bet it wasn't just Rita who was on his string. I was furious." Her chest heaved, and I suspected she was reliving that fury. She stared out at the ocean. "But I didn't kill him."

I processed what she had told me. She said she hadn't killed Oliver, but she was Mark's best suspect. I didn't see how the police could let her leave the country until they found who did murder Oliver.

"You are the Jane they were looking for."

"Yes. That's my name. Jane Lena Prior." She sounded defensive.

"I expect we can stay with Lena for this trip."

I didn't want the rest of the group to know about her problems, but with Mark singling her out for an interview, they'd know soon. "Did the officer put any restrictions on you?"

"He took my passport." She looked at me despairingly. "He took my passport."

There is nothing that makes a tourist feel so bereft as losing a passport. I reached out and held her hand. "You'll get it back, Lena. You'll be eliminated from his suspect list, and you'll get it back."

She snatched her hand away. "When!" She stood and brushed off her vest and jeans. "When it suits them." She answered her own question. "I will have to wait on some nitwit from the con-stab-u-lar-y," she drew out the syllables with sarcastic inflection, "decides I can go home. Until then I'm stuck here."

"If I can help, let me know," I said, quietly.

She stopped and turned back to me. "Thanks. This isn't your fault." Then she whipped around and caught up to the group.

I trailed behind her and slipped in with Kala, Deirdre and Sharon. The guide was just finishing.

"What did I miss?" I asked Kala.

"It's pretty cool, Auntie Claire. Smart crooks and dumb revenue agents. It probably wasn't like that, but I like the story."

Kala told me briefly about the history of the cave as we followed the group toward the entrance. We fell behind the others. I could hear the guide talking about the attitude of the community to smuggling in the past and today.

Kala tugged at my sleeve. "Auntie Claire, can you stay by Sharon. I want to get closer to the guide."

I raised my eyebrows. "Why should I get close to Sharon?"

"She can't hear very well, especially when there are lots of people around and the cave will echo a bit."

"I hadn't noticed her hearing loss." I was surprised that Kala had.

"Yeah. She's okay in the van and when we are eating because we are close. If she doesn't hear something, she just ignores it. I don't think it bothers her much but still....."

"Sure, I can do that."

Kala, for all her occasional contempt for her mother, was a kind girl. Deirdre needn't worry about her.

But I didn't get a chance to move up beside Sharon because Patrick came hurrying up beside me.

"I suppose the guide is giving the romantic tale of the past."

"That's what my tourists want to hear," I said.

Patrick snorted. "He should get with the times. These caves," he looked around. "Well, maybe not this one, but ones further east, are used by present day smugglers to bring in drugs and sometimes people whom they smuggle into the country. Even now, it makes sense to evade customs and the police by unloading from a mother ship onto a small boat and darting into the caves around here."

I remembered Carola Dunn's story about the illegal immigrants who were dumped into a cave and left to die, rescued by the heroic actions of a young man. Perhaps Dunn knew something.

Patrick stared at the entrance to the cave, bouncing lightly from foot to foot.

"Nott researched all that, so I expect he was right. He usually was.

Do you suppose he got too close to a drug operation, and the boss ordered him killed?"

I stared at him. I hadn't thought of that. Had Mark considered this?

"However, there are two things against that." He held up his first finger. "First, Nott didn't risk his skin for anything. If he'd gotten close, he would have backed off and," his second finger shot up, "second, modern smugglers run a business. They don't kill each other off. They just move to a different space or a different commodity."

Newspaper headlines refuted that statement, but I said nothing.

"Where is the detective? I have those research notes."

"He just left."

"I'll catch him later."

Mark would want those notes. I'd be sure to remind him that Patrick had them.

He dropped his hands and stopped talking as Kyle hurried from the parking lot trail with a camera in his hand and another hanging from his neck.

"Have they gone in yet?"

"Just going now," I said.

"This will make good copy," he said. "Look at that ocean. Couldn't be bluer. Great shot of a bird high up there."

It looked like an osprey, soaring on the wind. Magnificent.

We waited while Kyle took some video. The cove was more U-shaped than a half-circle and rock cliffs lined the edges. I could see the slipway where the boats had made their careful way into the cove and the stone jetty and steps leading up to the path above. It had been a convenient and well-organized shipping center.

We trailed after the group and entered the cave. Sharon was well ahead, so I couldn't keep my promise to Kala. I'd have to explain later. The ceiling was high and there was room for all of us but I didn't like it. Without the sunlight, it was gloomy.

We tucked into edge of the group and I counted heads—one of the things tour guides do automatically. Everyone was present. Deirdre moved up beside me.

"Are you okay?"

She knew I hated caves. I imagined all that rock above me suddenly letting go and crashing down. I know the earth isn't waiting for me to come along before it less loose in a deliberate and malicious attack, but I *feel* as though that is going to happen. I took some deep breaths and endured.

When we finally got back into the sunshine, I set out coffee, biscuits and chocolate on the picnic table and my group gathered around. Patrick and Kyle joined us but they were not paying tour guests.

Kyle munched a free biscuit. "Pretty clever of those Carters to keep the Revenue Agents away for thirty years. They must have been a smart bunch."

"Smuggling is still going on," Grace said. "I read about it. "

"Yes," Kyle said." Lots of smart people around today. It's drugs, though, not wool or whiskey."

"There's nothing smart about smuggling drugs," George said with some heat. "Murderers, the lot of them." George leaned toward Kyle, his eyes almost slits and his mouth in a tight line.

Kyle's eyebrows shot up and his hand froze, the biscuit half-way to his mouth.

"Uh."

"Are you blind?" George hissed. "Don't you realize what kind of menace today's smugglers are to us? They're a plague. A plague."

"Sorry, sir" "Kyle said. "I guess I got caught up in the stories."

"You didn't get caught up," George said. "You just don't care."

I moved between them. This was my tour, and I wasn't having any fist fights.

"Kyle, why don't you get some pictures of the beach and the slipway before the light changes?"

Kyle looked at me, nodded and moved away.

"George, can I give you some more coffee?"

Lena moved toward him. "Hey, George. Have some chocolate."

Kyle was now down by the shore. Good, a problem averted. I could see what Patrick meant when he said Kyle was annoying. It was as though he had never become an adult and continued to live in a Kyle-centered universe. I didn't think he noticed other people's antipathy, unless like now, it was obvious. He was no doubt perfectly happy with himself. He had found a profession that allowed him to do well without having to understand others. I didn't envy his girlfriend.

"Lunch at Ben's Cornish Kitchen, a short drive away. We can see St Michael's Mount from there."

I drove them quickly to Ben's and everyone soaked in the view. There was a sign post to the small village of Gulvan.

"They have a St Wolvela there," I told Grace.

"How do you spell that?"

I told her. She shook her head. "Only in Cornwall."

The dogs were tied outside the restaurant door with water and lots to interest them as customers petted them and seagulls taunted them. I passed out menus to the group and told them where we were going after lunch.

"Today is our day to visit St. Michael's Mount. The tide is advancing, so it will soon be cut off from the mainland."

"Do we have to hurry?" Holly looked worried. I don't suppose she ever hurried.

"No. Everything is governed by the tides in these coastal communities and the kind of access you take to St. Michael's Mount depends on the tides. If the tide is in, you take the boat. They run frequently. Just watch the tides when you are there. There are signs telling you when it is safe to walk back. If it isn't, you take a boat. I'll pick you up about six. Would that work?"

"What's there to do on the island?" George asked.

I passed out the booklet I'd put together. "There is lots to see. The history is fascinating and there's a pleasant café in the village at the foot of the Mount. You won't starve."

"And gardens?" Ellie asked.

"Beautiful gardens, even at this time of year."

"Is there transport up to the castle?" Holly asked.

I nodded. "You have to request it."

"Did anyone set a mystery on this island?" Lena finally showed some interest in mystery writers.

"You'd think Burley set one here, but I can't think of it." I said. "Grace, do you know?"

"I don't think so," she said, "although *Wycliffe and the Cycle of Death* has a picture of the Mount on the cover."

We drove to the causeway where I saw my group onto boats. Holly seemed a little dubious about stepping onto the bobbing craft, but she managed. George, bless him, helped her on.

I loaded Pike and Duff with me in the van and texted Mark. "Patrick is looking for you to give you the research notes." I realized he had more details to pursue than I did, so those notes were only one of many areas of his investigation. I had a short run on the beach. Then I took all the dogs to my room and had a nap.

CHAPTER TWELVE

The next morning, the group had breakfast at the hotel and were gathered in the lobby ready for the day's adventure. I studied them for a moment. Lena was back in hyperactivity mode. Her gestures were more rapid and more frequent than they had been yesterday. Mark had not contributed to her holiday. Sharon was her usual calm self, listening to others and waiting to hear what I had planned for the day. Holly and Ellie were conversing in low tones. Grace was reading her itinerary. George was a little apart, waiting. Deirdre and Kala were walking the dogs and would join us later.

"Are you ready to explore the great, historic Poldark Mine?" I asked.

"Sure," Sharon said. "Sounds like fun."

"Is it narrow in there? Will I fit?" Holly frowned.

I glanced at her body—a little plump, but certainly within normal weight. She probably over-estimated her size. I nodded.

Ellie was not impressed with Holly's self-degradation. "You," she said firmly, "see yourself as twice as big as you are. You have a perception problem."

Holly's swift intake of breath was audible. I'm sure all she heard was "You have a problem."

"Off we go," I said hurriedly. "Everyone has their walking shoes, vests against the chill, cameras and energy?"

They agreed they had and followed me to the van. I had called ahead and ordered hot Cornish pasties for their lunch at the mine site. The tenants of tour guiding are to keep the clients well-fed, well-hydrated and civil.

"'Poldark.' Isn't that a TV series?" George asked as he settled into the front passenger seat.

"It is, and it was filmed there," I agreed.

"It was a book first," Grace said before I could get that in. "or rather it was twelve books by Winston Graham. Set in the late eighteenth century."

"Adventure?" Ellie asked.

"And romance," Sharon said.

Having given a literary setting to the morning, we headed off.

I activated the mic and, during the fifteen minutes it took to drive there, gave the group a potted history of Poldark Mine.

"This site was mined in the Bronze Age which was somewhere between 2100 to 750 BCE."

"And it's called the Bronze Age…?" George queried from his seat beside me.

"Because they made bronze from melting copper and tin…at least they added tin at this site. In other places, they added arsenic or something else. Sorry, I don't know what else." I hurried on to get my spiel in before we had to leave the van.

"This mine is an eighteenth century mine and has miles of tunnels. You will be going with a guide, wearing hard hats and paying attention to his or her instructions. Look for the distinct veins of blue peach granite. That's unique to Poldark." I glanced into my rear-view mirror. They were listening. "There's been an underground tin mine here since 1493, but the first above-ground mines have been preserved here in the beautiful gardens, so leave enough time to have a look at them." The gardens were lovely. I hoped the weather cooperated and they'd have a chance to see them.

"Didn't Graham set one of his Poldark mysteries at the mine?" Grace called up to me.

"His last one in 2002 was set here and the TV portrayal of that book was filmed in 2015."

"I'll have to watch that one," George said. "It could be pretty interesting to watch a film after I've been to the site."

I was glad they were looking forward to it. I wasn't going in with them. It was another deep, underground menace that made me shiver with apprehension, although the bright lighting helped. I'd descended into the mine once to find out if tourists would enjoy it. Most would. The tour was well done and interesting. But once was enough for me. My group had a guide. They didn't need me. At least, that was my justification for avoiding the underground atmosphere.

I passed out the pre-bought tickets. Deirdre and Kala lined up to buy theirs.

"It's the one hour main-mine tour, Deirdre," I called after her.

"Is there a choice of tours?" Holly asked.

"Yes, there's a ninety-minute tour that descends another seventy feet. It has steep access to level four of the mine, about 230 feet below ground."

"That would be great," George said.

Holly looked worried.

I turned to him. "I'm sorry, George. We need twenty-five people to book it, and they didn't have that many today."

"Suits me," Sharon said. "Is it cold down there?"

"It's cool so you'll need a vest or jacket of some kind," I said, "but it doesn't get cold."

"Too much earth between you and the air up top," Ellie explained. "The earth would act as insulation."

Holly frowned more deeply. I hoped she was going to be all right.

"If you'd like to stay behind with me, Holly, I'd be glad of your company."

I wouldn't, truly, be glad of her company because I'd like some time alone. But I did want her to enjoy her holiday.

"No," she said with determination. "If I don't put myself into uncomfortable situations, I'll never learn anything and I'll turn into one of those boring old ladies."

"Well said, Holly," Ellie applauded.

Holly grinned.

I relaxed a little. Good relations between Holly and Ellie were restored.

I addressed the group. "Does everyone have trainers?"

They looked at me blankly.

"Uh. Sneakers, running shoes, secure footing," I translated.

All eyes dropped to their feet. Lena had heels on her boots.

She shrugged. "I'm okay with these."

I refused to take responsibility for her shoes as I had reminded them to wear appropriate shoes before we left the hotel. I also had printed those instructions in the booklet and it was included in the information about the tour.

"If I break my ankle, I'll sue you." She sent me a bright smile. I expect she was serious about that and she would entertain the thought of suing me.

Just you try it, I thought and waved them off.

I walked over to the Tea House to be sure the hot pasties would be ready when they returned. The kitchen staff reassured me that they had everything in hand.

"What's the mystery connection?" a staff member asked me. He was about twenty, head shaved completely, bright blue eyes and an engaging smile.

"My group are interested in mystery novels," I said, "and like to see the connections between the places they visit and the books they read."

He nodded. "Interesting. We had a writer here looking for information for his novel."

A writer. There might be more than one writer searching for information. "Was that Oliver Nott?"

"Yeah. The dead guy. Makes you wonder what he found out."

I agreed that it did. What had he found out? Or had he just been picking up stray pieces of information?

I released Gulliver from my van and Pike and Duff from Deirdre's car. She hadn't locked it, but I don't suppose anyone would try to get into that car with two big dogs defending it. Not that they would defend anything. A more affable pair I've yet to find.

"Come on, crew," I said and headed off to the far west area of the *Trenere Wolas Gardyn* gardens. I let Gulliver off-leash because he wouldn't leave me, but I kept Pike and Duff on leash. I didn't trust them to come to my call and I couldn't whistle the way Deirdre could.

I had just returned the dogs to the vehicles when my group exited the mine. I got some excellent pictures of them chatting to each other, their colorful vests intermingling and white hard hats bobbing. They reminded me of ducks at a pond, bustling and busy. I'd add these pictures to my website.

"Fantastic," Ellie said as she came up to me. "We got to handle pieces of ore-laden granite, and there were actors down there showing us how they mined in the nineteenth century. It was beautiful but eerie."

"It's nice to be up in the sunshine," Holly said, "but I did enjoy it." She patted my arm, assuring me that I hadn't made a mistake in offering it to the tour. That was a relief.

I waited while they deposited their hard hats and then led them to the Tea House. The pasties were ready for pick-up. So far, the day was going well.

I invited them to a round table. "Get a drink if you like. Just tell them you are on my tour."

There were few other people around. Some had brought picnic lunches, but this was the end of the season, when few tourists visited even this World Heritage site. The group got their drinks and settled around the table with their pasties. It might have been the intimate atmosphere of the tea room, or the emotional release of escaping the underground, but Lena led off with a litany of her troubles as if throwing them at us like stones.

"The police think I might have killed Oliver Nott," she said.

That was an attention-getter. The group stared.

"They do." She was emphatic. "I was at that party where he died, and I was furious with him. I'm a suspect."

"Are you scared?" Kala asked.

Lena turned and considered Kala's question. "Terrified," she acknowledged.

Sharon raised her head. "You didn't do it?"

"Of course, I didn't do it." Lena sounded irritated. That was more like her usual demeanor and somehow it took the drama out of her announcement.

Sharon was not offended. "So, who did? Maybe that's what we should find out? All of us are mystery fans. We know a lot about solving crimes. What do we need to know to prove you're innocent?"

"We need to know who really did it." Kala was enthusiastic. Her dark curls bounced and her eyes lit. It was a puzzle for her, not a tragedy.

Deirdre was quiet. She couldn't jump in with public speculations. She was an officer of the court; her participation could get complicated.

"Someone at the party killed him, is that a fact?" Grace asked.

"Someone at the party," Ellie offered, "or someone who slipped into the party unnoticed."

"Could they do that?" Sharon was giving Lena her concentrated attention, but I answered.

"Yes," I said. "They could have slipped in through the back gate, stabbed Oliver, and left by the same gate. If Oliver happened to be alone at that time, no one would have seen him…or her".

"Given Oliver's proclivity for promiscuity," Lena said. "It could have been a him or a her, anyone, really." She sounded bitter and angry.

"We can't consider strangers," Grace said, "even if they are a possibility. So, let's concentrate on the suspects we know. Who else was there?" She turned to me.

I was in what I think the Americans call the "hot seat." If I cooperated with my group, Mark would not be pleased. If I didn't, I could shut down the most cohesive group activity of the tour. In any case, I hadn't been at the party, so I didn't know who had attended

"Well, Lena might know." I passed the question to her. "Who was there?"

"I was there, but I was there as Jane Prior."

Everyone stared at her.

"It's my name," she said. "Jane Lena Prior."

"Why did you tell us your name was Lena," George asked.

"Because I stupidly was trying to hide from the police."

"It didn't work," Kala observed.

Lena, half-smiled. "No, it didn't work. You can still call me Lena. It's my name, after all."

There was silence for a moment. For one thing it is hard to identify someone by a name that is different from what you are used to and, for another, a person who admits to trying to hide behind a different name raises suspicions.

"So," Grace brought the conversation back to the question she had asked. "Who was at the party?"

"Rita and Patrick," Lena said. "It was their house. Kyle, the ad man, and his girlfriend, Alex something."

"Alexandra," I murmured. I brought her to mind: taller than me, thin, and blonde.

"That might be her name." Lena shrugged. Obviously, Alexandra hadn't impressed her.

"And there was a couple from London. She wore last year's shoes and gross makeup, but I never heard her name."

"It was loud with music and lots of yelling and talking. I could hear it inside my house." I verified that it would be hard to hear one another.

"And nobody really introduced themselves. It was just music, drinks, and joints. Oliver was outside in the garden because it was quieter there."

"Well, he's got it quiet now," George sounded as if he was satisfied with Oliver's death.

"Did you know him?" I asked. His satisfaction seemed personal.

He shook his head. "No."

Why the satisfaction at his death? Had Oliver stood for something he hated? Could he be lying and he *did* know him?

"All right," Grace said. "What about motive?"

"I know I was angry," Lena said, "but I've had many lovers and I've never killed any of them. Mary Wesley says the way to remove annoying lovers is to introduce them to someone else. I wouldn't have had to do that with Oliver. He found his own next lover. I would have calmed down and done something about him, but not murder. I'd just got to the stage when I realized I was well rid of him. I was still furious, but Rita could have him."

"Rita?" Holly perked up. "Another woman?

"Patrick's wife," Lena said. "She'd been having an affair with Oliver, but he was tired of her. He had another lover in view, a man this time, I think. Oliver was adaptable."

Sharon leaned forward. "Did I hear that right? He was chasing after a man this time."

"I think so."

Rita would not be happy that Lena had known all about her affair.

Sharon leaned back. Kala might be right, and Sharon was hard of hearing.

"Could Rita have been upset?" she asked.

I remembered Rita crying more over her own bad judgement than Oliver's death. Perhaps I was being a little harsh about that. She had been upset. If she'd knifed him, she *would* be upset.

Lena gave that question some thought. "She could have," she finally said, "but she's such a meek thing, I can't see her getting passionate enough to stab Oliver. I'd like to nail her as a suspect because it would let me off, but I just can't see it."

I could, but I wasn't going to say so. Holly and Ellie asked questions. Lena tried to answer them. George, for the most part, listened. I collected the garbage from the lunch and binned it.

"We have another hour here if you'd like to look at the machinery and the gardens. The machinery is interesting and the gardens are beautiful. The weather is good—no rain. Your tickets entitle you to wander wherever you like."

They arranged to return to the van in an hour. Deirdre and Kala decided to return to Penzance and take the dogs to the beach.

"You don't have tickets for the concert tonight." I reminded her.

"Who's playing?' Deirdre asked.

"It's *Tír na nÓg*, an Irish group. Kala would like them, I think. But it's sold out."

"No chance of tickets?" Deirdre was used to planning ahead. But she had joined my tour at the last minute. Therefore, I could not get her tickets.

"You could go early and stand at the box office. Someone might be selling their tickets."

I had a vision of my professional sister whose secretary arranged concert tickets, waiting in a crowd by the stage door, vying for a chance to attend. It would be different for her, certainly. On the other hand, she might enjoy it.

"Kala and I will talk about it. We might go and stand by for tickets," Deidre said.

I waved them off. "Have fun at the beach."

"I'm going to wade and find shells," Kala told me. "Can Gulliver come with me?"

I transferred Gulliver and sat in the sunshine to wait for my group. The sun was warm on my face, and I had nothing to do but think.

Lena insisted she hadn't killed Oliver, but then she would be adamant about that whether she had or not. Rita was quite capable, in my opinion, of shoving a knife into Oliver. Patrick? It didn't fit his personality, somehow, but Mark would tell me I was no judge of killers. Kyle? Alexandra? And there were probably others. What about the man Oliver was moving onto romantically? I almost dozed while suspects chased each other through my mind. The hour of contemplation was a waste of time because no stunning revelation came to me.

Gulliver slept off his beach run while I spent the rest of the afternoon in my hotel room working on my laptop: checking on reservations, answering emails and making inquiries on accommodations for my next tour.

Mark arrived at the hotel just as I was rounding up my group to drive them to the Acorn Theatre.

I was a little flustered. "I can't stop now, Mark. We are due at the theatre."

"Which one."

"The Acorn."

He could see Holly and Ellie standing by the door and Grace hurrying toward them.

He sized up the problem quickly. "I'll meet you in the Cabaret Bar at intermission."

"The concert is sold out. You won't be able to get a ticket." I worried aloud.

"I don't need a ticket," he said emphatically.

Oh, right. Police business. Handy that. He could arrive and gain entrance on his warrant card. Neither of us had greeted each other as lovers. He was the policeman and I was tour director. Sometimes, we would be doing our jobs when we met up. This was one of those times.

I love the Acorn Theatre. It is an old Methodist church, intimate and funky. I distributed the tickets and the group filed in. I was just turning to follow the group when Deirdre and Kala rushed up clutching tickets.

"Mum only had to pay half-price," Kala enthused.

"Excellent."

Deirdre flushed a little. It was always a thrill to get a bargain. Deirdre and I had grown up living on bargains and when we got a good one, we were delighted. I wondered if she remembered.

"The woman wouldn't take any more," Deirdre said.

I laughed and waved them in. I found my group and settled on a seat beside Holly.

She was studying the audience. It was eclectic: cashmere twinsets and pearls sat side-by-side with long, irregular hemmed skirts and kerchiefs binding up dreadlocks.

"My kind of an audience," Holly said.

"I hope you like it."

"Well, my dear. At my age, I'm prepared to enjoy just about anything." I thought about her determination to enter the mine this morning. What a wonderful attitude to have at any age. I hoped I would have more like her on my future tours. That curiosity, that willingness to try new experiences, gave tremendous vitality to life. I could learn from her about how to enjoy challenges.

She did enjoy it. She tapped her feet to the loud beat, sighed over the sentimental ballads, and clapped with enthusiasm.

At intermission, I left my tourists to mill with the locals and headed for the Cabaret Bar. Mark was waiting at a table near the far end, two drinks on the table.

I sat down opposite him. "Hi."

He smiled. "How is the tour going?"

"Pretty good." I took a sip of excellent vodka and lime. After a moment, I asked what I wanted to know. "Any chance you are going to spoil it by arresting Dr. Prior?"

"Not today or tomorrow. I'm trying to trace Oliver's' contacts in the area. He'd been busy researching around here. He'd even tried to meet with Tregere."

I couldn't imagine Detective Superintendent Tregere spending any time with a fiction author.

Mark confirmed my opinion. "Tregere thought Oliver was a waste of time and wouldn't meet him. He told him to go to the library." He pulled out a notebook, the electronic kind and scrolled down. "Aria Rowe, local librarian, supplied him with material. I thought I'd look through that material to see if there was any suggestion of where he might have researched or who else he talked to."

"Patrick's trying to connect with you to hand over the research notebooks of Nott's. Rita gave them to him."

"Yes, thanks. So you said. I'll look for him. They might give me some info."

It seemed to me that I was more interested in what was in those notes than Mark was. But he was used to assessing evidence and I wasn't.

Perhaps there wasn't anything of value in those notes. After a few seconds thought, I told him my group's assessment of the murder in terms of motive and opportunity.

We were talking when the bells chimed indicating the second half of the concert. We ignored them and stayed in the bar. I could hear the music which, even as a muted background, I really enjoyed. We had exhausted our discussion of the murder. The more important worry was his attitude to my legacy. I took a deep breath.

"Mark, please talk to me about my money."

He stared at me and then looked down at his glass. We both watched him rotate it slowly. Finally, he looked up. "I'm not sure it's rational. It just makes me uncomfortable."

That was frustrating as I did not know how to respond. A reason would be helpful. "I'm the same person I was before you knew about the money."

He shook his head. "I don't know why it bothers me. I feel cramped or oppressed or something by it, as if it's always there, something you can depend on other than me."

I had not considered what it would mean to a man who would want to take care of me. Depending on a man for my living, no matter how much or how little money I had, was not my experience in life. I knew I could depend upon money that a man left me. I had some thinking to do, too. Why are intimate conversations fraught with pitfalls? I wish I had something wise to say. I thought about Bert, the philosopher of the beach.

"Bert Wynne would say: Let those feelings go."

Mark snorted. "Bert's an Alcoholic Anonymous member. He'd also say "Don't give advice.""

"Is offering a suggestion the same as giving advice?"

"Yes."

The problem of my money would not be solved this evening.

I heaved a sigh. "Mark, I'm not giving the money away. Deirdre won't have it. My stepfather gave it to me so I would not have to worry about poverty. He knew that my childhood had been difficult. When I get home, I'll show you his note that was given to me upon his death. I honored his love for me by accepting this inheritance."

"I don't expect you to give it away. I'll mull it over what you just told me."

It looked as though it was out of my hands.

"Anyway, I have another four days to a week down here before my Superintendent in Hampshire hauls me back."

I would meet his superintendent some time--if we stayed together. She was a little older than Mark and ruthlessly efficient, so he said.

The clapping continued and then softly through the air came the strains of the Welsh hymn "All through the Night." Mark had sung me that song when we first started going out.

He met my eyes and reached for my hand. "I'll try, Claire. I really will."

I fought back the tears. We had tenderness between us, the beginnings of love perhaps. Mark was struggling with my legacy and I couldn't think of any way to help him with that. He would either work out a way we could be together, or he wouldn't. It hurt to think we might not manage to deal with this.

I gave him a hug and left him there and waited in the lobby. My group had enjoyed themselves and were ready to go back to the hotel. I transported them to the hotel, parked the van, escorted them into the lobby and bade them good night. I roused Gulliver from my bed, then the two of us joined Kala and Deirdre in their car. We drove to Long Rock Beach, about a six-minute drive. It was ten at night, and dark. Of course, there was no one there but us.

We opened the doors and the dogs erupted onto the beach. Pike and Duff tore off onto the sand while Gulliver galloped for about fifty meters, then turned and trotted back to me. It was dark and scary out there as far as he was concerned. I petted him and he happily tucked in beside me.

Kala ran after the dogs.

"Kala," Deirdre called after her. "Activate your light."

Immediately a pinpoint of red appeared in the dark.

"What's that?" I peered into the darkness, but I could only see the tiny light.

"My tracking device," Deirdre said. "It's attached to her vest."

In seconds, two more tiny lights appeared in the dark.

"The dogs?" I asked.

"Right. I put lights on their collars."

I'd consider that for the future. Tonight, Gulliver wasn't moving from my side.

We couldn't see the island of St Michael's Mount, even though I knew it was hovering just off shore in front of us, but we could see the strobe lights on the castle's stone walls and the warm lights of the cottages at its base. It was as though the castle and the village below floated in the sky.

The air was chilly and didn't tempt us to linger. We walked quickly along the sands, keeping an eye on the dancing lights of Kala and her dogs.

"We've had a great time, Claire," Deirdre said. "Thanks for letting us come. Kala has enjoyed your tourists, particularly Sharon."

"Sharon's pretty practical and straightforward," I said. "And she seems to enjoy Kala as well."

Deirdre sounded a little puzzled. "Kala treats her as if she is one of the dogs that she has to mind."

"She does, doesn't she?" I thought about Kala's revelation about Sharon's hearing loss and was about to offer that as a reason when Deirdre changed the subject.

"I've been talking to Michael on the phone every night," she said. "Somehow, he listens when I talk on the phone and we've been getting… well closer, I guess. Do you think I have to go away to get his attention?"

I thought about that. "What's your biggest complaint about Michael?" I asked.

"At home, he doesn't listen to me. I hate not having his attention. He used to listen and comment and help me work things out."

"*When*, doesn't he listen to you?" I insisted on more detail. I had an idea, and I was going to see if it was possible.

"When I come home from work, and I want to tell him about my cases, he just looks away."

"What else is going on when he does that?"

She thought about it for a moment. "Josh is likely coming in and demanding a ride to some sporting event. Kala is dashing through getting her books and clothes ready for the next day. The dogs want to pay me attention. At least the dogs care," she said bitterly.

"Any other time?"

"When we are out with friends at the pub. He'll interrupt me in the middle of a story. He doesn't get my order when I ask him for it."

"Is it," I said, "as if he doesn't hear you."

"That's it," she said. "As if whatever I said didn't matter."

"Back up to 'he doesn't hear you.' He just doesn't hear you."

She stopped walking and leaned closer. I could see her clearly.

"Doesn't hear me?"

"That's right. When Kala caretakes Sharon, I think it is because Sharon is hard of hearing."

"I didn't notice."

I let that comment lie in the still air.

Deirdre's head came up, and she put two fingers in her mouth and blew a shrill whistle.

In a few moments, Kala and the dogs trotted up to us.

"You called, Mother?" Kala said sarcastically.

"Yes. This is important." She looked hard at Kala. "Do you think your father is deaf?"

Kala stared back at her, with obvious derision. "Of course, he's deaf."

"What do you mean 'of course'?"

"Well, he's not completely deaf. He just doesn't hear you when there's noise around, or people are talking at the same time. If you sit where there is light on you, and he can see you and no one else is around, he can hear you."

"He can hear you on the phone?"

"That's right. There's just the two of us on the phone, so he can hear me. The phone is on his ear. He's not real deaf, just a bit deaf. Can I go back now? The dogs are jumping the waves in the dark. It's eerie."

"Sure," Deirdre said. She hugged her daughter. "Thanks."

"No problem." And she was off.

Deirdre turned to me. "Deaf," she said. "He's only forty-two. I hadn't considered that."

"Not *real* deaf," I quoted Kala. "Just a bit deaf."

She nodded and kept on nodding.

"Deirdre," I spoke sharply.

She let out a long sigh. "I will have to re-evaluate, for certain. Could I be wrong? Really wrong? Not a mistress; not disinterested—but deaf?"

Deirdre hated being wrong. She hated feeling that she had missed what her young daughter had seen. She had a hard time believing that, with all her brains, something so obvious as deafness, slipped past her. This trip was turning out to be one where both Deirdre and I were learning new and different ways to view our loved ones.

We walked on the cool sand, the waves slapping on the shore, the wind soughing softly and the dark like a blanket around us. Three pinpricks of light danced in the dark far off at the edge of the sea.

CHAPTER THIRTEEN

W e spent the next day in St. Ives, the quintessentially quaint, Cornish settlement on the sea, full of holiday independent shops where Holly could spend her money and Lena could avoid Mark. I hadn't seen him since he left the hotel last night.

The houses jostled in what my mother would have called "higgledy-piggledy" fashion, following narrow cobblestone streets and climbing the hill beyond the curved, sandy beach. Grace would, no doubt, find the bookstore, Lena, the trails along the shore to Gwithian's beach, and the rest could wander among the shops, the shore and the art galleries for the day. The Tate St. Ives was here, one of the four impressive Tate galleries of Britain, along with the Barbara Hepworth House and The Leach Ceramic Gallery. The town was rich in artists.

I walked the three dogs in the park above the town. Few people were about, but I kept all the dogs on leash. I didn't fancy chasing them. They were happy enough and loved the smells, no doubt pungent after yesterday's rain, and darted around me, investigating bushes, leaves and any piece of turf or mound of dirt they could find. I untangled those leashes many times.

I bought a late take-away lunch and sat in the van to eat it, then left the dogs for a check-in at the local tourist office, investigating the roster of shows and events scheduled for the spring and was back at the van to meet the group at five o'clock.

"I'd love to stay here a few days," Grace told me. "I hardly left the bookstore, and there is much more to see."

Holly chirped a hello as she climbed into the van. I noticed she had only one bag.

"No shopping?" I asked her.

"It's coming by mail," Ellie said, dryly. "Tons of it."

Holly grinned. "Very efficient, your post."

"Very smart, the vendors," George said.

The next day, I drove them around the peninsula toward Lands' End. I showed them the beautiful views along the coast and the Minack Theatre where plays were staged in the summer season. I pointed out the sign for St Levan to Grace. She nodded and wrote it into her diary, adding another unusual saint name to her collection. We stopped for a few minutes at the sandy beach nearby, managing a short, dry walk and some exercise for Gulliver, Pike and Duff. Deirdre followed us to lunch in Mousehole at the Rock Pool Café. We sent George and Kala to the beach with the dogs. Even though the Rock Pool Café was dog friendly, three dogs, two of them labs, would be intrusive. I handed George the keys to return Gulliver to his crate. Kala would do the same with her dogs, and they would join us at the café.

"Order me a beer and fish and chips," George said as he left. The varied menus of my carefully chosen pubs and restaurants were lost on George.

"Same for me," Kala said.

I laughed. Cheeky girl. "Sorry, no beer. Lemonade?"

"Okay."

We walked along the sea wall to the café which was getting the full benefit of the sunshine. The American women were fascinated by the English group: Deirdre, Kala, George and me as we pronounced the name of the town as 'Mowsel.'

"But it's spelled *Mouse Hole*," Ellie complained.

"There isn't any logic in many of our pronunciations. You might have trouble with Worcestershire and Derbyshire."

"How do you spell those?" Ellie asked.

When I told her, she stared at me her face showing incredulity. "Darb-i-sure?"

"So, the spelling is just a general guide to the pronunciation?" Grace said.

"That's often true," I agreed.

"I've been making assumptions that many place names were pronounced phonetically," she said.

I didn't answer her. It's England, after all, and we have a right to pronounce our own the language any way we like. I kept that opinion to myself, but I gave her another name.

"'Fowey' is pronounced 'Foy.'"

Grace stared at me. "That's not logical."

"No," I agreed. For some reason I felt a little glow of national pride that our version of English was not accessible to all.

George and Kala joined us and we tucked into the tasty food. One of the benefits of tour guiding for me was the quality of the food. But, since most tourists wanted to walk, I managed to burn off most of the excellent fodder.

"This detective," George asked me as we were leaving the restaurant. "He isn't around today?"

"I haven't seen him." That didn't mean he wasn't somewhere in the vicinity.

"He spends a lot of time near us. Who does he suspect?"

He looked at me directly from under his shaggy brows. I was reminded of an eagle's sharp penetrating gaze. I felt like a rabbit, waiting for the talons. I distracted myself by thinking of his incorrect grammar, I notice when a speaker uses "who" when they mean "whom". It's a lost cause trying to correct them. "Whom" is disappearing from usage.

"I'm sure he suspects everyone," I said. "But he has to have evidence."

"Not Lena? She's a little sharp, but she's not a killer."

"I'm not in the detective inspector's confidence," I lied.

"Looks like it to me." He leaned toward me.

George was tall, and wide. I wouldn't be able to push past him. The rest of the group had gone ahead and George was blocking my exit from the café.

"Uh, George, Mark and I are friends, but I am not an officer of the law, and I can't be part of his investigations. If you want to know anything, you will have to ask him." I spoke firmly, hoping that would satisfy him.

It seemed to, because he nodded and stepped back.

What was that about? Did he worry about Lena? Or about himself? What did I know about him anyway? Not a lot. He's lost his son to drugs. He hated the drug trade. I expect he was bitter and angry. I don't think he had been deliberately threatening, just unaware of his effect on me. I felt a sudden compassion for him. I was not a psychologist, but I wish I knew a way of making his life a little easier.

We returned to Penzance for the afternoon, and the group spent their last day there in the shops and galleries of the city. They were on their own for dinner.

Mark stopped to see me at the hotel where I was catching up on my correspondence and settling the bill. I was happy to leave my paperwork to join Deirdre, Kala, and Mark for dinner in the hotel dining room. After the meal, Mark and I offered to take all the dogs for a walk on the beach while Kala and Deirdre packed for their departure in the morning. It was raining, so Kala was willing to hand over Pike and Duff to us.

I wore rain pants and an anorak. Mark just had an anorak. He and the dogs got wet. We didn't have to go far for their romp, at least Pike and Duff galloped over the beach with their tiny lights showing us where they were. Gulliver stayed with me. He does not like the rain.

We rubbed the dogs dry in the lobby with towels supplied by the management and delivered Pike and Duff to Deirdre.

"I'll say goodbye now," Deirdre said, "as I want an early start in the morning." She patted Mark's shoulder and hugged me.

Kala reached up and wrapped her arms around me. "Thanks, Auntie Claire. It was brilliant."

"Fantastic," I agreed.

"Awesome."

We grinned at each other. Her curls sprang around her face, the moisture in the air affecting her hair the same way it did her mother's. She reminded me so much of Deirdre at that age. I hugged her tight. I was going to miss her.

"It was lovely to have you," I said and meant it.

We moved on to my room where Gulliver headed for the bed.

"Just a minute. Hold him, would you, Mark?"

I fetched a towel from the bathroom and spread it on the bed. "Okay. Now, he can come up."

Mark unsnapped the leash, and Gulliver leapt onto the spread, found the towel, curled around once and planted his chin on his paws. His eyes closed.

Mark smiled.

I looked at Gulliver, finally dry and comfortable. Then I looked at Mark. "Your pants are wet."

Mark glanced down. "So they are."

"I think you should get out of them and hang them on the towel warmer."

He put his hands on the snap of his jeans." I think you should get out of your wet clothes as well."

"I'm not wet."

"Pretend you are." His eyes held mine.

We had breakfast in our room, and Mark promised to see me later in the day. I had booked a tour of a smuggler's cave near Fowey, and he thought he'd come along. I felt a bubble of excitement. Sustaining, that's what this relationship was, or what I hoped it would be. I blinked, refocused and concentrated on business.

"Fine," I agreed. "It's popular today. I had a text from Patrick. He plans to join the group for the cave tour. Apparently, Kyle thinks it will make good footage as this is the area Oliver Nott was exploring."

"That's why I'm here as well."

I stared at him, my mind on Kyle's need for publicity but aware that Mark had said something important.

Mark continued. "Not because I want to promote Nott's books, but I want to know who he talked to here."

"Smugglers, you mean? Do you think there is active smuggling going on?"

"Of course." He was matter-of-fact about it.

"Drugs? People?"

"One of those. Possibly both, but probably drugs."

"Not in a tourist cave, though." That didn't make sense.

"Not likely, but I'll come anyway and see what I can find out. Your friend, Bert, lives around here. Keep your eye open for him."

"Do you think *he* has something to do with drug smuggling?" I couldn't imagine it. Bert?

"I don`t know. I'll look at anyone or anything. This tour might give me information. I'll pick up those notes from Patrick."

I nodded. He hadn't forgotten. It would take many pieces of the puzzle to put together the explanation behind Oliver's death. Drug smuggling might be part of it.

Fowey was about two and half hours from Penzance. I pulled onto the town quay at Fowey Harbour about eleven that morning and helped everyone unload and move into The Galleon Inn. It nestled along the River Fowey in the center of the lower town. The crooked streets, homes snuggled up to one another and crowding up the hill gave the impression of a settlement that had seen smugglers and Revenue men. I wondered if they used it as a movie set.

"We're scheduled on the smugglers tour at noon," I told them. "Could everyone be back here at that time? All right?"

They were back promptly. This time Lena was wearing trainers.

"This is Daphne Du Maurier country, isn't it?" Grace phrased it as a question, but it was more of an announcement.

"It is. She wrote about the smuggling and the wildness of the countryside. Her books abound around here—in the rooms and in the bookstores. You`ll be tripping over them."

"Not my favorite," Sharon said, "but she was an important writer. I get that. She lacks humor."

I glanced at her. She had definite opinions. I suppose when you get past seventy, you can be decisive and confident in your opinions—wear purple and learn to spit, as Jenny Joseph says.

"Fowey. It's a lovely little town," Sharon said.

"It's pronounced 'Foy,'" I reminded her.

Grace rolled her eyes. "I don't believe it."

I shook my head. "Trust me. It's Foy."

"I'll never get it," she said.

Archie Bennet, our guide for the morning, arrived. He was about five-foot-eight, wiry, pushing sixty, a little grizzled of beard and hair and almost bouncing on his feet.

"Good morning. Good morning. A nice crew you are this morning. Anyone been through this smugglers' tour before?"

We all shook our heads.

"Good. Good. We'll be off then."

"Where are we going?" George asked.

"East toward Looe," Archie said. "You're English?" It was an accusation as he reacted to George's accent.

"That's right," George said. "London."

"Welcome to the country of Cornwall," Archie replied.

George grunted. The slur was not lost on him.

"The rest of us, except for Lena, are from the Oregon," Sharon informed him.

"From America, then?" Archie said, making sure he had placed Oregon correctly.

"That's right," Sharon said.

"Good. Good. You've had a bit of smuggling history yourselves. Not so old as ours, but some."

"Prohibition, you mean?" Ellie asked.

"That's right. That's right. Back in the 1920s or so, wasn't it? You prohibited alcohol. What were you thinking?"

Sharon laughed. "It didn't work, in any case. Everyone found a way to get alcohol. You've had a longer history of it here."

"Yes, we have, we have."

And Archie was off on a history lesson. My group followed him, highly entertained by his information and his delivery.

I smiled at the hotel clerk as I left. She'd recommended Archie, and I think he was going to work out very well.

I caught up with them on the quay where, at this time of year, we were allowed to park.

"Were you born here?" Ellie asked.

"No, my dear, I'm a Yorkshireman. A man of the Dales, I am. But my wife grew up in Fowey and couldn't leave her parents, so we settled here, and I'm a happy man with a happy wife." He nodded several times and then added. "Nah then, I have to go roaming on the Dales at least once a year to keep my blood strong. It thins out in this climate—too much sunshine. Follow me, Missus," he said to me and hopped onto a motorbike.

He idled his machine at the exit, waiting for us. My crew piled into the van, taking their places without any discussion. I had placed a water bottle and some chocolate at each seat. On some tours, individuals became attached to one position in the van and didn't like to give it up. That meant another person objected. Rotating seats was the way to keep the peace. Lena was in the front today. As I turned the van to follow Archie, I saw Mark standing by a car in the lot, watching me. I nodded but didn't wave as I'm not sure he wanted the others to know he was there.

"There's the cop," Lena said.

"Mark," I said.

"He's following us," Lena queried?

"Perhaps," I said.

She bit her lip and blinked. I looked ahead, paying attention to the route Archie was taking. I knew she was worried. "You are no more suspect than anyone else, Lena."

"So you say," she snapped.

I stopped trying to ease her anxiety.

I followed Archie to a layby at the top of a cliff and parked beside his motorbike. The group was eager and escaped from the van quickly.

"Uh. Oh," Holly said as she stood beside me looking down to the sea. "Is it far to the cave?"

I stayed back with her as the others headed toward Archie. "It's down the cliff to the beach. Do you think you can do it?"

She stared out at the sea and at the clouds, scudding across the horizon. The wind gusted around us, lightly, almost gently. She pulled her knitted cap down and straightened her shoulders. "Let me try."

"Fine. You let me know if you need me to turn back".

"Claire, just stay by me, okay? I think I can manage the hike. I just hate heights."

I turned to her and met her eyes. "I hate caves."

She grinned. "Let's go then. A couple of wimps." We both laughed.

I saw the top of George's head, the last one heading down the trail to the beach.

It wasn't as bad as we'd expected because someone had put handrails along the worst parts and cut stairs into the steep sections. It wasn't long before we were on the pebbles of the shore. The tide was out, exposing a small cave, not deep, just a shelter from the waves and leading out from it, a road cut into the side of the cliff and trailed up toward the cliff top.

"Why didn't we come down the road," George asked.

"It's fallen away at the top, "Archie said. "Happened a few years ago."

We moved from the sea and toward the cave which, at this ebb tide, was free of water.

"Does the ocean come right in when the tide is full?" Sharon asked.

"It does, Missus, and right handy it was. A boat came in with the tide, unloaded the contraband and left. Then, the men on shore came down this road, loaded up the donkeys and trucked the contraband to hiding places all over the country."

"Is this cave in use today?" George asked.

"Well, no, man, but I probably wouldn't know about it if it was. If there are hiding places in use for smuggling today, they'd be secret. I'm from Yorkshire. No one would tell me anything. My wife, now, she might know. That kind of information gets passed in Cornish. She speaks it… well, she speaks a mish-mash of English and Cornish…and I don't. Not that she'd tell me, mind. Not good for me to know."

There were some people who spoke Cornish words, and I knew there was a push to revive the language, but, unless Archie had a unique group of Cornish-speaking relatives, he would understand his wife.

"I see," George said. "But you don't think they use this particular cave."

"Think on it, man, There's no road to it now."

"There's a path."

"Oh, aye. So perhaps," he said diplomatically.

"If it's not happening in this cave, it's happening somewhere around here." George was either fascinated by smugglers of today, or he was obsessed by them.

"You think so."

"Oliver Nott wrote about it. He researched here. It's happening."

"Aye, maybe so. Maybe so," Archie said peaceably. "Maybe further east around Looe. More possibilities there."

We stared at the cave while Archie pointed out the platforms and the rock jetties along the wall. From there, the smugglers must have tied their boats to the iron rings, loaded the contraband into carts, and urged the donkeys up the hill to the cliff top.

"It wouldn't take long, perhaps two hours, to unload and tote the brandy up the hill." Archie waved toward the cliff top.

"Who was the chief smuggler in this area?" I asked Archie.

"Many people over the years," he said. "Backalong, about 1840 or so, a lot of brandy headed to the local pub, the Crown and Anchor, where Richard Kingcup was the smuggler *and* the landlord."

"It was usually brandy they smuggled?" Ellie asked.

"Aye, or salt," Archie said. "They needed brae salt to pickle the pilchards, and salt had a crippling tax in the old days."

"No one wants to be taxed. So, people supported the smuggling, then?" Sharon asked.

"They did," Archie said "because they saw themselves as a separate state from England, a Cornish country, and," he shot a sly glance at George, "some still do. The taxes were rank unfair and the people as a whole were resentful of that, they were. Very resentful. The revenue officers were English. Not that there wasn't the occasional man considered a traitor here who informed on them."

"What happened to such a man?" Sharon asked. She leaned forward, trying to hear every word.

"He left…or he had an accident," Archie said.

A small silence followed this as we thought about what kind of "accident" might befall someone who betrayed the smugglers.

"If there is smuggling going on now," George said, "would an informant have an 'accident?'"

Archie looked at him and was quiet for a moment. "I wouldn't know, now would I?"

It was then that we heard the rattle of gravel falling from the path and the clumping of boots as two men descended. Patrick and Kyle. They had followed us here.

"Hello, all," Kyle said breezily. He stood looking around the cave. "Oh man, this is great." He pulled out his camera. He looked smaller here in the cave where the vast empty space towering above us diminished us all. It did not diminish his ambitious nature.

I was used to tourists with their mini cameras, but Kyle's was much bigger. He knew how to use it and started snapping shots.

"Hey," he said to Archie. "Tell me about this place."

Archie looked at me.

"No." I interjected. "Kyle, you can hang around at the back of the group, but you cannot ask questions. This is a private tour, and you are gate-crashing."

"Come on. It's just a tour. I can use the info."

"Back off, Kyle," This time, Patrick intervened. If I had it right, Patrick was Kyle's boss. "No questions."

"Sorry." He smiled at the group, sure of his charm. It didn't work on this group. They stared back, unimpressed.

Patrick was my neighbor, and it was hard to deny him, but they had horned in on my tour without regard for the group or myself.

Kyle wasn't curbed for long. He engaged Grace and Sharon in conversation.

"Oliver Nott's new novel is going to be a hit. It's set in caves like this one—in today's world though."

"What are they smuggling in the novel?" Grace asked.

"Drugs," Kyle said. "In this novel, it's a real business, a going concern. Nott did his research, everyone knows that. He was a pain to work with, but you could rely on his backgrounds."

"Leave it alone," Patrick said. "He wasn't God. He could make a mistake."

"Not likely. He could smell out a deal. People are getting rich on drugs."

"And people are dying from it," George said. His voice was quiet, but no less menacing for that. I hurried up to them.

"Kyle, I think you and Patrick should leave now. My group would like to have more time with the guide, and you are distracting them. Sorry about that. I'm sure you understand. This is my business after all."

"Your business?" Kyle said. "Oh, the guiding business. Yeah, I guess it matters. Sure, see you later. I've got my pictures anyway."

Patrick muttered a soft, "Sorry" and hustled Kyle away.

I breathed a sigh of relief when they left. Patrick, I can take. He can be quiet. But Kyle was another story. George couldn't stand him, either.

My group enjoyed Archie now that Kyle and Patrick had gone. I paid him when he had completed the tour and he received tips from everyone. He was happy and so were we.

"Anytime, Missus. Anytime," he called to me as he buzzed off on his bike.

I left the group at the Fowey Quay, drove the van up the hill, and parked at the Main Park. I could leave it near the inn for a few hours, but overnight required parking up the hill. Gulliver and I walked back, enjoying the cobbled streets, the narrow, crooked lanes and the ambiance of the romantic life of the past. I wondered what it would have been like to have been a citizen of this town all those years ago when everyone kept the secret.

Kipling's poem gave me some idea.

> If you wake at midnight, and hear a horse's feet
> Don't go drawing back the blind, or looking in the street,
> Them that ask no questions isn't told a lie
> Watch the wall my darling while the Gentlemen go by.

Every man, woman and child must have been part of the conspiracy. The tourist trade was capitalizing on it now. There was some irony in the Cornish people extracting money from English tourists in the celebration of smuggling, an activity that evaded English taxes.

I noticed the names of some of the stores: The Lugger which I think was the name of a smuggling ship, The Life Buoy Café, Du Maurier Literary Centre and Gift Shop, Mrs. Noahs. No apostrophe. I agree with Lynn Truss's book, *Eat Shoots and Leaves*, on the apostrophe question and other grammar problems. Apostrophes are disappearing all over the world.

I was approaching The Galleon Hotel and musing on the charm of the town when I turned a corner and bumped into Mark. He grabbed my elbow to steady me.

Gulliver bounced up, trying to get his share of attention.

"I see you, *ci bach*. Down," Mark said and squatted to pet him.

I noticed Mark spoke Welsh when he was feeling affectionate. I thought it meant "little one."

Gulliver almost twisted himself inside-out in ecstasy. I had a similar feeling tumbling about my heart. I took a deep breath.

Rising, Mark slid his arm around my waist and snatched a quick kiss. "Hello."

"The same to you," I said and smiled. "I thought you were going to join us this morning at the cave."

"I got called back to Penzance. The librarian, Aria Rowe, found the material Nott had been studying. I drove back to Penzance and had a look at it."

"Was he studying caves around Looe? That's where our guide said most of the smuggling caves were."

"Hmm."

What did 'hmm' mean? Was he going to keep back information? Highly likely.

I pressed a little. "Do you think he was really onto some big drug smuggling ring, or he was just looking for an imaginary setting for his own fantasies?"

Mark looked away and then back at me. "That's the problem. I don't know. But I'll follow it up. Want to look at caves with me?"

I don't suppose he expected to find anything because, otherwise, he wouldn't have invited me. I was starting to get some idea of how he both included me in his investigations and excluded me. He was a complicated person, and he had complex ethics.

I brought my mind back to the caves. "My people really enjoyed the one today, and I hear the ones around Looe are even better, but we don't have much time that isn't already allotted. If the cave is important, Nott might have been killed because he knew about it. If you know which cave Nott was looking at, I'd like to avoid it."

"Good plan, but I definitely want to find it. Can I take you out to dinner?"

I shook my head regretfully. "I'll be working tonight. We are going to dinner at The Ship Inn, an old pub from 1570: stained glass windows, tables, lots of wood, pub atmosphere and great food. You're welcome to join us."

He did join us and fitted in pretty well. I didn't expect Lena to be happy to have him there, but she was civil. Gulliver joined us as well and we crowded into a corner, ordering from the menu and having drinks all around. Gulliver got a bowl of water. There was a trio of violin, guitar, and bodhran, the Celtic drum, playing lively music. Gulliver stayed close to my legs, not quite sure about all the noise. Kala would have loved it, but they were no doubt home in Guilford by now.

I thought I saw Kyle come in, but I wasn't going to ask him over. I did see him later when I went to the restroom with Grace. He was sitting at a high table with Amos Gwavas, the man who had bid on the scholarship at the drug prevention auction. Detective Superintendent Tregere thought Amos was involved in smuggling drugs. Kyle was, no doubt, looking for color and film sets. He'd better be careful that he didn't get too close to the kind of information it would be safer not to know.

CHAPTER FOURTEEN

Early in the morning, I took Gulliver to the nearby beach called "Readymoney." I imagine there was a smuggling story behind that name. but I didn't know it. I fed him, then left him in my room and headed for the "included" breakfast.

Lena caught me in the hall to complain that the soap in her room was of poor quality and there was no shampoo. I told her I'd see to it. I kept a few toiletries in my van. Lena wasn't the only one I've ever had to deal with who had travel requests. My experiences included a particular weave count in the sheets, non-dairy, gluten free, vegan food, fish and shell fish free or a dedicated listening ear. It was how the travel business worked now. People had complicated needs.

My so-far reasonable group were gathered at the tables in the sunny pub overlooking the river. They had finished eating and were now drinking coffee. Holly was, as usual, encased in various scarves, skirts and shawls, Lena in practical but stylish leisure wear. Sharon looked comfortable in what was probably her uniform on her ranch: jeans, a loose polo shirt and a hoodie. George was in dark clothes, jeans and an open neck shirt. Grace and Ellie were dressed casually. They all looked rested and ready to be entertained. Other than a couple in the corner who were intent on each other, there was no one else in the room. Outside, three men sat on the terrace, enjoying the sunshine.

"Isn't that Bert over there on the terrace?" Holly asked me.

I took a closer look at the men. "I think so."

Amos Gwavas was sitting with him. Perhaps they both lived near here.

"I want to get another carving," Holly said. She turned to the group. "Would you wait on making plans until I return?"

They nodded.

I followed Holly. Bert had started to stand, but Holly waved him back to his seat.

"I'd just like another carving if you have any," she said as she got closer.

Bert nodded. "I can give you one. These are my friends: Amos, his brother, Dennis and brother-in-law, Jason Jones."

The men nodded.

"And this is Claire Barclay, the tour director." He introduced me to the men and looked at Holly.

"Holly, from America," she said.

"Hello, Amos," I said.

"Miss Barclay," He acknowledged me. When you had engaged in a fierce battle to win the bid at an auction as we had, you remember your opposing bidder.

The men had been drinking coffee and were in no hurry. Perhaps they met there every day. Bert fished inside his capricious pockets and came up with another puffin.

"That's lovely," Holly said. "I'll take it. Thank you."

Ellie and Sharon moved up from behind me and exclaimed over the carving. Holly had a good eye. Bert's carvings were unique.

"Any more?" Ellie asked.

"Sorry," Bert smiled.

I was glad I had my wooden shell. I wondered about Bert. He *couldn't* be as affable as he seemed, but he did radiate warmth and good humor. In contrast, Amos and his relatives were closed and reserved. The Cornish weren't known for the generous interest Bert showed. Amos was more typical.

"I wasn't expecting to meet you here." Bert looked from one to the other, including them. "But the unexpected can be a pleasure. Give up the expectations and trust the process." He must be quoting again. Was that in the AA Blue Book?

"We're here for another couple of days if you come back this way," Ellie suggested.

"Well, now, I'd have to work much too hard to have anything ready that soon."

Ellie said. "All right. I'm glad I already got one."

"We're making plans for the day," Sharon said. "Do any of you have boats?"

Amos nodded.

"Do you take tours?"

"No," Amos said. "Lots of tours going out, though. Check on the quay."

Amos was barely polite.

"You'll enjoy the tours, I'm thinking" Bert said. "The guides know the area like their back gardens. Most of them grew up here, they did, most of them, yes. So, they have the stories."

He smiled, and we were left to wonder if the stories were imaginative. No doubt they were entertaining.

We re-joined our group. Holly passed her puffin around for admiration.

"Did you get one, Claire?" Ellie asked me.

"Earlier," I said and rooted through my rucksack and found the wooden shell encased in a sock. I extracted it and passed it around. It was beautiful. I pushed the sock back in the rucksack but dropped the shell in my pocket. I'd wrap it later. We discussed options for the day. I handed out the booklet I had put together on Fowey. It included the boat tours that Sharon was interested in.

"There is a *Wind in the Willows* guided boat tour as well. Fowey is where Kenneth Grahame wrote the book."

Grace looked puzzled. "I thought it was set on the river Thames."

"There's a controversy about that, but he did live here, was married in the local church, and it seems reasonable that he was describing the Fowey in that book. The trip is lovely and the river an area... "

"Of outstanding natural beauty," Ellie supplied.

I grinned. "We do love to protect our beautiful areas."

"I'll go on that tour. I loved Toad of Toad Hall and Rat and the others," Grace said. "Anyone else want to accompany me?"

"I will," Ellie said.

The others turned back to the booklet and studied their options.

"I'll take the Fowey river tour," Sharon said.

"I'll go with you," Holly said.

"There's a bus tour of the town and surrounding areas. I'll take that," Lena said. "Mary Wesley must have known this country pretty well. I originally came on this tour to explore Mary Wesley's country."

"Is there a coastal walk?" George asked.

"There is. "

"Of outstanding natural beauty?" Ellie asked

"Of course."

"I'll take the walk," George said.

They agreed to meet for supper at The Ship Inn again which wasn't far from the Galleon.

"It's pub style, and the food is local and fresh," I reminded them. I had realized early on the tour that this group did not want fine dining with snowy linen and hovering waiters, but they did appreciate good food—most of them. George's tastes were not gourmet.

Here, at the Galleon Inn this morning, the pub was bright with a wall of windows, airy, and, even with the hovering clouds that dulled the sky, the ambiance was cheery and casual. The bartender arrived with a fresh pot of coffee.

"Tell us about the writers in this area," Grace said. "I know about Daphne du Maurier."

"Couldn't help but know about her," Sharon complained. "Everything in my room has 'du Maurier' on it. I expect to find cigarettes."

"You are right about the cigarette connection," I told her. "Her father was a famous actor and he sold the name to the tobacco company about 1929 to pay his taxes."

They stared at me.

"Really?" Ellie queried.

"Truly." I was sure about that.

"Who else wrote about this area?" Grace persisted.

"Janie Bolitho wrote seven books in the Rose Tevelyan series. Since her character is an artist who paints all over this area, she might have included Fowey at some time, although most of them are set in Penzance. She was born in Falmouth which isn't far from here."

"Good writing. A little too much romance," Sharon said. She always surprised me with her breadth of knowledge of the genre.

"I like that romance. It seems real and not, I repeat, *not* sentimental." Grace also knew her authors.

I continued. "There is L. A. Kent who wrote *Silent Gull*. That's more of a thriller than a cozy. W. J. Burley wrote about different places in Cornwall and certainly showed the village atmosphere of the area."

"I need a bookstore," Grace said.

"On South Street. It's a gem of a bookstore and specializes in Cornwall authors."

"Fantastic."

"Let's all go there first," Holly said.

"No," Lena was firm. "Let's go there last, so we don't have to cart books for the rest of the day."

"Some of the tours start in the morning," I said. "You might want to book your tour and then work out when you can go to the bookstore."

"I'm going to stretch my legs," George said. "I'll catch up with all of you later."

One by one, they gathered their various purses and rucksacks and left for the day.

I returned to my room to fire up my computer, check on my emails and do some correspondence. The day got progressively darker. It was not yet raining, but I stuffed a waterproof hat into the pocket of my quilted jacket before I set off later in the afternoon.

Gulliver and I walked around the town. It is beautiful, and I loved coming here. I had favorite places to go, but, now with Gulliver, I had to adapt my usual perambulations to include some grassy areas and cafes where he was welcome. We hiked out to Readymoney Cove again and then beyond to St. Catherine's Castle. The rain held off, but threatened with dark cumulous clouds on the horizon. Storms could whip up quickly as if racing from Newfoundland, impelled by thousands of miles of open Atlantic to hone in on the Cornwall coast. But today, it seemed hours away. We had time to join the Coastal Path and hike along the cliff tops.

I had to stop to give Gulliver a rest. He was young and not up to this prolonged walking. I settled on a flat rock, delved into my rucksack, found my thermos and poured both of us some water.

I saw George about a quarter of a mile away on the path to Polkerris. He had binoculars with him and was watching something. Birds, I expect. I tried to see what birds might be showing themselves but saw nothing of interest. He was looking at the cliffs. Perhaps there were birds perched on the cliff sides. Many had already left on their trek to the south, but the gulls stayed all year, and there were many different kinds. I left him to it and walked as quickly as Gulliver could tolerate back to the hotel.

Gulliver was happy to have his supper and crash into sleep on my bed. I left him there and walked to The Ship Inn. Everyone had arrived but George who walked in just as we were giving our orders. He slid into a seat where a beer awaited him. Grace had bought it for him.

"I hope it's what you like," she said. "I noticed you drank ale, and this is a specialty of the house."

"Thanks," George said and took a sip. "Very good".

Grace smiled.

It doesn't take much, sometimes, to make people happy. Just a little thoughtfulness. Could George accept Grace's benevolence and be generous to someone else? I pondered for a moment on the contagious nature of kindness and what it meant in daily life.

It's a good thing we didn't order food for George because he changed his regular order and asked for "Mr. Kittow's Pork & Leek Sausages, Mash,

Port & Juniper Gravy." I ordered the slow-cooked lamb and everyone indulged in delectable food in a relaxed atmosphere.

While we were waiting for our meals George pointed to a poster near the door.

"It looks like there's a lecture on tonight at the Parish Hall."

"What kind?" Ellie asked

"It's about preventing drug addiction. A big-wig police officer is going to speak."

I got up and walked over to examine the poster. Detective Superintendent Tregere was speaking. I wondered if Mark would attend. "The hall isn't far from here, about a block away." I hadn't planned anything for tonight.

"Not my cup of tea," Grace said. "There's an author presentation at the bookstore tonight. I'll go to that."

"I'll go with you," Ellie said.

"I'll go to that as well," Lena said.

"I'll tag along to the drug lecture," Holly said.

"Well, Sharon," I said. "What are your plans?"

Sharon didn't answer, distracted by the crab crusted cod the waiter was placing before her.

"Looks good, doesn't it, lover?" the waiter said.

Sharon grinned. "I live in beef country, far from the ocean, and never get any sea food fresh. It tastes different."

The waiter nodded. "Proper sweet when it's fresh."

"Good anyway."

I waited while she took a bite.

"Ah," she said with obvious satisfaction.

"A new experience?"

"Lovely. The older I get, the more I wonder what I've missed all my life."

I watched her take a few more bites.

"So, Sharon, what are you plans for tonight?"

She put down her fork and gave me her attention. "There is a football game on TV in the hotel pub. I thought I'd have a drink here, watch the game, and go to my room and start on one of the many books I bought today."

"Sounds good. You remember that 'football' here is soccer to you."

"Oh, that's right. Still, I think it would be fun to watch the game and watch the people watching the game."

Everyone seemed happy with their plans.

George, Holly and I walked to St. Fimbarrus Parish Church after our dinner and joined the people filing into the hall.

"I have never heard of St Fimbarrus," Holly said. "Who was he? Or she?"

"I looked him up," I told her. "There was a St. Barry who is apparently buried here, but he got confused with St. Finnbarr and somehow morphed into St. Fimbarrus. I doubt there is another reference to St. Fimbarrus in the world."

"Don't count on it," George said. "Someone, somewhere, will name their poor kid that just because it's unusual."

He had a point. I've heard some daft names for kids lately.

"Another saint, particular to Cornwall," Grace said, "even if he may not have been real."

I ushered George and Holly into a row of seats taking the last seat but one, leaving empty the seat beside me on the aisle. If Mark came, I wanted him to sit with me.

The room had filled and the moderator, a portly, bald man, tested the microphone.

Mark slipped onto the seat and reached for my hand, squeezed, released it and sat back.

"Hi," I turned, met his eyes and smiled. I was tempted to reach out and smooth those dark curls away from his forehead. That would not do. He has his dignity to keep in public. I forced my mind onto business. "Is Tregere here?"

"He's here. He's often here. He says there's drug smuggling going on nearby and he's determined to find it. This lecture is one of his ploys to combat the smugglers."

"What else is he doing?"

We were speaking in whispers and, with the conversations going on around us, were not likely to be overheard.

"He's taken to roaming the cliff paths with binoculars. He tells everyone he's bird watching on his days off, but he's watching for boats going into the cliff caves. He says the fishermen, a few he has his eye on, know what he's doing, but so far, he hasn't caught them smuggling. I think he wants the smugglers to know that, even on their days off, the police are watching."

"Amos," I said. "He told me he suspects Amos. He's here in Fowey."

"Amos Gwavas?"

"Yes."

"He lives here. Or around here."

The Detective Superintendent strode up the center aisle and took his place on the stage. He limped, but it didn't seem to slow him down or detract from his imposing presence as he swept onto the stage. He commanded silence and got it. He started mildly, talking about statistics, the kind of drugs that had been available in the past and the kinds that were available now. Then he began to speak about Fentanyl, the new and deadly drugs proliferating the world of addiction.

I glanced at George. His hands gripped his knees, the knuckles white. I wondered why he put himself through this pain. Was it a kind of penance, a way to assuage guilt? As far as I could see, all parents felt guilty about something, holding some regret about the way they had handled a problem, a decision of their child's they had influenced, but guilt about a child's death would be excruciating.

The Superintendent went on to talk about the possibilities of death from Fentanyl overdose. Then, he got specific and talked about the death of a fourteen-year-old boy in Fowey last month.

"You think drug deaths only happen to addicts? Not true. They happened to innocent, inquisitive boys and girls. We raise our children to be curious about the world, to be brave, and to try new things. That was all he was doing and he died for it."

The audience was silent.

"Either we dig out the dealers, the smugglers of drugs and the sellers of death, or we confine our children to our houses and make them afraid to live in the world. That would cripple them and make them unfit as adults. Parents need help. So do the police. The police can't do this alone. We need everyone to help us. Remember your fathers and grand-fathers telling you what it was like during the war? When Hitler was twenty miles away? Everyone was alert to the danger of spies and sabotage. Everyone reported any suspicious activity. That's what we need now. We need to know who is smuggling and who is selling—and stop them. It's ager!"

His voice rang over our heads. No one moved. He sat down. The moderator thanked him and the meeting was over. "Ager." Ugly. I agreed. It was ugly.

I took a deep breath and turned to Mark. "That was dramatic."

"It was. He's right. We need community help to stop this. The Super suspects many people know who is smuggling. He is appealing, mostly I think, to the women. They will, at some point, he hopes, have had enough and tell their men to stop."

"But the returns must be highly lucrative."

"They are. But the fishermen who are smuggling *live* here, and they don't want to take their money and move. If their wives, daughters, girlfriends and mothers come down on them, they may decide to live more peacefully with less money. If the women are determined, something might change."

I thought about it. Didn't the women of Sparta do something like that? I wondered if it had been effective back then.

I met Kyle and Patrick on the steps.

"That was terrific," Kyle said. "It'll make good copy."

"Did you check it out with the Superintendent Tregere?" Mark asked.

"I don't need to. This was advertised as a public event. Press can cover it and report on it."

Mark sent him a sharp glance. "You're not going to report on it, you're going to use it in a promo."

"Same thing under the law, as you might know."

"Not my area," Mark said.

Kyle smiled and moved off. He was clever and had obviously researched the laws around privacy so he could use the photos he wanted and stay within the law. He was young, ambitious and pushy enough to achieve fame. I half-admired his drive while I took care to avoid him as much as I could.

Patrick looked exhausted. "I wish Nott had written about the gardens of England or something. This is hard to take."

"You look tired, Patrick."

"I'm not sleeping. It's all getting to me. That idiot, Kyle, is getting to me. It's like spending time with an annoying twelve-year-old. I never wanted kids."

Mark left me to go talk to the Superintendent Tregere. George and Holly had joined the tea and biscuit line. I turned to Patrick.

"How bad is it for you, Patrick?"

"Really bad. I think I'm having a nervous breakdown, or a depressive incident, or a psycho avoidance episode or something. I feel crazy."

"What about consulting a doctor?"

"I have to wait weeks to get into my doctor. I'll probably be better by then. Something's got to give. Rita's nuts. She's been acting like Oliver was her best friend. I don't even think she liked him, but she's grieving, and it's driving me crazy. And then Kyle is dragging me into the digital world, and I don't want to go there."

Bert would say: don't give advice but I couldn't resist. "Book yourself a week at a farm or a B & B on the coast. Don't see anyone. Sleep, eat, and rest."

He stared at me. "And let the business go to hell?"

I nodded. "Call in and say you have the flu. No one would want to see you then for fear they'd get it."

He blinked, looked away, then back at me. "Not a bad idea."

My group plus Mark reconvened at The Galleon Inn pub.

Lena and Grace reported on a local author who read from her work.

"She was dreadful," Grace said.

Lena giggled, actually giggled. "Grace and I could hardly keep from laughing. Such purple prose. 'The slinky, inky, slimy hand oozed from the sand.'"

Mark laughed. "She *didn't* say that?".

"She did, and it got worse."

"Spare us," I said. I was smiling when I turned to Sharon.

"How was the game?"

"Manchester United won. That was not popular in the bar. I met a couple of gents who explained the game to me. While I had them talking, I asked them about cricket. Now *that* game is unfathomable. They explained it to me, but I still don't understand it."

"Very difficult to get, cricket," I said.

George collected his beer and brought it to the table.

"How was the lecture?" Sharon asked him.

"Hard to take," he said.

Sharon glanced at me quickly.

"Yes, Detective Superintendent Tregere laid it out for the audience that drug addiction and experimenting with drugs is a problem that everyone is responsible for. He almost demanded that the audience pull together and stop the importation of drugs."

"Is that going on here?"

"He thinks so," I said. I knew Mark didn't want to comment.

"We have more and more drugs in Oregon," Grace said. "It's scary. It's as if the drug barons are pretending they're legitimate businessmen and are amassing a monopoly on the world."

"What's the answer?" Ellie said.

They all looked at Mark.

"Decriminalize it. Make it a health issue, a mental health issue and get the cops out of the mix."

George stared at him." How would that help?"

"If your kid is on drugs and you know it, you could ask the health department for help. Right now, you don't dare because you'd be throwing your kid into the justice system which doesn't help your kid, just protects others from him. We have to change the system."

I thought of the fourteen-year-old boy who, if caught with Fentanyl, would have been deemed a criminal. That was ludicrous.

George nodded. "We have to clean up the mess we have. Like the Superintendent said at the lecture. It's up to everyone."

"He said that?" Ellie asked.

"Yes, he said it was like the Second World War where everyone helped to watch for sabotage."

"I see."

"The war was very close here," I offered. "France was occupied and only twenty miles away across the ocean. The possibility of invasion was real, the bombing was real and people were prepared to resist."

"So, the Detective Superintendent was telling the audience to resist?" Sharon asked.

"Instead of just letting the police or someone else do it" Holly explained.

"If I could get my hands on the drug barons or even one drug dealer, I'd kill him." George said quietly, but his voice was full of menace.

"I'm sure that's not what the cops want." Sharon was firm.

Mark agreed. "The Super wasn't advocating vigilantes. That would just be chaos."

"It's not a football game where one side gets to win," Sharon said. "It's life where we all have to help. The drugs dealers have to be part of the reconstructed society. Get with the program, George."

George stiffened, sat up straight, but refrained from retaliating. He was quiet after that.

I understood George's anger at those who sold drugs to kids. Was he patrolling the cliffs, looking for smugglers the way the D. S. Tregere was? Surely, he didn't think that because an author wrote about smuggling drugs, he was a drug smuggler? Did he think Oliver Nott deserved to die because he wrote about drugs? Was he looking for smugglers with the view of killing them? Had he killed Oliver Nott?

CHAPTER FIFTEEN

The rain drizzled all morning but didn't seem to deter my guests from exploring. They departed—some to search through more shops, some to walk through the town and George to tramp the cliff paths again. He didn't appear for lunch. Neither did Lena. Perhaps they had met at one of the many restaurants in town to have a private conversation. The others arrived at the hotel restaurant at noon in a flurry of packages, damp clothes and chatter.

"You should see the painting Holly bought," Ellie enthused. "A small thing, but beautiful."

"Of Fowey?" I asked

"It was an impression more than a representation," Ellie said.

Holly beamed. "By Sue Richardson."

"Let me see it." I liked Richardson's work, but it was expensive. Holly must have a few pounds. But I did as well, I reminded myself. Perhaps I could afford one now.

"I had it shipped, but I took a picture on my cell phone. Look."

She showed me a luscious composition of two women having coffee. They looked strong and powerful—a robust picture. I saw the price in the corner of the picture, twelve hundred pounds.

"A great buy," I said. "You'll love that picture for years."

"It's inspiring," Holly said. "And they included the shipping in the price. "

And well they should, I thought.

"Sharon bought one as well."

"A Sue Richardson?" I asked.

"No. I expect Fred would leave home if I brought another powerful woman into the house, even if she was just painted and hanging on the wall. No, I bought a landscape."

"A huge one by Tina Morgan." Grace informed me. I think Grace and Ellie enjoyed the art acquisition experience as much as Sharon and Holly.

I was interested. Morgan was well-known and had painted a seascape I had my eye on.

"The sea?"

"The sea is in the picture, but there is a woman standing looking out at it. The light on the water is …" she searched for the word and settled for, "*beautiful*. The contrast is intriguing. I mean the woman seems calm, and the water seems menacing. That appeals to me. It's as if she's challenging the ocean. I know I'll get philosophical every time I look at it, and Fred will see it as a nice picture of water."

Grace shook her head. "You might be surprised."

"Not likely," Sharon said with years of experience behind her. "And I bought a small one by George Hunt. Lovely thing."

I would make a point of stopping by the galleries to thank the owners for presenting my guests with what they wanted. Perhaps, they'd arrange private showings the next time I brought a tour this way.

"You'll have to let us know what Fred thinks at the next book club meeting," Grace said.

I thought about Sharon and her ranch. Ashland where she lived was in the interior of the state of Oregon, almost at the California border.

"Sharon, Portland is some hours from Ashland. How do you manage to get there for the book club meetings? And why go all the way to Portland?"

"She flies," Ellie answered me. "In her own plane."

I gawked at Sharon. I had never even *thought* of her as a pilot.

Sharon waved her hand as if to diminish the information. "It's just a small plane, a Cessna 172, and I don't fly it if the weather is crappy. I let the commercial pilots take me."

"She keeps her plane at her ranch," Holly offered, much in the manner of a proud owner displaying an unusual pet.

"I often go to Portland, and it was Powell's Bookstore where I met Grace and Ellie one day at the coffee house section. We got talking and… I just make the effort now and go to the meetings. They're only once a month."

Incredible. It was hard for an English-born woman, even one as well-travelled as me, to understand the American view of distance. They do not consider it a barrier. When I lived in Seattle, I once took the train to Portland, which I had thought an adventure. I spent one entire day in Powell's Bookstore. I ended up talking to a poet in the coffee shop. I could well imagine these women gravitating toward each other there. But to fly once a month for a meeting from hundreds of miles away? Perhaps ranch life was a little lonely. But Sharon, the pilot, was past seventy and hard of hearing.

"Can you keep flying? I mean don't you have to pass tests?"

"I can pass the yearly tests. They put ear phones on me to test for my radio competence and I can hear through the ear phones. I will have to give it up at some point. Soon, I expect. Fred stopped flying last year. I mean he stopped piloting. He still flies with me."

"It will be a new normal," Grace said firmly. "You can figure out how the rest of us live without a private plane." She grinned. "It will teach you compassion."

These women took some knowing.

They headed off to their rooms and then out on more tours of the countryside in spite of the relentless rain.

I passed through the entrance to the separate building that housed the hotel rooms and up the stairs to my floor. I glanced up as I heard my name. Mark stood at a doorway under the stairs to the next floor. I hadn't noticed that door before. I crossed the landing to him.

He held the door open for me, and I passed into a small snug, a private parlor—no doubt for private conversations. D.S. Tregere sat at the small round table, a pint of bitter in front of him. Mark's beer sat at his spot. The Super pulled up another chair.

"Want something to drink?" he said, somewhat inhospitably.

I shook my head. "I just finished lunch. I'm glad to see you both."

D.S. Tregere looked wary.

"It's about Dr. Prior's passport," I said. "She will be on to me soon about when she is going to get it back. The tour ends on Tuesday, and she will need it to board a plane back to America."

"Do we have it?" Tregere asked.

Mark nodded. "I have it."

"We can't hold her or her passport. No evidence."

"True," Mark said reluctantly.

"Better give it back."

"I'll bring it to you later," Mark said.

"Not much later," I said.

"Today."

I started to get up.

"Just a minute," Tregere said.

I stared at him. I didn't work for him. He could moderate his tone. He got my point. "If you please," he said with an attempt at politeness. I sat down.

"We are trying to glean more facts and are interviewing all over the place. The b'y here," he waved at Mark who, while he was younger than Tregere, was no boy, "says he interviewed you who lived next door to the site of the murder and said you knew naught."

"True," I said.

"And he interviewed your housekeeper, a Rose Jones," he looked at a sheet of paper he had in front of him, "who, garrulous as she was, didn't know a thing. In addition, he interviewed your part-time gardener, Peter Brown."

"And plumber."

"What?"

"He's my plumber as well as my gardener."

"As may be," Tregere said and glanced back at the paper, "and got nothing. We need more information."

"I don't think my guests know anything," I said. "Other than Dr. Prior whom you have already interviewed."

Was he going to ask me to spy on my tourists? Where do I owe my loyalty? Not to a murderer, that much was clear.

"We aren't thinking about your guests," Tregere said.

That was a relief. Perhaps none of them were now suspects.

Mark hadn't said a word. Tregere wasn't exactly his boss since Mark worked for the Major Investigations Team who had their own boss, but Tregere did outrank him. Mark was letting him do all the talking.

"We're thinking," Tregere continued, "of getting you to find out here in Fowey what people are talking about."

"They wouldn't tell me," I said. "I'm an outsider, an emmet."

"Of course. But you aren't police, and they may talk in front of you."

"I don't know anyone here who would talk to me. The only person I know in Cornwall is Aria, the librarian in Penzance."

"Who lives here," Mark said.

"What?" Now, it was my turn to be surprised.

"She lives here. Her husband is a fisherman, and she's from Fowey. Jobs are hard to find. The library here has a librarian, so Aria commutes to Penzance—four days on, four days off. She has this afternoon off and she is spending it at home. This is her address." He handed me a piece of paper. "Find out if she knows of any contacts Oliver Nott might have made down here."

"Talk to her," Tregere said.

I looked at Mark.

"Please," he said on Tregere's behalf.

Tregere continued with his agenda. "Find out if there is any movement afoot to turn in those drug smugglers. I made that speech to the public in the hopes that someone would decide to stop the smuggling."

"No one would tell me," I repeated.

"Just try."

I left quickly. I understood D.S. Tregere's position. He wanted to know everything he could. He wanted to make an arrest and stop the drug trafficking and the deaths. But he had no understanding of my position. How could I blunder around the community asking questions? Why would anyone confide in me? Why would Aria even want to see me?

I snapped the leash on Gulliver and stomped down the stairs and out onto the street. The rain had stopped for the moment. Gulliver cocked his head and looked at me.

"It's not you, sweetie." I leaned down and petted him. "You're fine." I shook my head. They had asked me to help. If I believed in their cause, protecting the public from murderers and drug barons, then I should help and not just by donating money. It seemed a bit simple, though. They must have tried to get some information out of Aria and not been successful. She wouldn't protect the drug trade, would she? Was her husband in on it? Tregere had said he was a fisherman.

With any luck, Aria would be away from home or busy, and I could have the credit for trying to help without actually having to do anything.

She was home.

Her stone cottage was on a steep street, with a tiny front garden and steps up to the front door which was painted a bright red. I flipped the iron knocker.

I heard music and then steps coming to the door. The door squeaked a little as she opened it.

"Claire? Hello! Come in. Bring your dog."

She was in jeans and a T-shirt, her red curls held back in a band. I followed her into the kitchen, a bright room with white fitted cupboards, an Aga that sent out welcome heat on this gloomy day and an amazing view of the river, the estuary and the sea beyond it. Clouds scudded across the horizon. I could see the rains squalls on the water far off shore.

"This is beautiful."

"Yes, we like it." She smiled and looked out at the view. "Coffee?"

"Love some."

She indicated a chair at the kitchen table. I sank into it.

She took my jacket and hung it behind the kitchen door. When she turned back to me, she looked at me quizzically. "It's nice to see you, but how did you find me?"

She hadn't given me her home address. We had a professional relationship. This was the awkward part.

"Someone who knew you said you lived here."

"Who was it? "

"Mark Evans."

"I can't recall him at the moment."

A slim black cat slid into the room and eyed Gulliver. He backed into my legs. I petted him and crooked my finger into his collar on the off chance he hated cats. He lay down and exposed his belly in true puppy submission. We laughed.

"I guess Samantha here is top dog." Aria smiled.

"She seems to be."

Aria filled a mug for me and offered milk and sugar.

I could see the green palms swaying at the edge of the road below us and the red of the acer, the maple, far off on the hills, but the river and the estuary beyond it dominated the view. It must be spectacular in the winter when the storms threw waves up into the town.

I sipped the excellent coffee. "Thanks for providing some activities for my group. It's sometimes hard to know what to suggest in the evenings. Most of the guests on my tours don't want clubs or loud music."

"An evening talking about drugs is preferable?"

"It was interesting. Did you attend the one at the Parish hall last night?" I asked her.

"I did."

"It appealed to George and Holly—George, in particular because he lost his son to an overdose. The others didn't attend."

Aria was suddenly still. "I am sorry," she said. "It touches us all, doesn't it?"

"You lost someone?" I looked at her.

"My brother."

"I'm sorry."

"Thank you. It was a year ago. He'd been an addict for ten years with periods of good times and periods of stepping out of the world. He was a good man. I loved him, and I miss him."

"It's a terrible thing," I said. "So hard for everyone."

"He was the reason I talked to Oliver Nott. I thought he might be able to expose the drug trade and help stamp it out." Her tone was bitter.

"He wasn't planning on doing that?"

"No, as a matter of fact, I think he was going to glamorize it, you know? Make it appear a romantic endeavor like the ones in the nineteenth century. Swashbuckling heroes defying the authorities. That sort of adolescent crap."

"Sick."

"Yes, well. He wasn't happy when I told him I thought he was an irresponsible hack."

I smiled, trying to imagine it. "It was probably good for him."

She smiled in response and sipped her coffee. "He was childish. Not a real man at all. More like someone who watched other people live and then moved them around on paper to pretend he wasn't really in the world like everyone else. I didn't like him."

"But I don't expect you killed him."

"No, I wouldn't have wasted more time on him. And no, I don't agree with murder. I'd like to help in some way to get rid of the drug dealers, at least in this area, but I don't plan on murdering them."

"Do you know who is smuggling?"

She studied me for a few minutes. "I saw you last night. You left with the constabulary. "

"I did."

"Mark Evans. I remember now. He's the Welsh cop. He sent you to me."

I might as well be honest with her, though there wasn't much virtue in it since she had figured it out. "That's right. They think you might know something, but they don't think you're involved. D.S. Tregere wants to know if his call to the women was effective. Are they going to do anything?"

She nodded. "Our lovely D.S. Tregere said it well. Because drugs are illegal, no one is going to turn in their relatives. But yes, the women have had enough. Most of us realized quite some time ago that the drug dealers were causing deaths. I have to say that the wives, mothers, and daughters were involved, too, in that they were well aware of the source of the money for their bobbles and beads, cars, and electronic toys. They all knew some people died, but I think they thought about it the way they thought tanning centers. The person who owns the center doesn't cause cancer. It's the person who chooses to use the tanning center that is responsible. So, deaths from drugs were seen as the fault of the person who took the drugs."

She spoke quickly and with a firm grasp of the subject. I was reminded that she was an educated woman and likely influential in this town. I expect D.S. Tregere knew that.

"What's different now."

"Now, they realize that the drugs themselves are polluted and dangerous and that it is unconscionable to pass them throughout the community. That boy was related to a drug smuggler, not closely, but he was second cousin to his wife. She was there last night. Nice woman. She's had enough. She's taking action."

"Did she tell you this?" I was surprised Aria knew so much.

"No, not at all. She just raised her chin, shot a look of pure determination at her husband and nodded once. That's a signal. I sat in primary school with her. I know her. I expect she is withdrawing favors and threatening divorce. She'll pass the word around. Other women will do the same. The message will get clearer to those smugglers every day."

I was fascinated. "What happens next week if he doesn't stop?"

She smiled. There was a certain wicked enjoyment in that smile. "He's going to find nothing works well. His truck won't start, his buddies won't be able to meet him at the pub for a drink, no taxi will pick him up, there is no money in his bank account, his wallet is lost, his dog disappears… although relax," she said when I reacted. `We'd take the pooch to St Ives for a holiday."

"And the next week?"

"Ah, the next week, someone will report his boat for a fisheries infraction, so the superintendent will impound it while they check it, then someone will report him for …" She shrugged. "We haven't got that far yet."

I finished my coffee. "Remind me never to get on your wrong side."

Aria grinned.

I envied her community. "You have a lot of friends here."

"I belong here," she said simply.

I thought of my travels through the world where I had few friends and no community like this one. I'd only lived in Hampshire for a short while, long enough to have about six friends. Friendship and a sense of belonging took time. Perhaps, I'd stay there long enough to become part of the community the way Aria was.

"No wonder you don't want to move to Penzance."

She shook her head. "Couldn't do it. My soul would shrivel."

"So, you commute to Penzance."

"One day, the librarian here in Fowey will retire and the job will be mine."

"I see."

I promised to let her know the next time I was coming to Fowey or Penzance and invited her to visit me in Hampshire.

I pondered on the different systems of justice that operated in Cornwall. The drugs suppliers were bringing death and corruption to the people of this area. They were ruining the lives of many. The constabulary was determined to find the smugglers and punish them. They did deserve to be found and removed from society. But the people here had other ideas. They wanted the smuggling stopped, but they didn't want the perpetrators taken away from the community and punished. They would control them in their own way. It took a death of the young boy to wake up the citizens to the devastation the drugs were spreading. Once they understood it, they planned action.

I texted Mark.

"The women are going to clean up the drug problem. Tell Superintendent Tregere to relax."

CHAPTER SIXTEEN

The rain moved off during the night. The morning sun had me up early, taking Gulliver for a long hike. We walked through town, climbed the hill above the ferry slip and joined a road running along the top of the ridge. We had a clear view of the River Fowey and the harbor and managed to return to the hotel without getting lost in the winding streets. As I was approaching the Galleon, I saw Kyle standing near the docks. I looked around for Patrick but didn't see him—just Kyle and two fishermen with their distinctive caps. They were too far away for me to identify the fishermen, but neither of them looked like Bert. Kyle was distinctive with his blond hair streaked gold by the sunlight. They moved toward one of the narrow streets that fed into the quay, turned a corner and were gone. I wondered if Kyle was looking for more caves to film.

I didn't have much time to ponder because Dr. Prior met me at the door.

She loomed over me. "Where were you? I need my passport."

I turned away from her and reached for the towel the management kept handy by the door. I wiped Gulliver's feet. He'd picked up some mud and moisture. I completed my ministrations and turned back to her. I ignored the first question and answered the second. "I asked for it, and the police said they would get it to you. I'll ask again."

"They'd better get it to me. I can't get on a plane without it, and we're leaving on Tuesday."

They were leaving Penzance on Tuesday, her plane left on Wednesday evening, but she was right. She needed it now. She was in Cornwall and, if Mark had it, so was her passport. The most efficient process was for Mark to deliver it to her.

I texted him. "Dr. Prior needs her passport."

He texted back "OK."

That wasn't helpful.

"When will you bring it to her?"

"When I can."

Still not helpful.

Lena had waited impatiently while I texted and read the replies.

"I'll keep trying," I said to her.

"Fine," she said. "See that you do." She headed for the sun room and coffee. I admired her brains, accomplishments, education and knowledge, but not her manners. I nudged my compassion. There was some excuse for her edginess. She must be anxious to leave England and the English police.

I left Gulliver in the room and went to find breakfast. I found everyone in the sun room already helping themselves to the buffet. George and Lena had a table to themselves and were talking intently. Before coffee? How did they manage to be coherent?

The rest of the group allowed me to have my coffee and a croissant before they began asking questions. At that point, Lena and George brought their coffee to our table. I passed out another booklet. This one had some history of the town and a description of the buildings.

"I'll take those who want to come on an architectural walking tour of the town. We will see the Place House. We can't go in as it's not open to public, but the same family has lived in it since the thirteenth century. Some of you have seen St. Fimbarrus church which was first built in the sixth century. I want you to see the Old House of Foye which is medieval, built in 1430. It's a shop now. We can go in and look at the beams and the fireplace which are original."

"That is impressive," Sharon said. "I can't get my mind around the fact that people live in houses that are six hundred years old and treat them, well, just like their house and don't put in a parking lot or a pool or tear it down to add a granny suite. Amazing."

"Probably shove Granny in the attic," Lena said.

"Probably have her serving customers in the shop," George said.

"We'll end up at the Daphne Du Maurier Literary Centre. I hope you'll enjoy that."

"We really do need to pay homage to her," Grace said. "This is her setting, after all."

The others nodded.

"It will be worth it. They have a film and some artifacts. It's interesting. After the tour, you're free to wander. If you like, you can reassemble here at four p.m. and we'll take the ferry over to view du Maurier's house and then the ferry back. I'll drive you up the St. Catherine's Castle and the blockade sites. "

"More war and smugglers?" Lena complained.

"War anyway," I said.

They did join me at four, and I took them across on the ferry for a drink at the Old Ferry Pub situated conveniently across the road from du Maurier's house and then drove them on a quick tour of the surrounding coastal area. They commented on what they saw and made plans for the next day. As Lena had reminded me, they were leaving tomorrow.

I texted Mark again for her passport.

"I know. I know," was his response.

I drove the group to Golant for dinner at the Fishermen's Arms. Golant is a short drive from Fowey and on the River Fowey. Gulliver was welcome there and I thought the group might enjoy the featured Celtic trio.

This tour group liked the down-home pubs with good food. They were charmed by the relaxed atmosphere, the wall full of pictures and the four dogs that accompanied the locals as they had their pints and pasties. We crowded around a table. The bartender came out to take our orders and general hilarity ensued as Sharon got into a conversation with the table behind her, and Holly engaged a group of young people near her.

The music began, the conversations got louder and everyone but me had several drinks. I was driving and had to be responsible. It's the down side of tour guiding.

Lena grabbed my shirt and pulled me close. "My passport!" she almost hissed at me.

"I'll get it, I promise."

She nodded sharply and let me go. "I like it here, but I don't want to stay in Cornwall forever." She looked around her. "I might as well drink."

I hoped she was not a mean drunk.

The food was delicious and most of us followed up the first course with a sticky toffee pudding.

We'd applauded the musicians who had played lively sets of jigs, reels, and a few pop songs. They smiled and announced they would have a break. The bartender lined up three beers and slid them down the bar to them. The noise level subsided a little, and we could hear each other talk.

George leaned in and said, "I'm going to stay on a while, ladies."

If he was going to stay at the pub, he could find his own way back to the hotel.

"George, can you get a cab home then?" I wasn't waiting up to fetch him.

"No. No. I mean I'll go back with you all tonight, but I've arranged with the hotel to stay on for a few more days when you go back to Penzance. I can take a train to London later on in the week. "

"Oh, well, it will be good bye then tonight," Grace said.

George nodded.

Lena seemed unnaturally quiet. She couldn't have been planning an affair with George. I just didn't see it. But then, I'm no expert in relationships. People can be surprising.

Everyone seemed to enjoy their evening and happily talked about it on the short drive to the Galleon Hotel.

I met George in the hall as I was taking Gulliver out for his nightly pee.

He put his hand on my arm. "Thanks. I had a good time. "

"I'm glad. I said. "I hoped it helped ease you a little."

"A little."

Nothing was going to make George stop grieving or forgetting what happened to his son. Time might lessen the pain, but George would be forever changed. I know I felt that when my mother and stepfather died.

In the morning, everyone, except George, was ready to go, a last day of sightseeing.

"Holly needs to buy another suitcase in Penzance," Ellie informed the group.

"Holly always needs to buy another suitcase," Grace said.

"I swear every time, I'm not going to purchase so much." Holly shook her head. "And then I do."

"There are worse vices," I said and helped everyone load.

"We are going to take a leisurely ride back to Penzance," I announced. "Your train leaves tomorrow morning. You'll have some time to do last minute shopping in Penzance. I thought we could take in some of the sights around here on the way."

They agreed. Grace was back in the front seat, and she pulled out the booklet I'd handed out this morning.

"The Tristan Stone," she said, "Tell us about it."

I engaged the mic and gave my mini-lecture on The Tristan Stone. "It's a sixth century Stone said to commemorate the life of Tristan, nephew of King Mark."

"Anything to do with Tristan and Isolde?" Grace asked.

"Yes, Wagner wrote his opera based on the Cornwall Tristan and Isolde's story."

"But there really was a Tristan and really was a King Mark?" Sharon asked.

"There really was," I assured her. "But their story of love, betrayal and death might have been embellished beyond credence by Wagner."

We stopped at the stone column and admired its endurance. Then drove to Restormel Castle. The approach is impressive as the castle is round and sits high up on a hill. It had been constructed around 1100 of wood but reconstructed in the 1300s of stone.

"You'd think twice about taking on whoever owned this place," Sharon said. "It looks like the owner would govern the territory."

We were near the castle entrance and turned around to survey the surrounding countryside. She was right. The owner in residence here would be able to oversee the populace for miles.

"The castle was given to the Duke of Cornwall in 1337 and is owned by the present Duke of Cornwall who is the Prince of Wales."

"You're telling me that this castle was once owned by a king in 1100 and it is still owned by royalty today?"

"That's right."

"Amazing," Sharon said. "And he lets us, the peasants, visit him?"

"It's run by the English Heritage. Do you have your passes?"

They searched in their rucksacks for their passes and entered. We spent an hour there, and then I drove them to Caolgeros in Lostwitheil, the nearest town to Restormel Castle. We had another delicious lunch and by three, I pulled the van into the parking space behind the Queens Hotel in Penzance.

"This is my last day for shopping," Holly said. "I'm off to do my best."

"Don't forget to buy a suitcase," Ellie said.

"I'll buy it first, so I can put my purchases in it."

"I want my passport," Lena said to me in the lobby, as I was registering the group.

I nodded.

I texted Mark again. "We are at the Queens Hotel. Where is the passport?"

I took Gulliver for a quick walk and then stayed in my room for the afternoon, checking into emails and taking care of business.

I had booked dinner reservations at The Old Lifeboat House, the upstairs section. We had a long table and everyone ate well and talked about their trip. Sometimes, guests were so polite I had no idea if they were happy or not, and sometimes they complained the whole trip and then told me what a good time they'd had. This group obviously had fun.

Perhaps Lena was the only one who hadn't enjoyed it, but then, she'd brought her troubles with her.

"This is for you," Grace said, "from all of us including George." She handed me a square package. When I unwrapped it, I found a lovely painting, small, but exquisite, of Fowey.

"It's one of the new artists," Holly said, letting me know that they hadn't paid a fortune for it.

"I appreciate your taste," I said, admiring it. "You no doubt picked someone who is going far. This is beautiful. It will go on the wall in my sitting room." It was a lovely thing and very thoughtful of them to trouble to get it for me.

She looked pleased.

"Does everyone have their train tickets for tomorrow's trip to Heathrow? Do you have what you need to get on the plane?" I would look after them until they departed.

Lena shot me a sharp look.

"You'll have that passport, Lena, if I have to spend all night tracking it down."

"We also have the map you gave us and the telephone number of the help desk at the airlines. We're good," Sharon said.

Where was Mark? Lena really had to have that passport. He hadn't answered my text. About ten that night, I saw him as I was leaving the hotel to take Gulliver for his walk. He was with Patrick. I ran up to him and held out my hand. He reached inside his jacket and pulled out the passport.

"Finally!" I was relieved.

"She can go," Mark said. "She was at the murder site, but we don't have any other evidence against her. We'll have to extradite her if we find anything, but it's not likely. She can go," he repeated.

"Hold Gulliver. I'll be right back." I turned and dashed into the hotel. Lena was in room 106, just down the hall. I knocked.

She pulled open the door.

"Yes?"

I handed her the passport. She stared at it, then reached out and slowly took it from me. She opened it, gazed at her own picture, then closed it.

"Thanks," she said, then shut the door.

Well! At least, she didn't yell at me.

I returned to the front steps. Patrick and Mark were talking, and Gulliver was patiently waiting for me. I took the leash.

"Just in time," I said.

"Was she grateful?" Mark asked.

I slid him a telling look. "In her deepest soul, I'm sure she was." I turned to Patrick. "Hi," I said belatedly. "How are you doing?" He'd been upset the last time I talked to him.

He shrugged, his thin shoulders moving under his jacket. "The Inspector here needed a hand. He thought Oliver might have mentioned something in his book manuscript that described the cave or the premises where the drugs were smuggled to. I'm not sure that it's relevant. The plot revolves around not just smuggling, but manufacturing Fentanyl, although he does put the site in a cave. You don't need to smuggle anything to do that. I think he was just romancing, you know? Putting the lab in a cave so it would resonate with the old smuggling myths."

"But he did talk about it being a Cornish gang," Mark said.

"Could be. Or maybe not," Patrick said. "Oliver was good at research. The cave probably exists, but he was a creative plotter and could have just made up the rest."

"True, but I'd like to find out what he knew about the area," Mark said.

I know Mark was frustrated by the lack of evidence for the murder. Finding the cave might lead him to someone with a reason to kill Oliver. It didn't look to me like a straight line to a solution.

"If the manuscript tells us where the cave is, it would save time. We could search the cliffs for years and never find it without some direction." He explained his reasoning.

Patrick shrugged. "I'm going in to register," he said, "and get a coffee. I'll come out and join you on the quay for a walk, if I may." He spoke to me.

"We'll walk along the esplanade."

"Patrick," Mark said. "The research notes. I need them."

"Oh, right." He stopped and turned back. "I have them. Rita gave them to me. I meant to get them to you. Just a loan, all right? They belong to his heir."

Mark nodded.

"I'll leave them at the registration desk." He nodded and left us.

We watched him as he returned to the hotel then turned and walked slowly away down the esplanade.

"I'm going to go back and wait outside his room." Mark was determined to get those notes.

"Do you really think you are going to find a drug gang at this cave?'

"Tregere thinks so. He thinks there is a London boss in the mix, a businessman with many interests. Tregere's heard he's operating here. If we can disrupt his operations, he will leave and go somewhere else."

I stopped and stared at him.

Mark shrugged. "Not an ideal solution, but it suits D.S. Tregere. I've got one more day in Cornwall, and I'm going to spend it looking for that cave in the vague hope that it will help my murder inquiry. I'll scan the notes in case I see something that might help. I'll study them later. But I need to look for that cave while I'm here."

"Good luck with that."

He kissed me briefly and strode back toward the hotel and the notes.

Patrick must have left the research notes for Mark, because when Patrick caught up with me, he was alone. Mark wasn't chasing him. We walked a short distance to the park and then back to the hotel. The sea slapped at the shore below the wall, but it was a calm night. No waves roared and reached up and over the wall to drench us. Those storms came later in the year.

"I'm fed up with it all," Patrick said to me. "I handed the notes over to your Inspector. I want nothing more to do with it. I'm going to take your advice and book into a B & B and do nothing for a week. Rita needs some time alone. I'm not sure anything is going to improve after this week, but I can't cope with Rita, the publishing business, or my life."

I wasn't sure if Patrick was indulging in his somewhat histrionic verbiage, or he really was at the end of his rope. "Things might look better in a week."

He looked around at the shops and bars lining the street, at the dark hills beyond, the black, at the velvet of the ocean. "There's something about Cornwall. I feel as though I can hide here."

CHAPTER SEVENTEEN

The tour group posed for a farewell picture under the palm trees at the railway station. They looked festive with luggage surrounding them, scarves fluttering in the breeze and brightly colored packages in piles around their feet. Holly had four pieces of luggage and various bags. I imagined the others would help her load onto the train. They had all bought books, so their luggage was heavy. They were an intrepid, good-natured, intelligent group and my heart warmed to them—except Lena.

"You have the directions to the airport train at Paddington?" I asked. They'd be transferring from the Penzance train to the airport shuttle.

"We do," Grace said.

"Are we on first class on the Penzance train?" Holly asked.

"You are," I reassured her.

"Lovely."

"Let the steward know when you want to eat, and he or she will reserve a table for you".

"How's the train food," Ellie said.

"It really is good in first class."

Sharon reached over and hugged me. "Thanks for everything. It's been great. Keep in touch".

"Yes, let us know who killed that bastard," Lena said. Her comment stopped the good-natured farewells.

Grace raised her eyebrows and shook her head. "I'm sure we will all want to know. You take care now," she said and hugged me.

Then they lined up and hugged me again. Very American that, and heart-warming. They also managed to slip me a tip as they did it. Generous souls, even Lena.

"Have fun on the train," I said as I tucked the bills into my jeans' pocket.

They waved and hustled into the station.

Another tour concluded, successful in spite of the disparate personalities. I drove to the quay, parked the van at the seaside and strode with Gulliver along the sea wall and down the steps to the beach. No rain today and the bright sun almost convinced me that, indeed in Cornwall, summer stays until Christmas. Gulliver found seagulls, hopping on the shore, to harass.

We climbed back up the stairs to the quay and stopped at a café with outdoor tables. The palms poking into the sky along the front street and the bright blue of the sea gave the illusion of the warm Mediterranean. Deceptive, because the temperature was English. But with my quilted jacket, it was warm enough to sit outside with my coffee.

I didn't have another tour scheduled until the spring—March in Yorkshire. The weather could be iffy then, but at least it wouldn't be crowded there in March. I hoped I'd get another group of intrepid women like this one. George had been fine. He managed to fit in with the group most of the time, but I'd be more careful about why someone wanted to join the tour. I'd put this group of women on my blog list and make sure they got updates of all the tours I was planning. I'd like to see them on another tour—well, perhaps not Lena. I breathed deeply of the tangy air, letting my shoulders relax, trying to release all the tension, albeit mostly normal business tension, of the past two weeks.

I petted Gulliver's silky head as he huddled against my legs.

"Want to move on?"

He sat up, alert.

I took my coffee with me and hiked toward Newlyn on the Western Promenade and Battery Road. The breeze off the ocean was brisk, but not wild; the sea was blue with turquoise and green patches where rocks hid and kelp grew. The gulls were abundant and ubiquitous, looked for handouts from walkers. I wondered if they ever bothered to scavenge their natural foods along the shore anymore, they were so used to chips and bread from tourists. I took deep breaths of the glorious salt air and felt rejuvenated.

We walked quickly, and I turned back in front of the Lugger Inn in Newlyn hiking back to Penzance, satisfied with the exercise. I loaded Gulliver into the van, nipped into the hotel for a top up of my coffee and settled back into the driver's seat. I knew Gulliver would sleep for a few hours in his crate. We headed home.

I'd driven the group from Heathrow to Hampshire and then along the coast when they arrived. Now, I was returning on the inland route. It was much faster. The skies were clear, the road was dry, and I moved along without traffic delays, construction halts or weather problems.

Midway, I headed for The Lacemaker's Café in Honiton, near Exeter. It's dog-friendly. But first, I took Gulliver to Mountbatten Park, so he could relieve himself and have a sniff of grass and fresh air. I poured him some water. He lapped it up quickly. I'd tried leaving some water in his crate once, but he spilled it and then had to sit in the wet. Now, I had to remember to give him a drink periodically. If I wanted coffee, I assumed Gulliver wanted water. That worked.

He trotted beside me into the café and elicited admiration from the server.

"Lovely, isn't he?" she said.

"Gorgeous," another server said.

"Yes," I agreed. "He is lovely." His multicolored silky hair, huge brown eyes and alert expression attracted attention.

I chose a window seat. It was out of the way of customers, and Gulliver wouldn't be tempted to get up every time someone arrived.

I ordered a sandwich which came quickly. Gulliver sat up when the waitress delivered my order, but immediately settled back down and put his head on his paws.

The waitress laughed. "He's a sweet one."

It was ridiculous how much that pleased me. I left her a tip.

Gulliver was happy to return to his crate, turned around twice and settled down to sleep. We were home by two-thirty.

It seemed a very long time since I'd left home. The roses at the side of the house were holding onto a few blossoms, but winter would discourage them soon. The lavender Peter had planted along the walk scented the air as I passed. It was Rose's day to clean, and she was just finishing as I turned my key in the kitchen door.

"My lord, you gave me a start," she said. She had a kettle in her hand and a very surprised expression on her face.

Rose is in her late twenties, blue-eyed, pale-faced with freckles splattered liberally across her face, and curly, red-brown color-of-the-week hair that she subdued with a bandana.

"Sorry, Rose. How are you?"

"Fair to middlin'. And you? How was the trip?"

"Good. Nice to be home, though."

"You oughtn't to have left."

"Why?"

"Robert Andrews, him who was sniffing around you, has found himself someone else."

"Really?" I was fascinated. Robert, who was Gulliver's vet and my sometimes companion on dogs walks and jaunts around the neighborhood, had been single for many years. His daughter, Sarah, was in university this year. Perhaps he felt he could now find a new life.

"Who is she?"

"You wouldn't know her. She's the new district nurse from Basingstoke."

"Good for him."

Rose snorted. If the new love wasn't from Ashton-on-Tinch, she no doubt wasn't good enough no matter how sterling her character. In Rose's opinion, Robert was a much more reliable suitor for me than Mark who tended to be come and go erratically.

"I hope I'll meet her soon." I hoped she was a gem. Robert was a decent man and deserved a good partner.

I let Gulliver out into the back yard but kept one eye on him from the kitchen window. He might find a small hole in the fence somewhere and disappear.

"And you missed the fight in the off-leash park," Rose continued to fill me in on the village information.

"What was that about?"

"Someone let their dog in heat off leash."

"Uh, oh".

"It was a right melee."

I could imagine it. Gulliver wasn't yet of age to be interested. Soon, I was going to have to make an appointment with Robert to take care of that part of Gulliver's life.

"A right melee," she repeated. "My mother said two neighbors aren't talking to each other. They come into the shop and don't speak. It's childish."

I expected her mother, Helen Taylor, who ran the local post office would have an opinion on it.

"I see Peter's been tidying up the garden." My small vegetable patch had been dug over and looked as if it was ready for winter.

"He said to eat that kale he left. It will be good all winter."

I could see the curly, green leaves at the edge of the garden. I suppose they would be eating bananas in Cornwall, but I was grateful for fresh greens.

"He spent a few hours. His wife will send you an invoice."

"I need to pay you as well, Rose. How much do I owe you?"

Rose whipped an invoice from her jean's pocket and passed it to me. I made out the check and passed it back.

In spite of her non-stop talking, she was worth every penny as a cleaner. I had no idea a house could be so tidy, clean and organized before I had Rose every week. Another blessing from my step-father, Paul, as I had never been able to afford a cleaner before he left me the legacy.

"I'm off, then, Claire. Welcome home. Oh, the dustman is coming today."

For some reason, Rose will not take out the garbage. It is one of the jobs she leaves for me.

"I'll get it," I promised.

"It's sitting right by the door."

I glanced to my right and saw the trash can on wheels waiting for delivery to the lane. I waved at her and let Gulliver back inside.

I toted my bag upstairs and unpacked, throwing most of it into the laundry hamper. I left my papers on my study desk to be sorted later. Every B & B and hotel had been paid, but I had to enter all the expenses and income onto my tax spread sheet, including the tips I gave out and the tips I took in. Those women had been generous. I put the money in an envelope, wrote the amount on the outside, and entered it onto the spread sheet. It was easy to lose track of cash. I'd put it into the bank later on today. I felt efficient and businesslike.

I'd better deal with the garbage, or I'd miss the truck.

It was easy to trundle the wheeled can along my garden path to the lane. It moved fairly smoothly. I unlatched the gate and pushed it through.

I settled it in its usual place, leaving it like the others along the lane, a patient testimony to consumption. I took a moment to notice the few yellow leaves on the alder tree, the rest stripped by the wind while I was in Cornwall. Winter was on its way. I heard the gate creak open nearby. Rita pushed her trash can into the lane.

"Hello," I said. She looked a little better: more color in her face, her long blonde hair pulled back into one neat braid. She wore her usual leggings and sweater. "How are you, Rita?"

She shoved the trash can into position and turned to me. "I feel as if I should stand beside the trash and let the dustmen load me into the truck."

"That bad?"

"Yes, Patrick isn't coming home for a week, so he says, and he leaves me with a mess at work….and…"

"Come on in for coffee and tell me about it." I wouldn't be much help to her, but she was my neighbor and I could at least listen.

She shook her head, then changed her mind. "Thanks. I could do with a coffee. Did you just get home?"

"I did and since I haven't settled yet, I can take time for coffee. Down Gulliver," I said as we walked up my path. Gulliver jumped up to greet her. He had yet to learn not to stand on his hind feet and leave paw marks on visitors' clothes.

"Down, Gulliver," Rita echoed and, for a wonder, Gulliver dropped to a sit.

"How about that?" I said marveling.

"Impressive," Rita said. "He is quite beautiful, isn't he? Smart too."

I was gratified by her admiration of Gulliver. I must be besotted.

I bustled around putting on the coffee, scrounging for biscuits and setting out the mugs. Finally, it was ready, and I sat at the kitchen table with her. She had been stroking Gulliver, and they both looked relaxed.

"You look good, Rita, but do you have a lot to do?"

"I can cope with work. I like work. I'm good at it, and I can manage it. In fact, without Patrick there, I can make decisions and keep production going faster than when he is there. It's the staff that drive me crazy."

I tried to remember what staff she had. "Kyle? Alexandra?"

She nodded. "Alex is angry at Kyle. Really angry. He isn't in much, but when he is, they go at it tooth and nail. I wish staff wouldn't sleep with staff."

She stopped abruptly and stared at me, then said quietly. "I should talk. I guess I should be more understanding but…"

I didn't want to get into a discussion about the morality of her relationship with Oliver Nott. "Kyle was in Penzance with Patrick when I was there, so he's been away for a few days."

Rita was willing to be diverted. "Yes, he's setting up a promo video using the setting of the next book. As much as he is a pain in the ass, Kyle gets results. The pre-orders are pouring in. We stand to make a lot of money on this book and maybe even push up the sales of his back list."

"Kyle seems ambitious."

"He's ambitious, but he doesn't respect boundaries so he's hard to work with."

"You mean emotional boundaries?"

"Sometimes, but physical boundaries as well. I caught him rummaging through the papers on my desk before he went to Cornwall. Imagine that? And he wasn't even embarrassed. Just said, he was looking for some of Oliver's notes."

"I asked him exactly what he wanted because I'm in charge of those notes. He backed off then. He's irritating, but I know he's good at PR."

At least I knew the notes had found their way to Patrick and thence to Mark.

Rita continued to talk about Kyle. "He *is* ambitious, but I guess he has reason to be. He's full of ideas." She sipped her coffee and reached for a biscuit.

"You know," she said, "an author usually has a blog online when a new book comes out. Well, Kyle has taken over Oliver's blog and gives updates of where he is in investigating Oliver's settings. He's keeping the online market perking."

"Isn't that a little weird, like Oliver Nott is still writing?" I wondered if, in the future, no one would really die. Their friends and relations would keep their social media going, post pictures of what they might have seen if they were alive, answer questions and engage in conversations as if they were living an online life. Perhaps in the future, we might be conversing with someone online who had died years ago. It was a strange idea.

"People know he's dead." She stopped for a moment, then continued. "But they like the fantasy that Kyle is giving them, that Oliver's ideas and his enthusiasms are living on. It's brilliant, really."

"And important for the company." I could see the marketing potential of that strategy.

"It is important for the company. I'm not denying that. We were in bad shape and this is going to help. Kyle knew he wouldn't have a job if this book of Oliver's didn't sell. He'd be the first to go."

"He knew that?" I didn't know Kyle at all well, but I doubted he'd believe he was dispensable.

"He had to know that. There's nothing wrong with Kyle's work. He's good, and we'd hire him back on contract, but right now he's on salary plus a bonus with increasing sales. We couldn't have continued that and it would be hard for him to get that kind of contract anywhere else in this publishing climate."

I recalled Kyle pushing for the shots he wanted.

"He does seem to know what will work and how to get it done."

"He's younger than we are." She included me in her generation. She's a little older than I am, but I didn't correct her.

"He has a different attitude to money. He thinks he should be one of those celebrity TV people with a rich and famous lifestyle. But he works hard to get it. He spends everything he earns, though."

"Did he tell you that?"

"No, but it's obvious; new car, all the new cameras, new electronic toys, vacations. Alex hassles him about it. She is more content with being middle class. She spends much less. All on herself, mind."

"It's hard to blame Kyle for forging ahead if his future is at stake."

"I don't, really. He's just annoying. If he gets a head of steam on this, he'll keep his job and get a raise. He has an expensive lifestyle, so he'd better succeed."

"Does he take on other jobs? I mean, if he is good at promo, does he take on contracts with other publishers or authors?"

She put her coffee cup down and stared at me. "I hadn't thought of that. Maybe he does."

"How do you feel about that?"

She was quiet for a moment.

"You know, he does what he is supposed to do for us and even more than we ask, so if he can work in another job, I guess I don't object. The young people really have to hustle to make it these days."

We sat there enjoying the warmth of the kitchen, the sunlight, pale this late in the day but cheerful on the yellow walls.

I finished my coffee. "How are you feeling about Oliver now?"

"As if I'm recovering from the plague."

I couldn't help it, I laughed.

She smiled. "I am better. Thanks"

She returned to her house and I turned to what needed to be done in mine. I checked the fridge. Nothing much there. I picked up Gulliver's lead, snapped it on, grabbed my jacket and bag and headed out the door. I had time to pick up a few groceries for dinner and make a bank deposit before closing. I'd do a big grocery shop tomorrow.

Gulliver stopped every few feet on my street to mark his progress, letting all the neighborhood dogs know he was back and then trotted happily beside me. I nodded to a few people, most of them members of my local Mystery Book Club. I should go to the next meeting and see what they had planned for this month. I had time for a quick hike up the hill at the edge of town. I crossed the river and hurried up the far side toward the trail to the hills. I met Robert Andrews as I passed his vet clinic. He was just getting into his vehicle but hailed me.

"Claire. You're back."

He stood waiting for me to get closer, a stocky man, about fifty, sandy hair he kept shaved close to his head. There was something different about him. Perhaps the new woman in his life created a new aura. No. I stared at him.

"You're not wearing glasses."

He grinned. "I got contacts."

"Very handsome," I said. I liked his glasses better but didn't say so.

"Look, Claire. I wanted to tell you that I've met someone." So, Rose was right. He had a love interest.

"Really? Who?" Robert had been a good walking companion and a reliable friend since I moved here and, occasionally, had tried to up the relationship into something more intimate. But he had recognized my involvement with Mark and stepped back into being my friend.

"Her name is Rosemary. Rosemary Stone. She is the new district nurse here. I'd like you to meet her."

"Wonderful, Robert. I'd love to."

"I'll host a pub night. Can you and Mark come?"

"I will for, sure, but Mark is a maybe."

"Mark is unreliable that way?"

"He is," I agreed. He was reliable in many ways, but I couldn't count on him turning up for a social occasion. That would be the night someone found new evidence, someone caused havoc or his Superintendent called him in.

Robert understood that. He could be called out on animal emergencies. "How is he getting along on the Oliver Nott murder case?"

I imagined everyone in Ashton-on-Tinch knew Mark was in charge of that case.

"He would say he was investigating all avenues," I intoned the official response.

Robert laughed. "Well, it couldn't be in better hands."

Robert was such a nice man. I hoped Rosemary Stone would hold his heart carefully. He squatted down and fondled Gulliver's ears. "Hello, young fellow. Aren't you looking healthy?"

"How's Sarah?" I asked after Robert's daughter.

"She's doing well at university. She's taking sciences. I thought she'd be taking humanities." He sounded puzzled.

I just nodded. Sarah had every intention of becoming a medical doctor, but she let her poor father think she was going to be a penniless writer. She had told me a little worry was good for him. I'd promised not to let on, but I could see he was starting to suspect she had ambitions he knew nothing about.

Gulliver and I had our walk. I deposited my hefty tip into my business account. I picked up some eggs, milk, coffee and butter from the post office store. Rose's mother, Helen Taylor, was the sole clerk left this late in the day. She was also the manager.

"Welcome back, Claire. Nice to see your face." She looked the definition of "matronly" with her plump, comfortable-looking figure, her bright, interested dark eyes. She didn't look much like her daughter, but they had the same chatty approach to conversation.

"Thanks, Helen. Rose kept everything ship-shape while I was gone," I told her mother.

"Well she might," her mother said tartly. "She's had lots of practice, and I will say she's conscientious."

"She certainly is," I said--except for putting out the garbage, but I said that mentally.

At home, I fed Gulliver his dinner and made myself an omelet. About eight o'clock, I got a text from Mark.

"Got new info. Going back to Cornwall tomorrow. Want to come?"

I looked at my tidy house and my dog settling comfortably onto his bed. I thought of the stacks of papers I had to attend to on my desk. I thought of Sharon stepping into her plane to pilot herself to a meeting hundreds of miles away.

I texted back. "Sure."

CHAPTER EIGHTEEN

When the alarm woke me in the morning, I dressed and staggered out for a quick walk of four blocks with Gulliver. I fed him and made sure I packed water, along with a bowl. I restocked his traveling case with dog food, got my overnight rucksack ready and was waiting when Mark arrived.

I handed him my van keys. "Could you get Gulliver's crate?"

It fit easily into the back of Mark's BMW.

"This isn't your car." I noted the improvement.

"Belongs to the department. One of the unmarked."

It was more powerful than Mark's, although I couldn't remember what make his was. Cars have never been a great passion of mine. I can tell a BMW from a Honda because they have different logos. It was easier to live with ignorance about cars than make the effort to distinguish them.

I stowed Gulliver's bag and my rucksack in the back seat, set my coffee travel mug in the holder in the front and slipped into the passenger seat.

"Thanks for being ready. I know it's early." Mark shifted gears and pulled out onto the street.

I glanced at my watch, waved a hand in acknowledgement and settled back for a couple of hour's snooze. I woke when he pulled into a coffee spot somewhere past Exeter.

"One cream," I said as I handed him my travel mug. "And something sweet."

I yawned, stretched and opened the door.

"Come on, Gulliver." I took him for a short walk along the road, poured out some water for him and had him settled back in the crate when Mark arrived with hot coffee and something Danish.

It was light now. I looked around finally taking some interest in the day. The pastry was delicious.

"So, what's the new information?"

Mark laughed. "It's the first time your curiosity hasn't won over your need for sleep."

"I know. I was tired, I guess. So, what's the info?"

"You know those research notes Patrick gave me?"

"Were they helpful?" I wondered what kind of notes a writer made. Would there be bits of creative writing in amongst the facts?

"Patrick *was* helpful because he gave me the notes, but he's disappeared. I can't get hold of him, and no one seems to know where he is."

"He might have gone to a B & B for a week to get away from it all. He was pretty nervy, and I suggested it."

"He could have his nervous breakdown *next* week," Mark grumbled. "I want him around *this* week. He's not answering his phone."

"He'll come back, Mark. I don't think he's skipped town. I think he just wanted a rest. Did you read the notes?" I changed the subject. It was, perhaps, my fault Patrick had disappeared.

"I had a quick look at them. Oliver described the cave where Fentanyl is being manufactured. I'm not sure where it is, but there are some details he mentioned that might make it possible for us to find it—if he didn't just make up the site."

I sat up. "Manufactured? The drug is manufactured? Not smuggled?"

"Not smuggled. They don't need to. It's easy to make".

"So, all that watching the coast for boats was a waste of time?" I thought about Tregere patrolling the cliffs.

"Not totally. The pilchards might take the Fentanyl from the caves for distribution by boat."

I smiled at his description of the criminals as fish, and stupid fish. It was a Cornish saying. He must have picked it up from Tregere. But what he said made sense. A fisherman's boat could travel up and down the coast, pulling into many bays, handing off drugs to other distributors. It could work like that.

"Did you get anything from Cst Pemberthy?"

Mark nodded, checked over his shoulder and passed a slow-moving lorry. When he was back in the correct lane, he answered me.

"The lad did a good job. Nott's nephew has a solid alibi."

I didn't think Mark had been considering the nephew seriously, but I suppose he suspected everyone. "Where was he?"

"At a play rehearsal and he was accounted for by several people."

"Too bad." I brought my mind back to Oliver Nott and his research. "Where are Oliver's notes?"

Mark gestured behind him. I leaned over the seat and grabbed the folder. I extracted a couple of notebooks. Inside were hand written notes. "Not on his computer?"

"No. He wrote in notebooks. He started off his career as a journalist, so that might be a habit he had from those days. In any case, you can read them. They're legible."

I ignored the rolling hills and the flat land we travelled through and scanned the notes. I tried to read quickly, looking for the word 'cave'.

About half-way through the first notebook, I found some references.

"Is this what you found?" I read, "The sea flows close to the entrance at high tide, and at low tide the entrance is almost hidden by a huge rock."

"That's it. I didn't get much further."

I read on. Six pages later, I stopped and re-read the information.

"Mark, he gave the coordinates of the cave. Look here, latitude and longitude."

Mark glanced over, then back at the road. "Keep that page open." He pulled over at a lay by and shut off the motor. "Let's see."

I pointed out the pertinent information.

"My God." He stared at the carefully written figures on the page. "I'll have to let Tregere know."

He hit a speed dial number, talked his way through the bureaucracy, and finally got D.S. Tregere on the line. The phone was on speaker mode. He didn't have to hold it.

"Where are you?" Tregere snapped.

"On my way to Penzance. I have the manuscript of Oliver Nott's last novel."

"Are you having a nice read, b'y?" He sounded impatient.

Mark's eyebrows rose. He glanced at me but didn't respond to the sarcasm which meant, in my opinion, he was the adult in this conversation.

"I have Claire Barclay with me. She's reading the manuscript as we travel, and she has discovered coordinates on the cave Nott describes in his novel. The one where he says Fentanyl is being manufactured."

"In the novel." Tregere said flatly.

"That's right, sir."

"And you think he might have known there was a real cave housing iniquity at those coordinates?"

"I think it's worth checking, sir."

There was a moment of silence. Then Tregere's voice come through almost quietly. "Do you have a GPS on your phone?"

"Yes sir."

"All right. Plug in those coordinates. Now, give them to me."

"Claire?" Mark asked.

I read them out.

Tregere grunted. There was silence for at least a full minute. Then Tregere came back on the air. "Evans?"

"Yes, sir."

"Those coordinates put the cave near Fowey. I'll meet you there."

"Yes, sir."

"And Evans?"

"Sir?"

"That ad guy, Kyle, was seen in Penzance last night with some of his friends from the press to take pictures of the caves. They may head off to Fowey to do some promotion for that very book your young lady is reading from."

Young lady? Forty-six? Perhaps young relative to Tregere.

Mark glanced at me, grinned and answered Tregere.

"You think he's going to Fowey?"

"Keep an eye out for him."

"Yes, sir."

I heard the crash of the disconnection.

"Will Tregere send anyone to check out those coordinates with you?"

"Likely. He'll send a sergeant and one more officer in case we do find the cave and find it occupied. It will take him an hour to arrange that."

"What was that about Kyle?"

"He doesn't want Kyle to find the cave we're looking for or to get in our way, so he warned me about him. He doesn't like Kyle. Too smooth. Too ambitious. Thinks he's too much the London man. Might be just a Cornish prejudice of the English."

"You escaped that with Tregere?"

"Yeah. But I'm Welsh."

We pulled into the very hotel we had left yesterday. This time I let Mark get the room. The receptionist, Carol, who ran the hotel from the bar, handed Mark the keys, and smiled at me.

"Back again, Claire?" I knew she wanted to ask me more but was constrained by her professional reception rule: Don't get too nosy about guests, and by the fact that there were others in the bar.

"I can't stay away from Cornwall," I said, which wasn't the explanation she was angling for.

"Hello, Gulliver." She reached her hand into a drawer and cocked an eyebrow at me.

"Yes, it's okay." I was a little more relaxed now about what Gulliver ate. He didn't seem to have any digestive upsets no matter what he gobbled down.

She flipped a treat to Gulliver who snapped it out of the air.

We dropped our luggage in our room and headed out the door. There were a few fishermen on the quay, docked after an early morning's catch, their nets empty now. Gulliver trotting decorously beside me. We could see a group of men further along on the sea wall.

"That's Kyle," I said.

"With his press colleagues," Mark agreed.

"And Archie," I said spotting our guide of the cave tour. "Maybe Kyle has organized a tour of the same cave my group saw."

Mark nodded. "That's likely. I'm going to tag along."

Gulliver pulled toward the group, recognizing Kyle, I think, but I tugged him in a different direction and took him on a short walk through the town. Most of the shops were open. I did a quick survey of the two dress shop windows and trotted Gulliver back to the hotel, left him in my room and then spent an hour browsing through the book store and chatting with the owner about the mystery writers of this area. When I returned, I met Mark striding up the quay toward the hotel.

"What did you learn?" I was sure I had a better afternoon in the book store than Mark had, following Kyle and his friends.

Mark grunted. "I learned that Kyle is an actor and can hold his audience. He used Archie's spiel about the caves to suggest that Oliver Nott's book brought the history of smuggling into the modern day. You could see those journalists peering into the corners looking for drugs."

"They knew the book was about drugs?"

"They did and were full of theories about why Nott died."

"Perhaps he was too accurate about the location of the cave in the book and the drug dealers removed him?"

"That was suggested," Mark said.

"Are you going to look for the cave now?"

"Yes, I got a text from Tregere. He has the team together, should be here any minute and then we're off. Nott may have gotten it right. What are you going to do while I'm gone?"

"I'm going to take Gulliver for a long walk up the Coastal Path and think about nothing at all."

He smiled. "Just stay away from the cave we're interested in."

"I don't even know where it is—I didn't plug the coordinates into my mobile, and I'm certainly not going to look for it. I'll hear all about it from you when we meet for supper."

He kissed me briefly and was gone. If he found the cave and the criminals and helped apprehend them, he might have time for supper. I reconsidered. That was unlikely. If he did find them, he'd be up to his ears in paperwork and wouldn't be finished in time for supper. If he didn't find them, I just might see him at the hotel later.

I threw on my quilted jacket. It's light enough so I could tie it around my waist if the weather was warm, but warm enough to cut the wind when the air cooled. I stuffed some dog treats in one pocket and the inevitable doggie bags in the other. I felt the rough edges of the shell carving Bert had given me and smiled. I'd leave it there. I shrugged into my rucksack, containing the dog water, my water and Gulliver's bowl. Gulliver and I headed toward the Readymoney Cove and from there to the Coastal Path beyond it. The tide was ebbing and we had the beach and miles of path to explore. There were few people nearby, only a mother with a small child on the shore. We jogged along until we reached the end of the bay and rounded the rocky outcrop into the small cove beyond it. Here, we found George. He was sitting on a rock, his binoculars to his eyes, apparently scanning the cliffs.

Gulliver bounded up to him as if he were an old friend, which I expect, in Gulliver's young life, he was.

"Hello there, Gulliver." George put down his binoculars and petted Gulliver. Gulliver wiggled, yipped and showed his appreciation of George.

I laughed. "You are a hit with him, George." I sat beside him on the rock. "Are you getting some relaxation?" I spoke as if relaxation was a scarce commodity, doled out by a capricious fate.

"It's surprising," George said. "but I am."

"Good."

"There's something about the sea," He gestured to the ever-rolling waves here where the river met the sea. "It makes you think that life just keeps moving in a direction, maybe a useless direction, but it doesn't stay still."

I wasn't sure I understood him. Perhaps he was talking about being reconciled to fate. I dug my toes into the pebbles at my feet and stared at the stones. They were mostly grey, but variations of grey, some with orange streaks, some with hints of purple.

George proffered two, smooth, oval white stones.

"Beautiful."

"Want one? They're like worry beads. You can rub your fingers over them. Kind of meditative."

I smiled at him. They were bigger than I would have chosen, but I took one. "Thanks." I rubbed my fingers over the almost glassy surface, then dropped it into my pocket.

"Where are you off to," he asked me.

"Nowhere, really. Gulliver and I are just walking."

"Me, too, but I think I'll sit awhile."

I got up and moved away. That was definitely a declaration that he wanted to be alone. It suited me. I preferred my own company and Gulliver's just now.

We rounded another cliff face and found ourselves in a cove with a small river which spread its water over the shore.

If there wasn't a bridge over the river, we wouldn't be able to go any further. But there had to be one. People walked this trail all the time. I turned toward the bushes at the shore. If there was a bridge, there should be a footpath from the shore. There might be a more used access before Readymoney Cove. After walking back and forth along the edge of the rock face, I found it.

"Come on, Gulliver, let's try this."

He happily followed me, marking a few tufts of grass to let any dogs following know how important he was.

We found the foot bridge. It was wide enough to take a horse and small wagon in the old days or a golf cart today. There was even a stone jetty with a small boat, equipped with an outboard motor tied up to it. There would be people on the trail, I assumed. On the other side of the bridge, the footpath headed up a slight rise in the ground.

"Let's follow this, Gulliver. There might be a view."

There was a view on a narrow bench, a little above the shore, allowing me to see down the beach. I pulled out my water bottle and poured a drink into Gulliver's collapsible bowl then had a drink myself. I stared at the beach. That must be George walking along. His binoculars hanging from his neck. He was studying the ground this time. As I watched him, he stood and looked toward the path where Gulliver and I had turned. He took the same path. He was following me? Why would he do that? Was he obsessed enough to be dangerous? I was alone here.

First things first. I slipped behind a boulder and had the relief Gulliver took for granted. I was not going to meet George with a full bladder. The woods around me gave privacy. I watched a chough squawk a complaint from a low branch, its orange beak opening wide with the sound. Gulliver watched me with some curiosity. I had straightened and put myself back in order when I heard men's voices. Gulliver turned his head toward the path.

"Here, Gulliver," I said, quietly. "Come."

He came and I held him. My hand over his mouth. "No barking." I whispered.

He looked at me but remained quiet.

CHAPTER NINETEEN

Whoever was talking was doing so only yards from me. I wasn't going to move, partly, because I was embarrassed to be caught peeing in the woods and, partly, because I didn't know who it was. I didn't think it was George. A man's deep voice came to me clearly. I didn't recognize it.

"We're going to stop this. My old lady's giving me grief and she's right. Poor Davey died. Could be one of me nippers. That's what she says, and, yeah, she's right. We'll go back to the whatever we can make money at, but not this poison."

"Nothing will make as much money as this." A second voice broke in. That sounded like Kyle, a posh accent. Not Cornish, that's for sure. He kept on. "This stuff costs peanuts to make and it sells fast."

"True enough," the man said. "But, *Fercrisaek*, it's killing kids."

"No more than cars do. Kids die driving cars, skiing, swimming, doing all kinds of things."

Another voice spoke, a lighter voice, but one that had authority. "No matter. We want no part of it now. You can clear out this stuff. Hear me true, now, y'bugger, if it's not gone by tomorrow. We'll chuck it in the drink."

The voices echoed. They might be nearby on the trail but their words sounded hollow as if they came from a cave. Every word could be bouncing around the cavern and out the entrance. Judging by the voices, there were at least three of them. If this was the cave that Mark was looking for, he would be here soon. Would he expect me to stick my head out, find the cave entrance and try to identify them? He might. Too bad. I wasn't going to do it. If these men were in a cave, I wasn't going there.

I stood perfectly still, one hand holding Gulliver and one hand in my pocket fingering the smooth stone George had given me. I needed some way of staying calm. I tried to keep my breathing slow and steady. I did not want to be discovered. I had to keep calm so Gulliver would keep calm. I dropped the stone back in my pocket and caressed Gulliver's head. "Good dog," I whispered.

"You can't just stop. London will send people down." Kyle was almost yelling.

"You bleddy tuss." The man was derisive. "Aye, they'll come, will they? And take a rock to me? Or a filet knife? Eh? And then what? You got me and my brothers and my cousins and my brothers-in-law? We'll take on any emmets. They'd be bait for the lobsters, they'd be. They'd be gawky to try." There was a short silence and then the same man said, "I's leavin'."

"Have a heart, man." That was Kyle again. "I've set up the distribution. It works smooth as silk. What will it distribute if we don't produce the stuff and move it out all over the country? If we stop producing here, nothing will get out and no money will come in."

I could hear every word. There must be air holes from the cave where the sound came through or I was very near the cave entrance.

"Not our problem," the deep-voiced man said. "We don't need you or your pills. We can use the cave to move out weed, alcohol, even folk. We've had enough of this. You can bugger off."

Kyle hadn't finished arguing. "This stuff is easier. It just gives users a high."

"As you say, but we know better. Fourteen nippers in Cornwall died—and one of our own. We didn't sign on to kill kids."

They'd finished talking and were leaving. I heard their boots on the stone coming closer. I wasn't going to risk peeping out from behind a rock even if a good detective would do that. I was an innocent bystander. I was not going to be heroic. Gulliver squirmed. I kept a firm hold of him and whispered in his ear. "Quiet." He stayed quiet. The boots stomped past. The men were silent. I didn't know if Kyle was saving his breath to talk to them later, or he'd given up.

If George had been following me, he would meet Kyle and the men. I heard nothing. Perhaps people on this path were not a threat to them. The cave might be difficult to find and they didn't expect George to discover it. That much inner speculation was just distracting enough to let Gulliver jerk and then drop from my hands. He darted around the boulder and onto the path. I was relieved there was no longer anyone in sight. He scurried ahead of me.

I scrambled after him around the boulder and saw the path stretching in front of me. No Gulliver.

"Gulliver," I called softly. I scanned the rocks and broken shale nearby but couldn't see him. I called again.

I heard him bark, but I couldn't see him. He barked again, and I turned toward the sound. It came from the cliff. I followed a curve in the rock. Behind it was a human-sized opening in the hillside. Not at all obvious from the path.

"Gulliver," I called. He barked again. I dropped my rucksack by the cave entrance to mark the spot and walked in.

At first, I couldn't see anything but a strip of light on the cave floor. I rounded another corner and the cave opened up. There were electric lights here, showing long tables set against the walls, packing equipment and small machines—and Gulliver, bouncing on his feet delighted to find a friend, Kyle. He hadn't left with the men. Of course. He had to do something about the drugs before the men tossed them in the ocean.

He stared at Gulliver and then at me. "What are you doing here? How did you find me?"

"Gulliver found you. I'd never have seen the entrance of the cave."

He patted Gulliver absentmindedly, staring at me.

I stayed by the entrance. "Come, Gulliver."

Gulliver ignored me.

"You can't leave here," Kyle said slowly.

I thought fast. "Did you just stumble on this? Or did you work it out from Oliver's notes? The police have those notes now and they are going to check out this cave. I guess you got here just before them. Good going." I prattled like a cartoon duck, frantically trying to think of something that would normalize this situation.

Praise. Everyone likes praise. Maybe, he'd believe I thought he was innocent. I didn't. Not at all. It sounded to me as if he was the one who gave orders to the fishermen to produce the Fentanyl.

"Yeah. I worked it out." His voice was slow as if he was thinking of something else.

I had to keep him talking and let him think I had no idea he was involved.

"How's the promo for the book going?"

I eased back toward the entrance.

"Good, he said, "It's going good."

"Are you going to take pictures of the cave?"

"No!" he almost yelled that. "You shouldn't have seen this."

"Relax. You're welcome to the story. I'm not a journalist. You can take all the credit. But everyone's going to see it soon. The police will find it the same way you did, from the notes."

"Yes," he muttered a little, "from the notes." He was quiet for moment. I eased back a little more.

"Don't move. I have to think."

He didn't have a weapon that I could see. I continued to move back as I talked. I glanced at the boxes packed in rows in one corner. Drugs ready for distribution? I noticed the almost clinical look of the cave. I wondered if the fishermen helped manufacture the drugs, or if Kyle had other workers who did that. I brought my mind back to the absolute necessity of getting out of there.

Gulliver continued to bounce up and down in front of Kyle, hoping for more petting. Kyle looked down, waved Gulliver away. Gulliver continued to hop up and down pawing at Kyle's leg. Kyle swatted at him with his hand.

"Gulliver!" I called but Gulliver insisted on being Kyle's best friend.

Kyle pulled back his leg and kicked. Gulliver yelped and darted away. I ran to him and grabbed him up in my arms. He whimpered. I turned on Kyle, furious with him.

"For God's sake, Kyle. That was cruel." My anger, quick to rise on Gulliver's behalf, was quick to drop. I was in a precarious position here. While I faced Kyle, I started to back away toward the cave entrance. I didn't like violence of any kind.

"Shut up," he screamed. "Let me think."

I wasn't hanging around. I whirled, and ran for the entrance, Gulliver in my arms. I heard the rush of Kyle's feet on the cave floor behind me.

"Stop. Just stop. I have a syringe of Fentanyl here. I can inject you before you move another step."

I turned my head and saw that he did indeed have a syringe in his hand, and he had moved up behind me, too close for me to escape. I froze.

CHAPTER TWENTY

Nausea welled into my throat. I fought it, taking deep breaths. He was not normal. No one could deal in drugs the way he did, send death out into the world and retain a normal conscience. *Keep that in mind, Claire.* I had to keep my wits about me if I was going to get myself and Gulliver out of this. I tried for a calm, soothing voice.

"The police aren't going to arrest either of us for being in the cave," I said. "They can't prove either of us had anything to do with the Fentanyl production going on here."

I wanted him to think that he and I were buddies here. He lowered the syringe. I breathed a little easier. The relief was too soon.

"They'll take fingerprints. They've got my fingerprints on file." The syringe moved up again.

That was true. They would take fingerprints and they had taken his at the start of the investigation. Kyle's would likely be all over this cave.

I thought quickly. "You could say you were investigating. Like a true journalist. You wanted to see how everything worked."

He considered that. The syringe dipped lower. I concentrated on being reasonable and supportive, as if I believed he was a good person.

"You've been a tireless promotor of Oliver's books. No one is going to think it odd you found the cave. You brought in a film crew to make promo for the book." I tried to sound admiring, even gushing. "Of course, you are going to be interested in what Oliver learned." I paused for a moment, curious. "What did he learn?"

Kyle put the syringe on the table and looked around him. "He knew about this cave. He got suspicious and followed me here. He didn't say a thing when he first worked it out. He didn't talk to me about it. Didn't try to deal. Just used it as the plot line for his book."

"I see." Kyle was revealing that he had organized this drug manufacturing and distribution. While he had been actively working for the publishing company, he was making thousands if not millions distributing drugs. No wonder he had the fastest car and the latest electronic toys. He could have a legitimate position in society while at the same time profiting from his crimes. He probably saw himself as a celebrity, an entitled man of the world.

"I didn't know he'd done that until the book was in production. I hadn't read it. I don't *have* to read the books, just sell them. I was promoting it, getting ads online, getting him blog spots and I hadn't even read the book. I don't read them all, you know?"

"Of course not," I said calmly. He could still reach that syringe and there might be more syringes around.

"It wasn't until the night of the party that he told me the plot. That's when I knew he'd found out about the distribution scheme. It was a betrayal, you know?"

He sounded aggrieved, as if Oliver owed him silence. I imagined anything that got in his way seemed unfair to him. Oliver had spoiled his plans. All that happened after Oliver wrote the book was then Oliver's fault. Even his murder was his own fault. Oliver had interfered in Kyle's business and Kyle blamed him. Kyle paced between the table and the cave wall while he expounded on his grievances. At some point, he would be too far from the table to grab the syringe. I braced to run when he reached that point, but he never went that far, turning quickly back to the table before I could move. I tried the soothing tone again.

"You think he should have talked to you?" I wanted him concentrating on the past, not the present. I didn't know if anything I tried would be helpful. I only knew I wanted that syringe away from me.

"Yeah, like this is a business, you know?" He waved his hand toward the walls of the cave. "He was going to wreck my business—and he didn't care. He said it would sell books. Sure, it would sell books, but book sales are peanuts. Books, even his books, don't make the money drugs do. It's fun promoting books, but it's a way to stay poor. He was stupid—blind really. He was going to break me and walk away laughing. It was the laughing that got me."

I supposed Kyle couldn't stand the idea that he wasn't important. Oliver's derision would be an affront. "Yes, I can understand that."

He shot a fierce look at me. I didn't move.

"I don't care if you can or not. Nobody laughs at me. He's not laughing any more."

I felt the chills up my arms.

"And now the men are abandoning me. I'm in deep shit here. Real deep. The boss expects performance. He likes me." Kyle preened a bit, as if he was a favored child. Then he shook his head. "But I know him. Business comes first. He won't let this go. He won't say, 'Too bad, just a mistake.' No, he won't do that." He was quiet for a moment, perhaps contemplating what the boss would do to him. "I can't just leave this. He'll expect me to clean it up. Everything."

"I can see that. Can you get other men to help?" At least, while he was talking, he wasn't concentrating on drugging me or killing me.

"No. They're like a union or a brotherhood or something. If those guys don't help me, no one will. They got some idea it's not right. Well, the laws aren't right."

That was too much for me. I couldn't help objecting. "Fentanyl is lethal."

"So's driving a car. People have to be careful, that's all. I don't know why those ignorant bastards got righteous all of a sudden."

It was the death of the fourteen-year-old and D.S. Tregere's plan to enlist the women that had made the difference, but I wasn't going to tell him that.

"They won't give me time to get it all out of here. They're coming back tomorrow to toss everything. I've got to get it moved. It's worth millions. It's worth some risks."

He cocked his head and considered me. "You can help me move everything."

If I helped him and worked very slowly, I might stay alive a little longer.

"I've got a small boat moored at the slip just below here. You can help me move all the packages into the boat. We could do it in an hour. That's it. That's what I'll do. Move everything. The boss with be happy to have the product."

And I will be sending more drugs into the world to kill kids. That was not going to happen. Could I help him move the drugs and then tip the boat? But he wouldn't let me get into the boat. He was going to kill me after I had helped move the boxes. Mark and the Penzance police might be here by then. But they might not be. I wasn't going to go along with his plan. I was going to stay alive and I was *not* going to send Fentanyl out into the world. Maybe I could delay him. Maybe arguing would take time.

"No."

"Oh yes." He picked up the syringe again.

Oh well, there was no arguing with the syringe. I shrugged. "If you say so."

"If I don't have the product, I'll have to pay for it. I don't have the money to do that. So, you'll pick up these boxes and load the boat. You'll do, it or I'll inject your dog with Fentanyl."

Gulliver. Oh crap. Gulliver was a hostage. "I'll help," I said quietly.

He needed help loading the boat. As long as I was moving boxes, I'd stay alive and Gulliver would stay alive, but there was no way he was going to leave me behind to inform on him.

"Think it through, Kyle. You'll never get away with it. If your fingerprints all over the cave and on the syringe, you'd be setting yourself up for a murder charge."

"I haven't killed you yet. And when I do, I can wipe off the syringe the way I wiped off the knife."

I didn't want to hear about the knife. I really didn't want him to admit to killing Oliver. That would be a death sentence for me. I suppose it didn't matter what he told me. It was becoming clearer by the minute that he wasn't going to let me go. All right. He was planning on killing me. My life was worth some risks.

I thought quickly. "You'd have to wipe off all the prints from everywhere in here. You don't have time."

"I'll use the excuse you gave me. I was investigating the cave. They wouldn't be able to prove a thing. I'd say you were dead when I got here." He moved a little closer. "Listen up. I can't go without the product because I can't pay the boss. So, it's *my* life on the line now. Start moving those boxes." He gestured to a row of boxes stacked against the wall of the cave.

If I put Gulliver down to help move the boxes, Kyle might kill him. Besides, I did not want to touch those boxes. I slid my hand into my pocket. I felt Bert's carving and then the rock George had given me. I clutched it, fitting it into my hand like a hard ball. I hadn't played cricket since sixth form, but I remembered how to bowl. Kyle turned his head to assess the boxes. I reached back and flung the rock straight at Kyle's head. It connected with a thud. I clutched Gulliver close and ran for the entrance. I had taken four steps when I crashed into a body. If it was one of the men coming back, I might be in worse trouble. I held Gulliver tight. He squealed.

"Out of my way!" George yelled. He picked me up, one beefy hand on each of my shoulders and set me aside. I held an immobile Gulliver close to my chest and fell back against the wall.

George flew into the cave. Kyle was not unconscious. That rock had only dazed him for a second. So much for my bowling power. He shook his head.

"What the hell?"

"I heard you," George screamed at him. "It's you. You are the one responsible for sending out this poison. You killed my son!"

Kyle shook his head again and stared at George. "Get a grip, man. It's nothing to do with you. I don't even know your son. Where did you come from? Get out of here."

Even in the face of a furious retribution, Kyle had no idea of the power of emotion. He ignored the volatile man in front of him and started to turn away.

George hauled back his fist and gave Kyle a mighty uppercut that lifted him off his feet and slammed him against the cave wall. He slid to the floor, still conscious and looking incredulous. One hand, miraculously, held the syringe. I suppose it was like holding a grenade—it was too dangerous to drop. With the other, he touched his face. "Jesus. Jesus. My jaw. You broke my jaw."

George reached for him, grabbing him by the shirt front, no doubt to do it again. Kyle looked down, pushed upright with his free hand and jabbed the syringe into George's arm.

And then the cave was full of people. Mark was there, holding George by one arm. George sagged against him. D.S. Tregere was there, holding Kyle while a female constable snapped handcuffs on Kyle's wrists.

People were so suddenly around me my mind couldn't keep up with the events, but one thing was clear to me and not to Mark or D.S. Tregere. I screamed for attention. "Kyle injected George with Fentanyl!"

Mark whipped his head around and looked at George, lying now on the cave floor. His face was pale and his breathing slow. His eyes were closed.

"Who's got the Narcan?" Mark demanded.

"I do" The constable reached into the front pocket of her vest.

She had the syringe with the naloxone reversal into George's arm in seconds. His lips had turned blue, but the reversal drug worked like a miracle. He blinked and shook his head. Then he struggled. Mark held him down.

"They often struggle for a few seconds," the constable said as she put away her rescue kit. She was standing over Kyle now, watching him, ready to subdue him if necessary. I stared at her: about twenty-five, athletic, blond hair cut short, wrapped in regulation armor—bullet-proof vest, pockets full of mace, radios, mobiles and clinking with keys. I focused on her, willing myself into a calm state. Hysteria would be of no use to anyone.

I stayed glued to the cave wall, Gulliver in my arms, both of us trembling. I could see Bert's carving in pieces. It must have come out of my pocket and dropped to the floor when I grabbed the rock. Many feet had stamped on it. Bits of the wooden shell had split and splintered. I stared at the pieces, thinking about the care and love Bert had put into making it, thinking about the care and love George had poured onto his son, thinking of evil and wickedness and all things sordid. I wanted fresh air.

CHAPTER TWENTY-ONE

Gulliver didn't want to leave my lap. He was curled there, occasionally looking up at me and then snuggling back down. Safety was vital. I felt the same way. Mark and Detective Superintendent Tregere and I were established in an elegant room, what would be a snug in a less upscale hotel than the Queens, and which had a door that shut and gave us privacy.

We had travelled back to Penzance where there was a substantial lock-up and more administrative clerks than Fowey and where D.S. Tregere could be sure he was in charge.

We had a view from the window of Mount Bay, the blue sky, calm sea and miles of beach, curving into a crescent from St. Michael's Mount to the headland before Mousehole. I appreciated the beauty and the fact that I was there to see it.

D.S. Tregere exuded confidence and humor. I didn't trust him for a moment. He seemed to me to be a man who was always on a mission and would use anyone to advance that mission. At the moment, I agreed with his mission—to rid the world of dangerous drugs—but I didn't trust his methods.

"Geddon me cock," he said with some enthusiasm, or at least, he said something like that. It sounded vulgar, but I expected it wasn't. I was sure my face must have looked blank, because he translated.

"This is satisfactory, very satisfactory." He smiled while he shuffled the papers around on the table in front of him. I almost expected him to start humming.

He looked up. "I need you to sign your statement, Claire, me lover. This is the one the clerk took down immediately following the incident."

I suppose that harrowing few minutes in the cave was a "police incident," just one of many. I suppressed a shudder. It was worse for me than for the police because I'd felt helpless. They'd arrived with firearms, experience and intention and did not feel helpless. Whereas, I'd cringed against the wall, impotent. I pulled the paper toward me with one hand and held onto Gulliver with the other.

I read quickly. It was just as I had dictated it. I reached for the pen.

"One moment." D.S. Tregere stopped me. "Now that you've had time to reflect on it, chew away on the ins and outs of it as it were, is there anything you can add?" He paused for a moment, then said slowly but with heat, "Anything that would nail down the bugger would be appreciated."

I grinned. He really wanted a conviction. I thought for a moment. "He did say he 'wiped off the knife' after killing Oliver. Is that going to help?"

"Just write it in, me lover, and we will let the Crown Prosecutor do what she can with it."

I wrote in the sentence that might help convict Kyle.

"Does the prosecution depend on my statement?" I was uncomfortable with that much responsibility.

"Of course, it does." Tregere gathered the papers. "But not exclusively. Bradbury's girlfriend, Alexandra Atley, is singing quite beautifully, like a glorious lark, she is."

"She's giving evidence against him?"

"Apparently." He smiled, the picture of complacency. "She decided he was not a nice man; she likes her job and he is a poor choice for her future."

"Does she know much?" I recalled Alexandra, a thin girl, blonde and waif-like.

"A little. Everyone knows a little. When we put it all together, we get enough ingredients in the pot to make a substantial stew."

I suppose that was as good a description as any of the painstaking compilation of details that the police must collect and present to the Crown Prosecutor.

"Patrick is going to need a new PR man," I mused. "Poor Patrick. Is he in the clear? I mean, did he know anything?"

"Didn't seem to," Tregere said, regretfully I thought. "His employee is safely in jail here and will stay with us unless he gets a particularly aggressive and competent barrister."

"It's not likely, is it?" Mark said. "His drug bosses are not going to want anything to do with him. They'll let him sink into the prison system without lifting a finger. He's a business loss."

Tregere nodded. "I'd feel sorry for him—if he wasn't such a self-satisfied dobeck better fitted for prison than decent company."

I searched my mind for a translation. "Dobeck". Stupid. It meant the stupid one.

He was quiet for a moment. "And he was spreading poison."

I watched Tregere square the papers preparatory to stashing them into his briefcase.

"Everything is tied up then? The Fentanyl distribution is shut down.?" I wanted it distant from Cornwall.

Tregere paused and looked at me. "It is gone from here," he said. "The fishermen who were augmenting their honest wages by renting out the cave and helping that bugger load and unload won't do it anymore. They weren't doing the manufacturing. The London organization had their own people doing that. But the fishermen were making the manufacturing and distribution possible—now they won't."

"Because Kyle got caught?"

"No," Mark said when Tregere hesitated. "Because their wives and girlfriends refuse to let them do it any longer. They're holding their men responsible for the death of the boy in Fowey last week and they are firm about it. It's like the measles."

"I beg your pardon?" I didn't understand that at all. I was tired. My brain couldn't relate measles to illicit drugs.

"Well, measles or any other disease that can creep into a community." Mark expanded on his idea. "Some people ignore immunizations and say they harm kids and refuse to do anything about it until their neighbor's kid dies from measles. Then they see the need for action."

"I see." I did understand what he meant. It sometimes took a graphic example to convince people to act. "Has the spread of Fentanyl stopped then?"

"Here it has," Tregere agreed. "The drug organization will move it somewhere else, but it won't be my problem."

That annoyed me. "It's somebody's problem. Somebody like George who lost his son. Other people have children who are going to die. You can't just say 'Not my problem.'"

I heard Mark take a deep breath. If he didn't like me arguing with Tregere, he could deal with it. Tregere was just as self-satisfied as Kyle.

"I'll give you that. I'll give you that," Tregere said. "I help where I can, but I can't run the world."

"Only this part of it," I said.

He smiled. "True, maid, true."

Mark changed the topic slightly. "I know you have enough to prosecute Bradbury on the drug charges, and attempted murder of

George Baker and Claire, but do you think we have enough to get a conviction on Oliver's murder." The murder charge was, after all, Mark's responsibility.

"Maybe, just maybe. We have the statement about wiping the knife handle thanks to our bird here. Alexandra Atley is providing a little collaboration on when Kyle Bradbury went to talk to Oliver Nott in the garden that night."

"Why did he kill him? I asked. "He told me Oliver had discovered the cave and the Fentanyl business. Was that the motive?"

Mark answered. "I think so, and from what I got when I talked to Bradbury, Oliver laughed at him. He didn't like that."

I remembered Kyle stressing that. "Yes, he thought he was too clever to be laughed at."

"And too smart to be caught," Mark said.

Tregere spoke slowly as if he was contemplating a mental picture. "I think he had that conversation with Nott where Nott laughed at him and then he left Nott alive, went to the kitchen, filched the knife and waited for his moment."

"When there was no one with him?" I asked.

"That's likely. Nott told him his career was finished because Nott was going to expose him, perchance not right away, but when the publicity would do the book the most good."

I thought about that. "When the first sales had died, he'd then reveal that Kyle was the villain he modeled his story on and let the ensuing court case keep his book front and center in the news."

"Something like that," Tregere said. "So, our devious tuss picks up the knife, stabs Nott, wipes the knife and thinks he is free as a gull."

Mark snorted. Tregere smiled. I looked at Mark for an explanation.

"Most people forget that when they wipe off fingerprints from a knife handle, they hold the hilt of the blade to do so, or brace their hand on the person. His fingerprints will be on the one or the other."

"He was wearing a leather jacket. If Kyle put his hand on the jacket, would his prints be there?"

"Yes. Easy to take prints off leather. Still, he could claim he touch the jacket at another time. I'm hoping the prints are on the hilt of the knife."

"Or on the wooden block that held the knives. Less conclusive, that, but helpful." Tregere said.

"It was premeditated then, "I said. "He didn't just stab him in the heat of the moment."

"Think on it, maid," Tregere said. "He would not be carrying a kitchen knife, now would he for any reason but murder?" He paused for a moment and then shook his head. "*Martesen,* a good defense will say it *wasn't* premeditated, that Kyle didn't bring the knife to the party, was in a blind rage for about twenty minutes and fetched the knife in that time. He might get away with that, even so. Me, I think Bradbury's a calculating sod and was nae in a rage at'all."

"One of Kyle's problems," Mark said, "is that he doesn't think anyone, including the police, *especially* the police, is as smart as he is."

"I don't think either Kyle Bradbury or Oliver Nott were particularly evolved humans," I decreed.

Tregere laughed. "Lots of that about," he said.

"Is George all right?" I had seen him for only a few moments before the ambulance took him away, but he had been conscious.

"Just fine. That Narcan works wonders." Mark answered me.

But, Tregere had to put in his opinion. "He is a civilian, and he shouldn't have interfered."

Again, Tregere annoyed me. I wasn't sure why. Perhaps he handed out decrees as if he had more wisdom than anyone else. Condescension. I guess that was what I didn't like. Condescension. "You are inconsistent, Superintendent. You want the women of Fowey to interfere in the drug trafficking as civilians, but you don't want George to do that. You can't have it both ways."

Tregere sat back and pursed his lips. He stared at me for a few seconds. "Perhaps. *Martesen.* Perhaps. We need public education. The citizens need to do their part, but I don't want them deciding they're vigilantes, handing out justice as they see it. There's anarchy that way."

I nodded. He had a point. Nevertheless, I was grateful George had arrived in time to help me.

We left the hotel and headed for the sea wall. Gulliver could use the walk, and I needed the cool, cleansing air off the ocean. Mount Bay seemed to pull the blue of the sky into the sea until I wasn't sure I could distinguish them. The slight breeze was crisp and I was glad of my jacket. Gulliver flapped down the stone stairs to the beach, almost tumbling over himself to get to the bottom quickly. He began his quick and inquisitive investigation of every piece of seaweed left behind by the receding tide and every rock that interested him. He was happy. Mark and I followed him in an aimless, desultory way. We had no real agenda this evening.

"I will have reams of paperwork to do on this but I should have at least a day free before I have to start on it," he said.

Mark had a free day and I was not on duty with tourists. We should make a plan. But I was still turning over in my mind the perfidy of Kyle.

"Do you think you'll get a conviction on the murder charge?" I asked.

"It's not my job to get the conviction, but I'll do my best to get in all the evidence I can so the prosecutor can get it."

"What would his sentence be?" I tried to imagine Kyle in prison. It should be a humbling experience.

"Hard to know. He hasn't been caught at anything before, but the courts are anxious to stop the Fentanyl trade and may throw the maximum at him." Mark picked up a pebble and spun it into the water. We watched it skip and then sink.

"Does a stiff sentence really deter criminals from trafficking?" I hadn't read much about the effect of sentencing.

Mark was quiet for a moment. "Not usually. There are different ways of thinking about that. Some people think retribution is a kind of justice. That the anger people feel around the criminal act demands satisfaction, and that a stiff sentence will make the victims or the loved one like George feel satisfied that their love mattered."

"And what do others think?"

"Others think that retribution is a childish response to anger, and that adults need to channel that anger into creating a better society. That would mean setting up sentences that give the criminal a chance to reclaim his or her life and become someone different."

"Would that happen?" It seemed idealistic, but perhaps society just need to think about prisons and criminals differently.

"Possibly. We don't have a system now that offers a new path for criminals. Usually, they just put in time until they get out. In some countries, they learn to be better criminals in jail. Here, it's not too bad, but I wouldn't say we have programs that give them hope of a different life."

"It's imperfect." I sighed.

"It's imperfect," he agreed. "I'd like to see something different than trying to catch drug lords and slimy dealers. We should try something like Portugal."

"What's going on in Portugal?" It was a small country. What had they tried?

"Drugs are not illegal there."

"Truly?" I was surprised. I was used to thinking of drugs as illicit, illegal and somehow inherently evil.

"Yes, and when they decriminalized drugs, their juvenile use went down by 50%."

That was impressive. "So, it works."

"It works, but I can't see it happening here."

I thought about it. "People would have to change the way they think about drug use—from considering it a crime to considering it a health problem?"

"That's right, and that wouldn't be easy. But if we managed that, we could do what Iceland does."

"Which is?"

"Put the money we save from chasing illegal drugs into youth services and sports."

I stared at Mark. I could not imagine politicians supporting that process. He was looking out at the sea, thinking, I supposed, about how much of his time was spent uselessly pursuing drug dealers and importers and how much his life would be improved if politicians and the public changed their thinking.

He was a man of principle. I would have to remember that and support that part of his life. It might be uncomfortable at times. I was sure there would be days when his commitment to justice would be hard for me to accept. I suppose every woman wants to be first in her lover's life. But I was forty-six now, not twenty, and could be more realistic about relationships. His commitment was part of what I loved about him.

I took his arm and moved closer to him. "What would you do with your time if drugs were legal?"

He looked down at me and grinned. "Just chase the everyday murderers. There is no end of weirdos in this world. "

CHAPTER TWENTY-TWO

Mark spent a long day wrestling with paperwork and trying to find the correct forms on the computer, so he told me, and generally putting his evidence in order. I spent the day taking Gulliver on a long walk to Mousehole.

The emmets had disappeared for the most part; there were only a few couples who were obviously not local with their cameras and rucksacks, bundled against the October chill. They stared at the tiny harbor and peered into the few shops that remained open. It was different here in the height of the summer heat when thousands surged through, buying souvenirs, ice-cream, Cornish pasties and pounds of scones and clotted cream. I never brought my tourists here in the summer. They would be frustrated at the long lines for food and drink, and I would be frustrated by the lines of cars and lack of parking. Mousehole was a tired old lady today, content to shake off the bustle of the frantic, long days of July and August and settle back into the ease of winter.

At this time of year, it was beautiful. The sea was never truly blue here on a bright day. It was turquoise, aquamarine and a deep purple where the eel grass grew close to the surface. The cliffs rose abruptly and the tiny village with its crooked lanes and cobblestones settled into the landscape, bound by centuries of tradition.

Gulliver and I sat in Penny's Pantry. I sipped her excellent tea and munched on her carrot and walnut cake while Gulliver gulped up the water she'd provided, yawned and settled at my feet.

Penny's mother was here again. I haven't been in the café when her mother, immaculate in twinset and pearls, wasn't chatting away to whomever was around—to Penny as she bustled in and out or to herself if no one was close by, keeping up a melodious chatter whether anyone listened or not. It was comforting to find the same people doing the same things—a kind of antidote to greedy opportunists like Kyle rushing through life grabbing what they could. Penny's mother was content,

Penny was happy to have her visit and the customers were willing to add her presence to their day. Kyle could take lessons from them.

The three-and-a-half-mile walk from Penzance had tired Gulliver, so we rode the bus home. Several ladies flashed their free bus passes at the driver, boarding for a shopping trip to Penzance.

"What's up, Mother?" the driver asked, nodding at the woman's basket.

"My Samuel is coming home for a visit, and I need some bits and pieces from the Penzance co-op."

"Finished in the Middle East then, is he?" the driver asked.

The woman heaved a long sigh. "That was a terrible time, it was. I wished he hadn't joined up, my ansum. I did indeed, but there was no talking to him. You know what a stubborn child he always was."

"Aye." The driver nodded. "A right stubborn boy, I remember. You got to be careful of that PPSS now."

There was silence for a moment while I and the other ladies on the bus tried to translate 'PPSS'.

"Post traumatic, you mean?" Samuel's mother offered.

"That's it." The driver nodded.

"Aye. I know. I've been reading up on it on the Internet. If he screams in the night or starts to shake, I'm going to ask him what he needs. Maybe some kind of pills. That's what they said to do."

"Oh, and that will help?" One of the ladies leaned over her basket and asked the question with obvious interest.

"So they say. But then if it doesn't, I'll send him fishing with his dad, digging in my garden and chopping wood with his brothers. He'll be that tired he'll drop off to sleep."

Everyone nodded. Having settled Samuel's future, we rode in silence to Penzance.

I spent the afternoon in the room at the Queens Hotel on my computer, entering figures on my business spread sheet and setting up next year's tours. I wouldn't lead another tour until next spring, March in the Yorkshire Dales. It would be beautiful there, but I'd like to come back to Cornwall, perhaps the next year in daffodil season.

Mark arrived at the hotel about six.

"I've booked a B & B in Fowey. Want to spend the night hiding out from D.S. Tregere and my office?"

"Sure." I packed quickly and loaded Gulliver. We took the A30 and turned off on the A390. Then Mark took a narrow road toward the cliffs. We stopped in a farm yard. There were no other houses around and the view over the sea was spectacular. The sun was setting, reflecting off a few low clouds, filling the sky with orange, purple and golden light. We left the car, walked to the edge of the cliff and stared at the sky. I couldn't move for a moment, captured by the magic of it.

Gulliver nudged my knees, and I turned to Mark.

"Amazing."

"Yeah." He put his arm around my shoulder and I leaned against him. We stood like that until the brilliant colors faded, then walked toward the house and our B & B hosts.

In the morning, Mark headed back to Hampshire and his headquarters in Alton. I rented a car in Fowey because I wanted to take more time on the return trip. I left the car and took Gulliver for a walk around the town and up onto the coastal path. There was an overlook there, with a bench and a view of the ocean. It was another cool but sunny day, and I wanted to enjoy it. I wasn't the only one there. Bert sat there carving another bird.

I smiled at him and sat down.

"I'd forgotten you live near here. Another puffin?"

"No, this is a chough. My friend likes them, and I have time now that the emmets have left us."

"My guests loved your carving." I wouldn't tell him what happened to my sea shell.

"Good."

We sat in silence for a while. Then I prodded a little. "The drug traffickers are gone, and the men have gotten away from them." I let the statement hang in the air. He could ignore it, or he could satisfy my curiosity a little.

"True. They didn't think very far on that one."

"They didn't realize how dangerous Fentanyl was to the users?"

He looked away for a moment and then nodded. "Perhaps. Or didn't care. The kirk isn't as strong as it was. The need to make money is stronger than the need to live well."

I wondered how much Bert had done to point Tregere in the direction of the caves. He wouldn't want to betray the fishermen in their smuggling. After all, it was a tradition, and he lived here, but he might not have been willing let it go on either.

I stopped at the bakery and bought a pastie for lunch. I could live on those. I sat outside St. Fimbarrus on the bench in the church garden and ate it, feeding Gulliver a few pieces of the chicken from the filling. The garden was beside a path that created a short cut from the town quay to the houses straggling up the hill beyond the church. I saw Aria climb the few steps from South Street and start up the path. She stopped quickly when she saw me.

"How are you, Claire? Still here? What's up?" She plopped down beside me.

"You're not working today?" I eyed her few bags of groceries.

"Just picking up some missing items from the post office," she said. "No, I'm home today."

The post office, I remembered, had groceries, sundries and lotto tickets.

"The women did a good job on the Fentanyl problem," I said. "Congratulations."

"We were late with it, and we're all bearing the guilt of Davy's death. The money was tempting, you know. There's not a lot of work around here, but it isn't worth Davy's life. Not to any of us."

We were silent for a few minutes. She was right.

"What will the families do for money?"

She snorted. "Smuggle something else." She gathered her parcels, and stood, hesitating for a moment. "Maybe the new separation of Britain from the European Union will keep foreign fishing boats from taking our fish, and the men will fish again. We live in hope. It's easier for me with a university degree and a librarian`s job. We`ll eat. Some will have a tough time, though."

I watched her walk briskly up the path and then disappear behind the church.

People had lived here for hundreds of years, doing what they needed to do to stay alive. I had faith they'd turn to something that would feed the community but wouldn't kill anyone. Or, more accurately, I had hopes that would happen. I was beginning to appreciate the courage it took to face poverty. I had never been without a pay check. I often worked when I didn't want to, but I'd never faced the prospect of no salary. I didn't have to wonder where the groceries were going to come from next week. I didn't have to worry that the police would be at my door for anything other than support. I was definitely on the right side of the law and I was going to stay away from any confrontations with the criminals.

Well, honesty prevailed. I was going to stay away from any murder investigation, unless it was too big a challenge to my curiosity. Mark was in my life, so crime was in my life.

I shrugged. Today, Gulliver and I were free of it all. We drove home to my comfortable cottage and my incessantly talking Rose. I felt lucky.

To follow the progress of the writing of the next in this series, click onto emmadkainauthor.com and click the *Join My Newsletter* button.

ABOUT THE AUTHOR

© Duke Morse

Emma Dakin lives in Gibsons on the Sunshine Coast of British Columbia where she enjoys the seals, whales, mergansers, eagles and wildlife of the ocean and where she is an enthusiastic, if somewhat amateur, violinist. She has over twenty-five trade published books of mystery and adventure for teens and middle-grade children and non-fiction for teens and adults. Her love of the British countryside and villages and her addiction to cozy mysteries now keep her immersed writing about characters who live and work in those villages. She introduces readers to the problems that disturb that idyllic setting.